MW01136295

Mike
Bailey

Printed in the United States of America

First Printing, 2015

ISBN-13: 978-1517223526

ISBN-10: 1517223520

Michael Bailey/Innsmouth Look Publishing
www.innsmouthlook.com

Cover illustrations Copyright © 2015 by Patricia Lupien
Cover design by Patricia Lupien

Book production by Amazon Create Space, www.createspace.com
Edited by Julie Tremblay

*The Adventures of Strongarm and Lightfoot*
*Scratching a Lich*

# Act One
## In Which Unlikely Heroes Come Together To Undertake an Epic Quest

# ONE
## Ill Fortune, Undeserved

Greetings and welcome — welcome! to Ne'lan, a magical, fantastic world that will no doubt seem strange to your eyes — a world full of wonders and horrors and mysteries awaiting discovery and, yes, on occasion, the dreary mundanities of daily life.

What can I say? No world is perfect.

Now sit you down and prepare yourself for an epic tale of danger and daring-do, of friendship gained and loyalties tested, of tragedy and loss — indeed a tale for the ages, starring two humble men who shall, in time, come to live ever on in legend —

What? No, I will not *hurry it up*. I'm trying to set a mood here. Now shush.

(People these days...no respect for the art of storytelling.)

This grand adventure starts, as grand adventures often do, with a single small story — the kind of trifling distraction that strikes no one in the present as significant, but through the lens of history, will stand revealed as the spark that ignited the fire in which the very world was re-forged.

This single small story begins with two small men: would-be adventurers of fortune who, as of late, have seen adventure aplenty but a dearth of accompanying fortune. To wit — let us look now upon these gentlemen's current exploit, which sees them fighting their way up Mount Rihon, a long-extinct volcano upon whose south face sits a great ugly boil in the form of an ancient keep, the name of which has been lost to the ages.

(It's Castle Cramm-Rankor, by the way. As a narrator I know these things; one of the perks of the job. But I digress.)

As we join our heroes, they have already successfully, and with a minimum of fuss, dispatched several sentries who sought to bar the adventurers' way, starting with a pair of Hruks guarding a rickety wooden bridge that no longer served its intended purpose, as the river it spanned long ago had dried away to dust.

(An aside — one of many in which I shall indulge throughout my tale — regarding the savage Hruks, a race of vaguely human creatures that has plagued Ne'lan for centuries. Bestial and simple-minded, Hruks are often sought out by powerful but evil men who prize the Hruks' two greatest skills, the first of which is their uncanny ability to follow orders to the letter — particularly when those orders involve inflicting terrible violence upon other living creatures. The second is their proficiency at inflicting terrible violence upon other living creatures. A further aside: their common name was coined following man's first documented encounter with the race. A poor, hapless hunting party scout was ambushed by a lone Hruk, and upon his return to camp, as he lay dying in his wife's arms, he responded to an inquiry as to the nature of his attacker with, "hruk." His comrades mistook his dying grunt for a proper noun, and the rest, as they say, is history.)

Once past the first set of sentries, our protagonists hacked and slashed their way past several more Hruks patrolling the anemic forest of twisted, skeletal trees ringing the base of Mount Rihon — with no harm to themselves, I add, for such was their skill with blade and bow. Hruks are most dangerous in large numbers, but individually they are no match for the duo of Derek Strongarm and Felix Lightfoot — respectively a warrior whose battlefield experience belies his youth and a thief who honed his skills as a young apprentice cut-purse under the tutelage of Lars of the Gentle Fingers, a master rogue whose name unfailingly provoked juvenile tittering but whose exploits could fill this tome and several more besides. However, another narrator has been employed to chronicle his adventures, so I shall speak of him no more lest I incur my colleague's litigious wrath.

Felix, an ace archer, next dispatched with a single arrow to the eye the massive troll chained to the front gate like a guard dog — were that dog in fact a hulking humanoid with fists the size of its own head, a leathery wart-pocked hide, and a taste for human flesh. The Hruks, overconfident in the troll's ability to ward off intruders, had posted no additional guards beyond the front gate, and so the men ascended unhindered to the keep's upper level. There they located a portcullis separating the keep proper from an upper courtyard of sorts, an expansive crescent-shaped lip of rock edging the central crater. On the far side of this courtyard sat the penultimate obstacle: a guardhouse, crudely constructed of wood scavenged from disparate sources, sufficient in size to hold several dozen bodies but — according to the detailed scouting reports shared with Derek and Felix before their departure on this errand — generally unoccupied during daylight hours.

Two Hruks stood outside the guardhouse, though their postures suggested they were loitering rather than on a scheduled watch detail. Reinforcing this notion was the presence of a dented steel stein, large enough to hold as much blood as one would find in a single infant — its express purpose — which the Hruks passed back and forth.

(I am pleased to report they were not partaking of baby's blood but brandy stolen from the very same caravan that ferried the object of our heroes' quest.)

Derek pressed his face to the rusted portcullis and scanned the courtyard. "Just the two," he reported.

Felix set an arrow on his bow, a simple yew longbow that had served him very well since he acquired it — that is to say, stole it — in his fifteenth year. The first shot would be simplicity itself, but the second posed a greater challenge since speed would be of the essence. Felix waited until one Hruk took the stein, until he tossed his head back to drain it, before loosing his first arrow. The Hruk lowered the stein, beheld his companion's state, and thought, *Huh, that's weird. He didn't have an arrow in his throat a second ago* — that keen observation coming a split-second before Felix's second shaft entered the Hruk's ear canal.

"Nice," Derek said. The portcullis, as it turned out, was not attached to anything. "And check this out.

Boy, this has been an easy one."

"A little too easy," Felix said.

"Pessimist."

"Realist."

"But you can't argue the intelligence has been spot-on so far," Derek said. "Now, Lord Spendle said there are maybe a dozen Hruks around at any given time, and we've taken out about that many between the bridge and here..."

"So, what? Maybe a couple more inside?" Felix said. "That's doable."

They dashed across the courtyard and took positions on either side of the entrance, a plain slat door held in place by wooden peg hinges. It invited kicking in, and Derek was ready to oblige.

"I'll charge in, take care of any Hruks near the door," Derek said, "you take out any others. Sound good?"

"We could just seal them in and torch the place."

"That's a little inhumane, don't you think?"

"It's efficient."

"It's cruel."

"Oh, so now *you're* sympathetic toward Hruks?" Derek gave him a look. "*Fiiiiiine.* We'll do it your way."

"On three. One. Two. THREE!"

The door fell under Derek's thunderous kick. He charged in as planned, his longsword ready to taste Hruk blood. Felix followed, the first of many arrows nocked and drawn. Their screams were a horrible harmony that foretold of death and destruction and would forever haunt the dreams of any Hruk who might somehow survive the onslaught to come.

Fifty Hruks froze in the midst of their midday feast and stared at the men stupidly — their default mode. Derek and Felix froze and stared back just as stupidly — which was not their habit, generally, but in this case understandable.

Felix summarized this unexpected scenario thusly: "Well, shit."

The brightest of the Hruks pointed damningly at the interlopers. "HOO-MUHNS!!" he bellowed, and his fellow Hruks rose as one and roared their intent.

Felix, ever quick-witted, formulated a cunning new strategy. "Retreat!"

I assure you this was not the whole of his plan, for upon entering the guardhouse, Felix noticed a series of oil lamps hanging from iron hooks set into the walls. He fired, shattering one such lamp and spraying flaming oil across the walls, a feasting table occupied by a dozen or so Hruks, those self-same Hruks, and the dirt floor beneath them. The latter of these was the only object that did not ignite instantly.

Felix led the strategic withdrawal. Derek cleared the door, spun, and ran through the first Hruk in pursuit. The hapless Hruk unwittingly aided the battle that followed by crumpling in the doorway, giving his comrades something to trip and fall over; four toppled and pig-piled onto one another in sequence, and each received a sword blow to the back of the neck. Felix dropped several more as they charged the entrance, adding to the dam of greasy mottled Hruk flesh.

The Hruks' screams of rage changed to screams of panic as the fire spread and consumed the guardhouse, aided and abetted by several Hruks who — in a rare, well-intentioned, and ill-advised display of creative thought — attempted to extinguish the blaze by blowing out the flames or dousing them with brandy.

At first, despite the unexpected turn, our brave adventurers believed they had snatched victory from the jaws of defeat — ah, but often do noble men fall victim to the sin of hubris. Had they thought to properly reconnoiter the premises, perhaps they would have taken steps to barricade the second door on the guardhouse's western face. And so it was that a handful of Hruks escaped the growing pyre, and within the span of a few seconds they surrounded the men, their weapons drawn — and fearsome weapons they were: wicked swords with broad blades and flattened tips with a sharpened edge, hence their name among men: chisels. They were crude weapons for a crude race with a crude style of fighting based entirely in wide, wild swings that would most certainly do great harm if they connected with their target.

*If.*

And that uncertainty was only amplified against a swordsman of Derek's caliber; clumsy blows were expertly parried and deflected, leaving the Hruks vulnerable to precise retaliatory cuts and thrusts. His armor, a mismatched patchwork of steel and leather, was not once tested by a Hruk chisel. Felix, having at this point slung his bow for a pair of matching short sabers, fared as well, though he was less in his element with hand-to-hand combat than his comrade; he greatly preferred stealth to direct confrontation.

The battle, such as it was, did not last long and ended with a score of Hruks dead upon the courtyard. They were the fortune ones; their suffering was trivial compared to those who perished within the blazing guardhouse. To his credit, Felix resisted an open boast over the ironic turn of events.

"We *were* told a dozen, right?" Derek said.

"We were," Felix said. "I think when we get back, we should have a little discussion with our employer about the quality of his intelligence. And negotiate a bonus for the extra trouble."

"Sounds reasonable to me."

In time, the guardhouse collapsed to ash and embers, granting Derek and Felix clear passage to the final leg of their journey. As is often the case with yawning chasms, the only way across was over a rickety footbridge assembled from dry planks laid over a network of thick but frayed hemp rope.

(Explorers throughout the world of Ne'lan have thus far failed to document a single rope suspension bridge in trustworthy condition. Historians have theorized that these constructs have always been of questionable physical integrity, made that way by early bridge-builders who were universally corrupt and padded their bottom line through the use of substandard materials.)

"I hate these things," Felix said, peering past the bridge and into the crater that, centuries ago, held a roiling lake of molten lava. He estimated a half-mile of open air beneath his feet — enough of a plummet, should one take an unfortunate tumble, to give one time to seriously contemplate the series of decisions that led to such a miserable demise.

"Yeah. But think of it this way: if the Hruks could cross it to stash the horn, it should be safe enough for us."

Felix was unconvinced, but at this late juncture,

turning around and going home empty-handed seemed a far less desirable option than a headlong plunge to certain death — which speaks strongly to the lean times our heroes had as of late fallen upon.

The men ventured across at a modest pace, balancing caution with the strong desire to cross as quickly as possible and reach solid ground — specifically, the solid ground of a vast column of rock jutting, against all logic, from the center of Mount Rihon like the axel of a wheel that had lost all but one delicate spoke.

"So far so good," Derek said.

"You're determined to jinx us, aren't you?"

Yet jinx them he did not; they crossed without incident and marked the occasion with deep sighs of relief.

A high stone dome, a natural formation, capped the pillar. As daylight did not want to stray far past the black cave mouth, Derek paused to withdraw from his pack a travel torch — a short shaft of wood wrapped in pitch-soaked burlap — which he set ablaze with flint and steel and no small amount of profanity over how long it took him to set a travel torch ablaze with flint and steel. When the torch at last caught, the flickering flame revealed a wondrous sight that made the entire day worthwhile: wooden chests, large and small and in-between — and behind the chests, something that made their eyes pop and lips spread into unbreakable grins.

"I think we just got our bonus," Felix said.

"First things first," Derek said, forcing his voice of reason to do its job. "The horn."

"Yeah. Right. Horn."

Felix tore his eyes away from the mountain of gold coins and picked at random one of the chests, one secured by a heavy iron padlock that looked easy enough to spring. From a leather belt pouch, he removed his picks, and then he set to work.

"Bring the torch down, I need more light."

Derek stabbed the butt of the torch into the ground next to Felix, who grunted a thank-you, then turned his attention to the gold. There was so much here, more money than he'd ever seen, too much for him and his partner to carry off in a hundred trips — a hundred *lifetimes*. The gold glittered in the torchlight, tiny reflections of the flame dancing in each coin. Derek bent to scoop up a handful for closer inspection; they were not the square coins common in most lands but oval in shape and, it appeared, oddly convex.

"Hey," he said, feeling the pile, which did not shift under his touch as he'd expected. "The coins are warm."

"Uh-huh," Felix said distractedly.

"And they're stuck together."

"Great."

"...And they're not coins."

"Trying to work here."

The treasure raised its head and blinked the sleep from its eyes.

"Felix..."

"Ha!" The lock popped open under Felix's gentle ministrations. He raised the lid and beheld the prize within: a black bull's horn, as long as his arm from fingertip to elbow, polished to a nacreous finish and inlaid with intricate gold swirls cascading down its length.

"Derek my man," Felix said, closing the lid with

the greatest of care, "I do believe our luck is changing."

"It isn't," Derek said. "It really isn't!"

Drakes are a distant branch on the family tree of dragon-kind. They share a general aesthetic, but drakes are smaller and wingless. They are highly adept at scaling the most terrifying of ascents to reach their mountain lairs, where they live solitary existences. They interact with few creatures that do not immediately become the evening meal, and Hruks, curiously, are among the rare exceptions. Scholars have theorized this is due to the Hruks' atrocious flavor — though how these scholars discovered this fact is best left unsaid. Consequently, drakes and Hruks have been known to form if not friendships, amicable truces. In terms of disposition, drakes are not very pleasant under the best of conditions — and when rudely roused by obnoxious humans intruding upon its den? They're rather surly, to say the least.

"Ohhhhh," Felix said as the beast rose to its full height; its shoulder was on level with Derek's head, and Derek by most measures was not a small man.

Have I mentioned that drakes could, on a less impressive scale than their gargantuan draconian brethren, breathe fire? Not many people are aware of this ability.

Derek and Felix certainly weren't.

Fear not, dear reader. I have not brought you so far only to end my tale aborning with the untimely and unseemly demise of our good heroes — nor have I glossed over their harrowing fight for survival against the irate drake but merely spared you the disappointment of witnessing one of Derek and Felix's decidedly less impressive battles.

Despite the drubbing received by the leads in our drama, Derek and Felix escaped with their pride more bruised and battered than their bodies, and that is the sort of injury that may be easily soothed with a pint or three at the local pub (as you shall witness momentarily).

For now, however, let us look in on the adventurers as they return to their point of origin for this more or less successful assignment: Ambride Manor, the opulent and extravagant home to Lord Spendle, he who sent Derek and Felix upon their errand with the promise of a reasonable reward.

"The horn!" Spendle cried as Felix opened the chest with a lack of ceremony, for exhaustion from the long journey to and from Mount Rihon — and all the fighting in-between — had claimed as its first victim Felix's sense of the theatrical. Spendle gingerly lifted the horn and held it up to the late afternoon light beaming through a series of tall windows lining his great hall, where the kindly lord of Ambride regularly held magnificent feasts for esteemed guests. The horn appeared as it did when Lord Spendle first packed it away for transport to Lord Paradim of Somevil: gleaming and spotless — the polar opposite of our heroes, who had yet to rinse away the grime of their labor. Ne'lan is not such a magical world that hot baths are readily available in its forests.

"And not a scratch on it," Spendle said as if he were expecting otherwise. "Well done, gentlemen! Well done indeed!"

"All in a day's work, m'lord," Derek rasped, his throat raw and parched. His mouth tasted like he had polished off a severely overcooked steak — as well as the ashes of the fire upon which it was severely overcooked.

"You have no idea what this means to us," Spendle said. "This drinking horn has been in my family for generations, and I promised the horn to Lord Paradim as a dowry for marrying my daughter Alyssa."

Alyssa was pretty enough, but she had a face that seemed most at home set in an expression of sour disapproval — and in this moment her face was extremely comfortable. Lord Spendle's chamberlain Elmore, unusually young to hold so important a position within a warden's household, smiled as would a man who'd received a birthday gift of questionable taste, yet as a matter of decorum, he could not allow himself to make the appropriate retching sound. Conroy, captain of the household guard, might have had an opinion, but one would never know it by his face, ever an unmoving mask of stern indifference.

"Paradim refused to proceed with the marriage unless he received the horn — a matter of pride, you know — but now that you've retrieved it, the marriage can proceed!" Spendle turned to drink in his daughter's thin, forced smile. "Isn't that wonderful, my dear?"

"Marvelous."

Felix felt the chill through his worn leather cuirass.

"I'm going to send a message to Lord Paradim right now to tell him the good news!" Spendle said, clapping his hands like a little boy who just discovered the entertainment value of daddy cursing after striking his thumb with a hammer. "Elmore, please see to these gentlemen's payment. Captain Conroy, if you'll kindly secure the horn..."

Conroy moved, dispelling any notions that he might have in reality been a remarkably lifelike statue.

"One moment, Lord Spendle," Felix said.

"Tactfully..." Derek said.

"Why weren't we told about the drake?"

"The what?" Spendle said.

"The drake. The one guarding the horn. You told us about the Hruks at the old river and in the woods, and the troll at the front gate, and the guardhouse — even though there was a *teeeeensy* discrepancy between how many Hruks you said would be there and how many there actually were — why did you not mention the friggin' drake in the cave?"

"Tactfully," Derek said.

"I knew nothing about a drake, Mr. Lightfoot," Spendle said in earnest. "Elmore? Did your sources mention a drake?"

Elmore cleared his throat. "That particular detail might have slipped my mind, my lord."

Felix reddened. "Slipped your —?! You motherfu —"

"Tactfully!"

"Oh, dear. I wonder if that's why the first four expeditions never returned," Spendle pondered aloud. "Did you defeat it?"

"Let's just say there were no real winners in that fight," Felix said — tactfully.

"Mm. Well, what matters is you're returned and you've recovered my horn! Now, if you'll excuse me, gentlemen, I have happy news to share. Elmore, their compensation?"

"Of course, my lord."

Spendle departed, mumbling merrily to himself about weddings and feasts and grandchildren and advantageous political allegiances.

Conroy bent to take the chest, only to have the lid slam shut under Felix's boot. "Mr. Elmore," Felix said. "I'm sure your...*memory lapse* was completely accidental, and you fully intended to tell us about the drake, but seeing as you didn't, I think that violates the conditions of our original contract — and as such, I think we're entitled to a little extra compensation. You know, so our payment is commensurate with the increased risk we faced. Say, double?"

"No," Elmore said. "You'll receive two hundred gold coins, as we agreed on, and you'll be grateful for it."

"Yeah? Then maybe we won't hand over the horn until we renegotiate the contract to our satisfac—"

For a man who did not move frequently, Conroy, when suitably motivated, could move quickly and fluidly; Felix did not realize Conroy had drawn his sword until it was resting on the back of his neck, right below the shallow depression where skull and spine met.

"Maybe we'll take our payment and be on our way," Felix said airily.

Elmore threw a sack of coins at Derek's feet. "A pleasure doing business with you."

Felix held his profane tirade in check until he and Derek exited the great hall and entered the safety of the grand foyer, which boasted bold acoustics that lent Felix's outburst a certain majesty.

"I know, I know," Derek said.

"That wasn't an unreasonable request, was it? I mean, all I asked for was something extra for our troubles, y'know? A little show of gratitude?"

As Felix said this, Alyssa, followed by Elmore as closely as by her own shadow, burst through the great hall's grand double doors. "Wait!" she called out, sprinting up to the adventurers.

The flickering ember of hope for a more profitable conclusion was cruelly extinguished when Alyssa's dainty hand landed broadside on Felix's cheek and, like a flat stone on a still lake, skipped off and landed again with equal force on Derek's cheek, leaving behind clean spots in their second skins of filth.

"Do you know how much grief I went through to get rid of that damned horn?!" Alyssa screeched. "Now I have to marry that fat, sweaty, hairy oaf Paradim thanks to you two IDIOTS!"

Her dramatic exit was very dramatic indeed — and yet undermined by Elmore sliding into a parallel course of travel and, with no hint of subtlety, laying a hand upon her firm left cheek.

"That's gratitude for you," Derek sighed.

## TWO
## A Pale Woman on a Dark Path

Allow me to indulge in a tried and true technique of the storyteller's craft and detail a moment in time concurrent with the events that I have just described. This is an example of, as we say in the trade, a non-linear narrative. It's a wonderful way to convey artfully vital information that, really, one should have presented a bit earlier.

I take you now to the road leading from — well, from many places, for no road leads to but a single destination, but for our immediate purposes, this road leads from Oson, the grandest of cities in Asaches — the largest, most advanced, and most civilized of the six continents of Ne'lan — to the smaller but, in its own way, quite magnificent city of Ambride. It is a well-traveled road, but like many paths in life, it has its periodic barren stretches.

It is upon one such barren stretch, in the fading light of sunset, that a pivotal event within the greater scheme of this story occurred while Derek and Felix were feeling Lady Alyssa's, *ahem,* displeasure. This event involves a dark lady by the name of Erika

Racewind — and by dark I refer to her demeanor, not her complexion, for Erika is of the elves of the Clan Boktn, a rugged, bellicose, some say nigh-barbaric segment of Ne'lan's elven population. Most elves are fair, but those of the Clan Boktn have skins the colorless hue of a winter frost, and for this simple quirk of the cosmos, other clans roundly shun them. Humankind is not so unfair and instead chooses to resent the elves of Clan Boktn for their reliably unpleasant dispositions — a more reasonable stance, say I. After all, one cannot choose to be pink or pale, but one *can* choose not to act like an ass.

Yet there are those who prize a no-nonsense, all-business attitude and will not hesitate to put these energies to good use — for example, High Lord Ograine, ruler of all Asaches, who years earlier took our lady Erika into his employ as his personal bodyguard. Her temperament has proven a benefit to High Lord Ograine, for during her tenure as his protector, she has personally and without aid slain four assassins — and severely injured one innocent soul who came at her master wielding in a threatening manner what she later learned was a pie server. She has not been allowed back in that particular restaurant since.

Erika would normally never leave her lord's side, but these were not normal circumstances, and High Lord Ograine deemed her talents necessary to safeguard a very precious cargo, now secured inside the hulking horse-drawn carriage upon which she rode. Next to her sat a driver whose name she'd not bothered to learn, for that might have invited the mindless chit-chat that often accompanies long journeys. She needn't have worried, for he was very businesslike and preferred to focus on controlling the four thundering destriers pulling the carriage. The sextet of mounted guards flanking the transport were too far away to engage them in conversation, so Erika enjoyed relative peace — a peace broken only by the rattle of carriage wheels on the compacted dirt road, the steady tattoo of hoofbeats, and the choked scream of a guard as he took an arrow to the face.

She cursed to herself; she hadn't expected this so soon...

"AMBUSH!"

Her cry alerted her companions to the danger but also acted as an attack signal for her unseen assailants. Numerous shafts shrieked out of the dark woods from all directions, stinging the guards who had brought with them only their swords — useless weapons against distant attackers. Erika was not so shortsighted; she took up her longbow, a slender but deceptively powerful elven bow capable of punching an arrow through stout plate armor at impressive distances. She scanned the woods for flashes of movement and, with a speed and fluidity of motion of which only elves are capable, returned fire — but she knew luck would only favor her for so long against such odds.

"Get us out of here!" Erika screamed.

"Summon Lord Spendle," Erika said to the young footman, who stared in awe at the mighty destriers. The horses had shown more fortitude than their human companions had by ignoring the many arrows jutting from their bodies just long enough that they might dutifully ferry their cargo to safety. Their task completed, the animals sank to the ground and closed their eyes.

"Who may I say is calling?" the lad stammered. Such inquiries were proper protocol, but in this instance, it felt foolish to ask.

"Tell him Erika Racewind, sworn protector of High Lord Ograine, is here and requires sanctuary."

The footman shifted his gaze to Erika and continued to gawk; he'd never met an elf of the Clan Boktn before. He led a sheltered life.

"Hey! Am I not speaking English?" Erika barked.

(Technically, she was not speaking English but the common tongue of Asaches, which has been liberally translated for your convenience. You're welcome.)

She jumped down from the carriage, which now resembled an expertly hand-carved pincushion, and stood nose-to-nose with the footman. "I said get your ass inside and get Lord Spendle. Now."

The footman glanced past Erika to the driver, who sat bolt-upright in his seat, his face surprisingly placid in light of his recent experience. "Is he okay?" the footman said.

As if in answer, the driver pitched forward to display his newly acquired collection of arrows, which he carried in his back.

"He's fine," Erika said.

Elmore studied Erika with the quiet disgust of a man who'd chanced upon fresh roadkill — or of a priss whose early bedtime had been thwarted by a very rude elf who looked like she counted barroom brawling among her hobbies. She was a striking young woman, admittedly, with long white hair shot through with streaks of black, presently twisted into a braid that fell almost to her tailbone. Her face reminded him of a porcelain doll's, pale and perfect, save for an odd tattoo: a design in gray that described a gentle arc below her right eye and ended in two small prongs that suggested eyelashes.

"I suppose I should offer you some refreshment," Elmore sniffed. "Would you care for anything? Wine? Beer? Puppy blood?"

"Boy, you'd better lose the attitude," Erika said. Elmore stiffened; the threat *Or else I'll snap your spine over my knee* was implicit.

Satisfied that Elmore was in his place, Erika took a seat on the edge of a massive banquet table, one of three curved tables that ringed the great hall to form a sort of arena in the center — a performance area for bards and jesters during formal dinners. She did not rise, as etiquette demanded, for Lord Spendle as he bustled into the hall, wearing an enormous fur robe that could still fit the grizzly from which the hide had been forcibly taken. Conroy drew his sword upon spying Erika and moved to intercept her. She held her peace.

"Remove your sword belt," he said in a most impressively commanding monotone.

"Oh, Conroy, really," Spendle said. "That's utterly unnecessary; I know this woman."

"But my kind can't be trusted," Erika said in Conroy's direction, almost as a dare. "Everyone knows that."

"Nonsense," Spendle said. "What brings you to my house, Miss Racewind?"

"Four dying horses," Elmore said, "which are

bleeding all over the courtyard."

"What?"

"My carriage was ambushed," Erika said, "in the woods about five miles outside the city. My driver and escorts were killed. I need sanctuary for the night, four fresh horses, and a dozen armed guards — your most trustworthy men — to accompany me to my destination."

"Now see here..." Elmore began. Erika silenced him with a look.

Deciding that a touch of politesse might be in order, Erika said, "I realize I'm asking a lot, Lord Spendle, but I'm on..." She paused; *important business* was a fantastic understatement, yet she hesitated to divulge the sensitive details of her mission — at least in present company. "I need to speak to you in private."

"I trust Elmore and Conroy implicitly," Spendle said.

"I don't," Erika said. "I can't. I mean no offense, Lord Spendle, but I shouldn't even trust you — but if you insist on knowing the nature of my mission..."

"I'm afraid it's a moot point, my dear. I could provide a horse or two, but most of my personal household guard are with my wife in Idlerouh. Visiting family, you know," he added by way of an explanation.

"You have *no one* you can spare?"

"We're running on a skeleton crew," Conroy said, "and I am not about to leave the manor unmanned, for you or anyone."

Spendle shrugged as if it were not within his power to override the man.

"I need to be on the road at first light. Are there any reputable mercenary guilds?" she asked, loathe to consider that avenue but lost for another. It would take a courier several hours to return to Oson to fetch replacement guards, a few hours to ready a new escort, and several more for them to return — assuming neither courier nor guards were caught in the same lethal crossfire that had created her current predicament.

"Not in Ambride. The nearest guilds are in Somevil, but I wouldn't regard them as reputable," Spendle said softly, as if fearful one of the thuggish guildmasters might overhear his assessment. "But perhaps you could inquire in some of the local inns and publick houses. Adventurers pass through regularly, looking for work."

"Just look for the drunkest of the drunken idiots in the room," Elmore said.

"No no, that's not — oh!" Spendle said with a snap of his fingers. "The two gentlemen who recovered my horn! They did excellent work, and at a very reasonable price."

"Competent men?" Erika said, resigning herself. "Trustworthy?"

"Very competent, very trustworthy. Wouldn't you say, Elmore?"

*No* was the answer that first formed on his lips, but then Elmore considered how Derek and Felix's unexpected success had so neatly confounded the plan he and Alyssa had laid — a plan devised to thwart an arranged marriage neither of them wanted consummated.

"This mission of yours — exceptionally dangerous?" Elmore inquired.

"I lost six of High Lord Ograine's finest guards already."

"Then I can think of two people no better suited to aid you," Elmore said with a devilish grin, "than Derek Strongarm and Felix Lightfoot."

## THREE
### Gazing into the Future through the Bottom of a Glass

Ambride is a city of quality known throughout Asaches for its many academic societies, both mundane and magical; its stately residential manor houses; and a thriving, if pretentious, artistic community. Any work, fine or performing, that did not bear the labels *minimalist, experimental,* or *interpretive* was regarded as culturally worthless. It was the kind of city in which even its most lowbrow culinary establishment was ten times finer than the finest of restaurants in a lesser city.

It is in Ambride's least respectful publick house, The Perfect, that we now find our heroes as they partake of the time-honored tradition of drowning one's sorrows in tankards of beer deep enough to drown a cat in.

"To getting screwed again," Felix said, too exhausted to properly hoist his tankard for the toast. Derek, the son of a career blacksmith from a long line of career blacksmiths, did not share that problem.

"To making it out alive again," he said, tipping the mug to his lips.

"Barely."

"We've had closer calls," Derek said, accurately, "and even you have to admit the pay was decent this time, all things considered."

"Not decent enough for almost getting barbecued. And I'm sick of *decent* being the best we can do," Felix grumped. "And I'm sick of always getting sucked into other people's horseshit. Did you see that little thing with Elmore and Alyssa?"

"I saw. They weren't what you'd call discreet."

"And they practically confessed they were behind the theft in the first place."

"I don't think they —"

"Oh, come on! Think about it a minute: Alyssa and Elmore have a thing going, Alyssa gets thrown into an arranged marriage, her father offers up something irreplaceable as a dowry...she knows if the horn got stolen or went missing, the marriage would be called off..."

"You don't think Spendle wouldn't just offer something else for the dowry?"

"He might want to, because he's looking at a political deal that would give him a foot in the door to expand his reputation into Somevil — though Gods know why; the place is a dump — and Paradim might accept something else, because he'd still be getting a hot trophy wife out of the deal...but!" Felix said, raising a finger for emphasis. "There's the matter of their personal honor to consider. You know how these wardens are: they'd sooner lose all their money and land than let their poor fragile pride get bruised. If Spendle promised the horn, a priceless family heirloom, he wouldn't back out of that promise, and Paradim wouldn't allow himself to accept anything less."

"Hm. Compelling theory," Derek said, "until you get to the part where Alyssa and Elmore hire a bunch of dumb Hruks to steal the horn."

"It's possible."

"But unlikely. Those things can't count to twenty-one unless they're naked."

"They raided a small caravan, Derek. A bunch of ten-year-olds armed with sharp sticks can raid a caravan. All someone needed to do was send word that a carriage carrying something valuable would be at a certain place at a certain time, and let the Hruks do what they do best: raise hell and steal stuff. It's actually brilliant in its way."

"It's unlikely is what it is."

Bullmoose — a beefy black mastiff that acted as The Perfect's mascot and chief peacekeeper — plopped a head the size, weight, and approximate shape of an anvil into Derek's lap, quietly demanding his leftovers — but as his dinner had yet to arrive, Derek could only give the dog a vigorous scratching behind his ears. With this, Bullmoose was satisfied for the present.

"My point is we got played for suckers, again, and I've had it," Felix said. "Really. Had it."

"What do you suggest we do? Retire?"

"*Pft*. If that were remotely an option..."

"But it isn't. So maybe what we need to do is simply be more discriminating in choosing our clients. Most of the time we take work from whoever has money to throw our way, so we're bringing this on ourselves in a sense."

"We can be as choosy as we want, it won't stop clients from lying about why they're really hiring us," Felix said, and on this point Derek could not disagree.

"Besides, we're not rich enough to enjoy the luxury of picking and choosing our work." He snapped his fingers, announcing the arrival of a revelation. "One big score, that's all we'd need, something to give us a, what do you call it, a nest egg."

"Well, look," Derek said as Bullmoose's contented drool soaked through his pants, "we got two hundred from this job, and that'll last us a while if we don't go crazy with our spending. You need to buy some more arrows, but the rest of our equipment is intact — dirty, but intact — so all we have to worry about is room and board. If we keep an eye on our money, we could go a month, maybe six weeks before we'd *have* to take another job. Let's use that time to put out some feelers, see what's out there for work, and check out potential clients before we accept anything to make sure the job's legit. If we don't find a nest egg job, then we look for ones with a good return for low risk to keep us on our feet until our big score comes along. What do you say?"

"Or," Felix said, retracing his thoughts, "we call it quits."

"You're not serious."

"Maybe the Gods are trying to tell us we're not meant to be adventurers and we're too stupid to listen. What if all these close calls have been a warning? Some higher power trying to give us a chance to get out before we get ourselves killed?"

"I don't buy that," Derek said, and he doubted that Felix, a dedicated agnostic, truly did either.

This heady philosophical debate consumed the next few hours, during which time our heroes consumed several cold lagers. When Erika Racewind at last arrived at The Perfect, they were in fine shape to make an indelible first impression.

Erika's entrance made its own impression upon The Perfect's clientele, whose respective conversations fell to a hush and, regardless of the previous topic, immediately turned toward the elf of the Clan Boktn — a rare and not necessarily welcome sight in Ambride. Long accustomed to such reactions, Erika approached the bar and addressed Fenster Dott, The Perfect's endearingly gruff proprietor — one of only two known varieties of innkeeper; his father Oscar, the original proprietor, had been of the endearingly jolly variety.

"Can I help you?" Dott said with the same uninterested tone he took with everyone.

"I'm looking for Derek Strongarm and Felix Lightfoot," she said. "Lord Spendle said they'd be here," she added, hoping this would grease a wheel or two.

Dott nodded in their direction. "Don't start trouble," he warned, "or you answer to Bullmoose."

Bullmoose, on cue, delivered a headbutt to Erika's buttocks and *wurf*ed at her softly.

"I'll watch my step," Erika said, more to Bullmoose than Dott.

"See you do," Dott said. "Bullmoose hasn't eaten yet, and he isn't fussy about white meat."

"Funny," she said.

Erika wondered if Spendle and Elmore might be playing a cruel joke on her. Derek did not look like a professional warrior; he looked like someone on a tight budget attempting to impersonate a knight errant. She could discern little about the man's partner, who from this angle appeared to be merely a head attached to a ratty cloak, that head resting precariously on the edge of his tankard.

"Derek Strongarm?" Erika said, approaching the table.

"What? Yes. Hi! What?" Derek said, turning a mildly unfocused gaze toward Erika. Up close she could see that Derek was of sturdy physical stock, but he had a face that could not hold an intimidating expression if his life depended on it — a country boy, if she wasn't mistaken (which she wasn't).

"My name is Erika Racewind. I'm in need of men to accompany me on a mission of great importance and urgency. Lord Spendle recommended you."

"He did? Hey, that was nice of him," Derek said to Felix, who was deep in his beer coma and beyond hearing. "Sit down. Tell us what you need."

She remained standing. "Shouldn't you wake him up first?"

"Yeah, good idea. Felix? Hey. Felix. Client. Felix."

Receiving no response, Derek yanked away the load-bearing tankard. Felix's head struck the heavy oaken table with a disturbing thump and, with the resilience of a child's rubber ball, bounced into an upright position. "What?" he said. "Yes. Hi! What? Ow."

"We have a client."

"*Potential* client," Erika corrected.

Felix followed the sound of the voice. His jaw fell open.

"She wants to hire us," Derek said.

"Uhh...okay. For what?"

"I need men to help me guard something I'm

transporting cross-country. That's all you need to know and that's all I'll tell you. The pay's two thousand gold, each, and part of that is payment for keeping your mouths shut. This is a no-questions-asked deal, so take it or leave it."

"Uh-huh," Felix said. "I see. Well. Um. Do you mind if I, y'know, talk this over with my partner in private?"

"Go ahead."

"I don't like it," Felix told Derek. "She's one of those ghostface elves and they're not trustable...wait, trustable? Trustworthy? Trustable? You can't trust 'em. We shouldn't take the job. Tell her to go piss up a rope."

Derek did the only thing he could in this situation and buried his head in his hands to hide his shame, for Felix had forgotten the cardinal rule of shielding your conversation from unwanted listeners: don't hold the conversation with the unwanted listener standing right there.

"Shit!" Felix said, starting. "Derek! She was eavesdropping on us! Told you y'can't trust her!" he said in a conspiratorial normal speaking voice.

"This was a bad idea," Erika said.

"No!" Derek leapt to his feet and grabbed Erika by the arm. He towered over the elf by two heads; she had to look up to glower at him. "No, look, I'm sorry about Felix, he's a little drunk."

"Yes I am," Felix said.

"I suspect that's a normal state for the two of you," Erika said.

"No, no, it isn't," Derek said. "We were celebrating not getting killed. We're normally perfectly sober."

"Because we normally can't afford booze," Felix said.

"Not helping..."

"Sorry."

Derek released Erika and held his hands up, the universal gesture for *Please hold on while I get my thoughts in order, sorry for the wait, your business is important to me.*

"Here's the thing: my partner has nothing against you personally. Really," Derek said, praying Felix would hold his tongue. "But we've had a run of clients hiring us under deceptive circumstances, so when you come to us with a mysterious no-questions-asked job offer, you can understand why we'd be skeptical, right?"

Erika made a *come here* gesture. Derek bent that she might reach his ear. "You'd be protecting something *very* important," she whispered. "Something I have to deliver, intact, to Hesre by the end of the month. I can't tell you anything more. Two thousand gold each to get me there safely. Take it or leave it."

"...Hesre," Derek said.

"*Hesre?*" Felix said. "Oh, no way in hell. No. Absolutely not. No. Way. In. Hell."

"Four thousand gold each," Erika said.

"Now, when I said 'No way in hell...'"

## FOUR
## The Journey of Several Hundred Miles
## Begins with a Single Misstep

Erika's generous offer fell on many a deaf ear within The Perfect and in the neighboring inns; when she returned to Ambride Manor to check on her cargo — which had been left in the care of Captain Conroy and the remaining house guard, a small but formidable force — she had secured the services of Derek and Felix and no more. They were unsatisfactory in quantity and quality, she decided, but they would suffice until they passed through the next populated town on their route, where she could make fresh entreaties.

Our heroes, as instructed, rose at dawn, packed their few belongings, and trudged up the hill toward Ambride Manor. That is to say, a bright-eyed and bushy-tailed Derek marched up at a smart pace, whistling merrily, while Felix attended to the trudging, burdened by the unwanted farewell gift the previous night's revelry had bestowed upon him.

"I hate that you're never hung-over," Felix said, not more than a little jealous.

"You could never be hung-over too if you didn't

drink so much."

"You drank as much as I did."

"I weigh more than you," Derek said, which was true by about seventy pounds — most of it muscle — but Derek's heritage also imparted upon him the ability to imbibe heroic quantities of alcohol with, at worst, modest immediate or lasting effects. He was among the latest generation in a long line of hearty drinkers, but he never cared to boast about this trait, especially not in front of Felix on those occasions when he was in a state to complain how bright and loud everything was.

"This feels like a bad idea," Felix said.

"You didn't think so last night."

"That was drunk, greedy Felix talking. Now I'm sober Felix, and sober Felix thinks this is a bad idea."

"If this is because she's Clan Boktn..."

"It's not," Felix half-lied. "I think we're setting ourselves up again by taking a job we know nothing about."

"We *thought* we knew everything about our last job," Derek pointed out. "We've taken a lot of jobs where we thought our employer was being completely up-front. So in a way, Erika's being more honest than most."

"That's a twisted way of looking at things."

"Sorry, am I stepping on your toes?"

"Ha."

"Do you want to back out? It's not too late to back out, you know."

Felix, thinking about the hefty reward, let out a long sigh. "Yeah it is."

"All right, then. Let's get to work."

This morning the front gate was closed, chained,

and protected by two armed guards; none of this was true yesterday when Derek and Felix returned from their quest. One of the guards demanded their names and made them wait outside at a respectable distance from the gate. He ran inside while his companion and his pole axe enforced the buffer. He returned immediately with Erika, who was dressed and armed, her sword and knife hanging at her hips, but not yet in her leather armor.

"Let them in," she said. The guards complied. Once the partners were inside the perimeter, they resealed the gate.

"Good morning," Derek said.

"You're on time," Erika said, barely masking her surprise.

"What's first on the agenda?"

"Come with me. I want to show you what we're up against."

Growing up on a farm, Derek was adept at recognizing many scents particular to an agricultural setting that might escape a layman's notice. Ambride Manor's stables smelled powerfully of horses, of their natural musky scent, of dirt and hay and manure — nothing at all out of the ordinary. But beneath that, Derek detected an out-of-place odor, sharp and warm and coppery.

"Did you lose horses?"

Erika stopped short and shot Derek a look. Her face softened, and she said, "Four."

"Did they go quickly?"

"I made sure of that."

Derek nodded solemnly.

Erika led them to her carriage, secluded deep within the stables by a team of household servants. Rolling the carriage away from prying eyes was no mean feat, for this was a Wensley Moste Grande.

Its creator, master carriage-maker D. Richardson Wensley, designed the first Moste Grandes to be practical, not pretty; he intended the carriage as a transport for valuable material goods rather than people, so his earliest renditions were plain and dull. An early commission for a custom Moste Grande led to the aesthetic changes that are now standard for the model. The less visually appealing version, which is still in production, was redubbed the Wensley Grande.

The redesigned Moste Grands quickly became a favorite among nobles, high-ranking city officials, business magnates, and other Very Important People (real and self-styled) because of its stately appearance — and for the security it provided. The frame was stout oak. The veneer was two-inch-thick mahogany treated with a special lacquer — the formula for which was a proprietary family secret — that added to its armor-like qualities. The treated wood was also remarkably resistant to combustion. Heavy steel mesh covered its few windows, and those screens could be covered both inside and out by thick shutters.

These, Derek knew, were difficult vehicles to damage.

He ran his fingers over the countless nicks and gouges marring the carriage's otherwise mirror-smooth finish. Some were long and thin and superficial, the kind of damage that could be removed by a vigorous buffing; others were like miniscule pinpoint craters; still others formed small, deep, perfect crosses — signs of arrows that had, respectively, struck at an unfavorable angle and glanced off the surface or had struck true but failed to pierce the chassis. Several shafts had achieved some degree of penetration and remained lodged in the wood. Had this been a lesser carriage, they would have punched through the walls and continued on to strike anyone inside.

"Close-range shots," Derek said to Felix, fingering one of the deeper scars.

"Or arrows shot from a more powerful bow," Felix said.

Derek turned to Erika for clarification, but she did not indulge his curiosity. "Lord Spendle said he could spare us a couple of horses," she said.

"You're going to need more than two horses to move a Moste Grande," Derek said.

"He offered two, we'll make do with two. We don't have much choice," Erika said, repeating what was fast becoming the slogan for her journey.

"Then you'll need a lighter carriage."

"Not an option. As you can see, we need the protection."

"Okay, but you have to know even a pair of solid destriers won't be able to get up too much speed," Derek said, circling the carriage. "Not enough to cover the distance to Hesre in four weeks. You'd work them to death. Then you have this problem..."

Erika followed Derek's pointing finger to the right front wheel. Three of the thick wooden spokes had lost chunks the size of Derek's thumbnail while the wheel itself still had an arrowhead lodged in it.

"This wheel's been weakened," Derek said. "Not a lot, but that damage is going to get worse over time.

That's a common flaw in earlier Moste Grande models, before they switched to iron spokes."

"Will it make it to Hesre?" Erika asked, getting a shrug in return.

"If we take it easy? Maybe...but if we're running on two horses we'll be taking it easy whether we want to or not."

"Damn."

"Question."

"Was there something about *no questions asked* you didn't understand?"

"Does that apply to questions that might affect our chances of successfully delivering your cargo?"

Erika chewed her bottom lip in irritation. "What?"

"Your cargo. You're trying to transport it secretively, correct? Without drawing attention to yourself?"

"That's the idea."

"Then you might want to consider removing that very large and colorful family crest."

The crests, one on each door, were exquisite examples of the woodcarver's art. Ribbons of wood swooped and swirled and spiraled around a central oval, quartered in alternating red and blue. Upon this was carved a disembodied hand that, thanks to an equally skilled paint job, looked unnervingly like an actual human hand had been attached to the carriage. Felix pressed his face close to the crest. By the way the scrollwork glowed under the morning light, he determined that the ribbons surrounding the crest were gilded, not simply painted gold. The whole of the design was undeniably eye-catching — a veritable beacon.

Erika's cheeks turned a shade of hot pink made

all the more vivid against the backdrop of her white skin. Derek reckoned she'd been so absorbed in planning the larger elements of her trek, she'd overlooked that minor but revealing detail and now felt a fool and an amateur for it.

"Get me an adze and I'll take care of it," Derek said. "It'll ruin the carriage — "

"Fine," Erika said after a moment's hesitation. "Do what you have to."

Opulent manor houses are continually maintained to preserve their all-important air of affluence, and repairs are affected immediately and often by skilled tradesmen kept on retainer by the owner. Such is the case with Ambride Manor, which had on-premises a large and well-stocked tool shed belonging to the home's on-call carpenter. Derek stripped off his armor to allow greater freedom of motion, in the process revealing a muscular physique developed through a life steeped in farming and blacksmithing and later in warfare. He went to work, lopping off great chunks of hardwood with each swing. The hand lost its fingers with the first blow. The scrollwork followed. Felix, under the pretext of clearing the area, collected these bits, intending to salvage as much of the precious gold leaf as possible. Within a few minutes, one crest had been removed. The resulting scar was as prominent as the crest, but at least it was anonymous.

"WHAT ARE YOU DOING TO MY CAR-RIAGE?!"

The young man who shrieked this, in such a high register that every dog within a quarter-mile cocked its head in alarm, gawped at Derek with a mix of shock and fury. He temporarily lost his voice and gesticulated incoherently at Derek, at the coach, at the pile of fresh excelsior at Derek's feet, back at Derek, then at Erika as if expecting her to translate his spasms.

"The hell!?" he managed.

"Gentlemen," Erika said. "Meet my cargo."

# FIVE
## Large Headaches are Often Born of Small Annoyances

The boy, a lad of no more than fifteen, turned his slack-jawed expression on Erika. "THIS is my new guard?" he said, flapping a hand at Derek. "This...this *lunk*? Where did you find this? On a dairy farm?"

"I grew up on a farm," Derek said. This did not impress the irate young man one whit.

"What happened to the guards Spendle was supposed to provide?"

"Lord Spendle can't spare anyone," Erika said. "I had no choice but to hire mercenaries."

"Adventurers for hire, if you don't mind," Felix said.

"And what are you supposed to be?" the boy demanded.

"I'm guessing I'm supposed to be one of the guys protecting your scrawny ass, you little snot."

"Hey! You can't talk to me that way! Do you know who I am?"

"*No,*" Erika said, "and he doesn't need to know who you are."

The boy narrowed his eyes and uttered a contemptuous grunt. "Great work, Racewind. Really. Bang-up job. Now will you tell me why the big goof with the axe is defacing my carriage?"

"It's an adze," Derek corrected.

"A necessary evil," Erika said. "The *big goof* rightfully pointed out the crests drew too much attention and should be removed. For your safety."

The boy considered Derek in this new light. "It can use tools, it talks, *and* it thinks for itself. Wow, what *can't* it do?"

"It can't bring itself to throttle a small child," Felix said. "Me, on the other hand..."

"Knock it off, the two of you," Erika said.

"I need breakfast," the boy announced and, with a final sneer, spun on his heel and marched back into Ambride Manor.

"And isn't he a bucketful of sunshine! Are we going to have to deal with that attitude the whole time?" Felix said.

"Yes," Erika said, turning to follow her charge. "So don't say you aren't earning your money."

"I don't know who that kid is, but I'll tell you right now, man, he smarts off to me one time too many and I'm cutting his tongue out and feeding it to Bullmoose."

"You don't want to do that," Derek said. "You don't know who he is? Seriously?"

"Should I?"

"He's only the most famous kid in Asaches." Felix shrugged. "How can you not know who he is?"

"I don't pay attention to current events, you know that."

"I'll give you a hint," Derek said in a hushed voice. "This crest I'm chopping into tinder? The Ograine family crest."

Felix processed this information immediately, but it took a second or two for his sense of belief to catch up. "Ograine? You mean that kid is —?"

"Uh-huh?"

"And he's en route to Hesre?"

"Uh-huh."

"Shit!"

"Uh-huh."

"Okay, taking this job? Officially the worst idea we've ever had. We need to bail out now."

Derek resumed chipping away the crest.

"Derek, no...the money isn't worth —"

"Not thinking about the money," Derek said. "Last night you wondered if our all our bad luck was because the Gods were trying to warn us that we weren't meant for the adventuring life. I'm wondering if the Gods are trying to tell us we're in this for the wrong reasons."

"Oh, please do explain this," Felix said, settling against the carriage.

"We've been accepting jobs from people acting out of selfish motivations," he said, the adze *thunk*ing in syncopation. "Lord Spendle wanted his expensive drinking horn recovered so he could marry off his daughter and increase his holdings. Lady Biscont wanted us to clear out her hunting lands of Hruks so she could go out and kill deer for fun with her rich friends. Governor Hispiel —"

"I get it, I get it. Your point?"

"My point: we *are* mercenaries. Sure, we've

drawn a line at taking thug jobs and assassination, but we haven't done anything all that noble — and ultimately, we *are* just doing it for the money. Maybe what the Gods are trying to tell us is that we need to start thinking past all this selfishness and pursue a more righteous path."

Felix never cared for Derek's occasional introspective forays; they usually rang of a wisdom belying his rustic origins but meant their already difficult path in life was not about to get any easier. Life, Felix mused, was so much less complicated when he lacked an annoying conscience whispering into his ear.

"You're following through on this no matter what I say or do," he said.

"Uh-huh."

"Fine," Felix muttered. "But when this job is done, you're buying me a tankard of ale I can bathe in."

"Fair enough," Derek said.

They found Erika and the boy in the great hall. The former sipped a mug of strong, bitter coffee grown in the warmer climes of Necic — Ne'lan's fifth largest continent for you geography aficionados — the latter ate with the gusto of a starving hog from a plate heaped high with bacon, eggs, and toast slathered in jam.

"Wow, that's quite a breakfast you have there, little fella," Derek said, taking a seat next to the lad. Derek threw a chummy arm around him. "My dad always said breakfast was the most important meal of the day."

"Get your hand off me," the boy said through a mouthful of eggs.

"Shouldn't talk with your mouth full, son," Derek said cheerfully. "It's not polite, especially in front of a lady."

"Stop touching me."

"Is the carriage ready?" Erika asked.

"As ready as it can be, unless we can find a replacement for that wheel, but Moste Grand wheels don't exactly grow on trees," he said, adding with a laugh aimed directly at the boy's ear, "well, I guess they kind of do, huh?"

"You're sweating on me," the lad groused.

"Little honest sweat never hurt no one, that's what my pa used to say," Derek said, dripping with more homespun charm than sweat — but only just. "Hey, you know what? We were never properly introduced. I'm Derek Strongarm and that's my friend Felix Lightfoot. What do we call you, buddy?"

"You can call him David," Erika said.

"All right then. Nice to meet you, Davey."

"David!" David squawked. "Racewind, get this oaf away from me!"

She was tempted to leave him right where he was; she was convinced Derek's excessive friendliness was a deliberate effort to needle the lad. "Mr. Strongarm, if you don't mind?"

"Sure thing," Derek said. He rose, leaving across David's back a stain like an impressionist artist's interpretation of a human arm, lovingly rendered in perspiration.

"Strongarm?" David said. "What sort of stupid name is that? No one's named Strongarm."

"That's my adventurer name."

"Your what?"

"It's some weird tradition for adventurers to adopt colorful names," Felix said. "Strongarm, Racewind..."

"Racewind is my real name," Erika said.

"Seriously?"

"It's elvish."

"Huh. Cool."

"Then what's your real name?" David inquired.

"Bla'smith," Derek said. "Casual form of Blacksmith, which is what my family's been for generations."

"Blay-smith?" David *tsked*. "That's even worse than your fake name. What about your partner? What's his adventurer name?"

"Lightfoot," Felix said, "but that's my real name too. It's not elvish."

"Uh-*huh*."

"Well, it's sort of my real name. See, I was an orphan so I never —"

"I didn't ask for your life story." David snatched up his plate and stalked off. "I'm going to finish this in my room. Let me know when it's time to go."

"We'll hit the road as soon as you're ready," Erika said.

"Sure acts like a spoiled rich kid," Felix murmured to Derek.

"So you figured it out," Erika said.

"I have no idea what you're talking about," Derek said. "I'm just a simple country boy, I don't —"

"Don't give me that. You're not as dumb as you look," she said — and coming from her, it did not sound much like a compliment. "But for your sake, let's pretend you are. Believe me, you're better off acting like you don't know anything. As of this moment your job is to keep your mouths shut, your eyes open, and your weapons ready. Is that understood?"

"Yes sir, ma'am, sir," Felix said, flicking a salute Erika's way.

Within the hour the quartet had gathered back at the carriage, to which had been attached by Lord Spendle's stablemen two massive shire horses: Bravia and Titania. The sight caused Derek to rethink his prediction of a slow journey; a typical destrier was an imposing beast to be sure, sturdy and strong, built to easily transport a man of war in full armor, but a destrier would have been dwarfed by these animals. David would need only to stoop slightly to walk beneath them.

"Look at you," Derek said with admiration, stroking Titania's muzzle. The female was a rich chestnut from head down to her legs, which ended in white. "You are a beautiful girl. You going to take good care of us? Huh?"

"At least we'll have a couple of friendly faces with us," Felix said. "Probably be better conversationalists, too."

"If you're done fondling the livestock," David said, trying to suppress his fear of the animals, "take your positions and let's go."

"You're on the box with me," Erika said to Derek. "Lightfoot, you're watching the rear."

"What's our route?" Felix said. "Oh, sorry, that was a question, wasn't it? Oops."

"I've mapped out a series of back roads that runs along the Grand Avenue. It's not as fast, but it'll keep us out of the public eye."

"Is that the smartest thing to do?" Derek wondered. "Traveling secluded back roads?"

"You'd rather we parade down the Grand Avenue in plain sight? Surrounded by people that might be looking for David?"

"That's my point: we'd be surrounded by people on a large, open road. On the back roads we'd be all by our lonesomes, and surrounded by woods where attackers could easily stage an ambush."

"You know," Felix added, "like the one that killed all your men."

Through gritted teeth Erika said, "Gentlemen, your input is neither requested nor appreciated. You were hired to do a job, and that's to protect him," she said, jerking a thumb at David.

"In other words," David said, "no backtalk from the help." He strode up to the men, hands behind his back, chest out, head up, frowning like an imperious general inspecting troops he'd decided well beforehand were failures and washouts. "You two are hired goons. Remember that. You handle the fighting, and leave the thinking to those of us skilled in it. Racewind!"

With that, David swept into the carriage and slammed the door shut.

"We're burning daylight," Erika said, offering no apologies on behalf of her master. "Let's get rolling."

## SIX
## The Uneventful First Day,
## Which Could Also Be Called the Calm
## Before the Storm

A word or two, if I may, about the Grand Avenue. This is the main thoroughfare in Asaches, a road an eighth of a mile in width and fourteen hundred miles in length, stretching from the capital city of Oson to the western city of Wecride. It was not laid through any conscious plan; early travelers discovered a relatively clean and uncluttered natural path — truly a path of least resistance — carving through the continent, and they followed it. For generations they followed it, and over those generations the grass was scoured away and the soil packed down until it was as hard as stone. Mankind assisted this evolution where needed, constructing sturdy stone bridges over intersecting rivers to save man and beast of burden alike an unnecessary mid-journey bath. Many towns and cities rose up along the Avenue to take full advantage of this natural trade route. On any given day, one will find the road bustling with those traveling on foot, by horse, by carriage.

The Grand Avenue also sprouted several shadow roads running roughly parallel to the main. These, for the most part, were safe enough and did not as a rule attract trouble, but bandits were more likely to haunt these secondary streets so far removed from the Grand Avenue, thus so far away from any passing commuters who might stop and offer assistance. This was not lost on Derek, but Erika had made it clear she did not desire his further advice on the matter, so for the present he would not offer it.

The Moste Grande rocked gently beneath them, the worst of the ruts and pits in this rougher stretch of road absorbed by an ingenious undercarriage constructed of thick steel strips layered one atop another to create a springy cushion. Felix, his bow resting across his lap, sat in the rear seat reserved for attendants. Erika sat at the reins, her focus on her surroundings rather than her borrowed horses; her eyes, so dark that they appeared as two black dots against the pale slate of her face, scanned the area constantly. Derek thought, woe be unto any cutthroats or ne'er-do-wells hiding in the sprawling fields of ankle-high grass that surrounded them on all sides. The nearest tree line was several hundred yards distant, within the range of a good longbow, but only just, and he had yet to meet an archer who could shoot with appreciable accuracy at such range. Rather than advising his elven companion to relax — advice he sensed would not be welcomed or heeded — Derek opted to begin chipping away at the dense wall of metaphorical ice separating him from his employer.

"Sooooooo," he said. "Clan Boktn, eh?"

"Obviously."

"Never been to City Boktn."

"I'd be stunned if you had."

"Nice place?"

"It's a big elven city."

"Hm," Derek said as if this was a point of great interest. "You have any family there?"

"..."

"Erika?"

"Technically. Look, I hate small talk. It annoys me."

"We're going to be on the road a long time..."

"Which is all the more reason for you to keep your mouth shut, because I don't want to listen to your inane prattle this entire trip."

The barb slid off Derek, who smiled in a gentle, disarming way that made Erika want to kick his teeth in. "You don't think it's important to get to know the people who're going to be watching your back?"

"No one watches *my* back."

"*No one* takes exception to that remark," Felix called out.

"No small talk," Erika reiterated. "End of discussion."

Derek leaned back, resting his elbows on the carriage roof. "*Ooooooohhhhhhhhhh,*" he began, tuning up. "*The road, the road, the road ahead is long and lonesome...*"

"All right! One thing," Erika said. "You get to tell me *one thing* about yourself."

"One thing each day," Derek said.

"Then you're quiet for the rest of the day. No talking, no singing — especially no singing."

"If that's what you want."

"Him too," Erika said gesturing toward Felix.

"Like I want to talk to you," Felix said.

"Agreed," Derek said.

"So go ahead and get it over with."

"Any requests?"

She shrugged. "Tell me how you two met."

"Oh," Derek said, disappointed. "I'm afraid that's not a very interesting story."

Indeed, it is not a very interesting story. If it were, this volume would have presented that adventure instead of the one I am now sharing now, yes?

Derek Strongarm and Felix Lightfoot, prior to their first meeting, had not insignificant experience in their respective trades — Derek as a member of the militia for the hamlet of Fath in the eastern Anstl region, Felix as — as I mentioned earlier — a protégé of Lars of the Gentle Fingers. Pivotal events in their separate lives, toward which I shall only hint for the nonce, drove them to seek new paths in life, and that in turn drove them quite coincidentally to answer a general summons for skilled adventurers to participate in what is known colloquially as a "dungeon dive." The mastermind behind this ill-fated expedition, the late Lord Darius Maxus of Ull, discovered on his land an ancient subterranean lair of unknown origin, and personally led a dozen men into this mystery with the promise of generous shares of the long-lost treasures he was certain they would locate within. The party had been in the labyrinth less than an hour before disaster struck in the form of a den of terrible creatures, the likes of which no man had ever seen before. The horrors overwhelmed the party, and of the dozen and one who descended into darkness, only Derek and Felix emerged — not unscathed but alive and grateful for that much.

Lord Maxus's son, Darius Maxus II, paid the men for their troubles and sent them on their way, and it was over the first of many drinks to celebrate their continued survival that Derek and Felix bonded. A fast friendship formed, and that became a partnership that has, as of this tale, lasted eighteen months.

"You're right," Erika said at the end of Derek's story. "That isn't very interesting."

"They can't all be winners," Derek said. "What about you?"

"What about me?"

"You want to tell us how you came to be in Lord Ograine's service?"

"He bought her," David said. Derek followed David's voice and saw his face pressed against a side window screen. Judging by his expression, he'd also found Derek's tale extremely dull.

"Bought her?"

"David," Erika said, "I'd appreciate it if you didn't —"

"What? Don't tell me you're ashamed of your culture," David said.

"With all due respect," she said, a threat in her voice, "that's my story to tell, not yours."

"*Pfft*," David said, disappearing into his carriage.

"Don't say a word," Erika said to Derek. "Don't say a damned word."

Around noon they rolled into Warow, a small but robust town at Ambride's western border, and had done so without incident, which Felix did not regard as a positive sign; an adventure without a little trouble at the outset only meant that, when the first challenge did at last arise, it would be that much worse. Felix liked his adversity doled out in frequent small portions.

The companions — I would not call them all friends at this early juncture — took lunch at a small publick house while the horses rested and took water. The mealtime conversation was lopsided. Derek and Felix chatted amiably, trading jokes for which only they knew the full context, recalling amusing episodes from past escapades, while Erika and David ate in silence, contributing nothing and wishing that their escorts would shut the hell up so they could eat in peace. David expressed this wish vocally and repeatedly but went ignored.

Erika had them back on the road within the hour for the express purpose of reaching before dark the town of Elesy, an affluent community in which High Lord Ograine had friends who had agreed to provide Erika and her entourage with comfortable lodgings for the night — possibly the last good beds they would sleep in for a long while. Their path would take them past but not into the cities of Newo and Aming for the same reasons Erika chose to eschew the Grand Avenue. Aming would also be the last major city they'd pass before adopting a more westerly tack toward Hesre. As they progressed westward from there, they would pass through and by countless villages large and small and growing ever smaller, many of them with no wardens of their own — local governors supervised these, if that much.

Before their departure, Derek paused to check the damaged carriage wheel. He saw nothing to suggest its state had worsened in their first few hours on the road, but he remained concerned for its long-term integrity. He recommended finding a wheelwright in Elesy. Erika said she would take it under advisement.

"In other words," Felix said to Derek on the side, "don't hold your breath."

Yet when they arrived in Elesy a half-hour after sundown, Erika instructed Derek to inquire about local wheelwrights. A few minutes in a tavern picked at random produced several recommendations for a gent by the name of Turner Goss, a master wheelwright whose work was on the higher end of the scale pricewise but of impeccable quality. More importantly, he worked quickly.

Not so quickly that he could produce a brand new wheel by the next morning, however, for Moste Grande wheels were of a unique design, and so he had none at hand to fit the carriage perfectly. There were several near matches in his stock that Goss said he could adapt to the Moste Grande, but that would delay their departure by a day — which impressed Derek, who knew what sort of work was involved, but not so the impatient Erika, who opted to have braces installed to reinforce the wheel.

They left the carriage with Goss and proceeded on foot to House Miggis, the stately home of Clarence Miggis, a dear old friend of High Lord Ograine who'd agreed to shelter Erika and her companions for a night. The footman on duty informed Erika that Miggis and his wife were not home at present but would return later in the evening, and in the meantime they had the run of the manor.

Felix took full advantage of this and, after locating the kitchen, hauled several cuts of meat out of a large steel chest for the purpose of making sandwiches — mainly for himself.

"Hey, Derek, check this out," he said. "It's one of those magic coldboxes I've heard about."

Derek stuck his hand inside. It was as chilly as a late fall morning, but unlike mundane coldboxes that used ice packed between an outer and inner wall, the cold here was maintained by a simple spell - though, in truth, there is little about magic that is simple. I shall expound upon this momentarily.

"That's neat," Derek said.

"This thing must have cost a small fortune."

"It did," David said. "My father paid ten thousand gold coins for his. It's much larger than that one, of course."

"Of course," Derek said.

"Man, isn't that a sweet racket?" Felix said. "Hell, we should learn magic so we can make coldboxes and soak rich rubes."

"My father is not a *rube*," David said hotly, "nor was he *soaked*. Magic is not a cheap service; he was charged an appropriate price."

"Horseshit he was. The guy who enchanted your coldbox? Betcha anything he wasn't the guy who actually crafted the spell. Betcha he just bought the info off someone else and now he's using it over and over to crank out coldboxes at an insane profit margin. What's it cost to make a steel box like this?"

"Three, four hundred for a standard coldbox, depending on the size, and that's mostly for the materials," Derek said, speaking from experience; he'd helped his father craft a few back in the day.

"There you go," Felix said. "A guy pays a few hundred for a coldbox, lays his whammy on it for no cost, sells it to daddy at a *ten thousand percent* profit margin — like I said: that's a sweet racket."

David rolled his eyes. "You know nothing about magic," he said.

While our heroes partake of their evening repast, I shall take this time to educate you about the nature of magic on Ne'lan. You might think that magic is a widespread knowledge, ancient in nature, that grants wielders of sufficient skill nigh-omnipotent power over all things, but that is not so. Magic is a relatively new phenomenon, an art less than four centuries old and still in its infancy. Practitioners are few and far between, for magic is not without risk, and only so many are willing to jeopardize life and limb in its service; thus the magical arts have evolved slowly. Early magic allowed simple manipulation of the basic elements, with lifeless air, earth, and fire falling into line before water, which teemed with life unseen — and had the first wizards known this, they might have come to realize sooner that living things do not bend to magical manipulation as readily. It should then come as no surprise that healing magic is the youngest and most unreliable of the schools.

Over the generations, as mankind delved ever deeper into this new realm of knowledge, cooperative bodies of wizards formed the first academies. These research hives attracted men and women of like minds on the nature of magic and how best to advance their craft, but soon the academies developed heated and often bitter rivalries. They took to hoarding their discoveries; each academy developed proprietary spells — sometimes achieving by differing methods the same effects as those of a rival academy, others resulting in wholly unique outcomes — and shared that information only with carefully selected students sworn to keep what they learned in the strictest confidence. But it was not unheard of for a wizard to breech this contract and sell or trade secrets with another — sometimes in service to the more noble pursuit of enlightenment and truth, sometimes for base mercenary reasons; as you've learned, a fellow can live comfortably indeed off the profits of a half-dozen coldboxes.

Let us return now to our protagonists who have finished their meal and been shown to their rooms by the butler, who did so with the expected level of snoot-iness and disdain. Though he too was a recipient of this treatment, David expressed his admiration for the but-ler's professionalism, marking the first time he had of-fered anyone anything resembling a compliment.

Felix, a night-owl by inclination, did not turn in. He stripped off his armor and weapons in his room and, after some wandering, stumbled upon the perfect place to unwind: the manor's impressive library, a re-pository for hundreds upon hundreds of books. A cav-ernous fireplace held audience for a set of high-backed chairs and, best of all, a liquor cabinet stocked with crystal decanters of exceptionally expensive brandy and single-malt whiskey. Felix chose one at random and poured a liberal serving into a snifter then grabbed the first book his hand fell upon: a treatise by a dwarven author on the vicissitudes of speculating in commodities — gold, iron ore, coal, et cetera. It was ex-ceptionally dry reading that, coupled with the brandy (which was marvelous), lulled Felix into a half-sleep —

from which he was awoken hours later by a piercing scream.

## SEVEN
## Spilling Blood is a Good Way to Wear out One's Welcome

The labyrinthine mansion baffled the source of the scream and stymied Felix's attempt to locate the same. It was by luck he found her sprawled across the carpeted foyer — and looming over her, a stranger holding a bloody hand axe. A fellow brandishing a sword entered the home behind him and a second sword-toting man behind him. He wondered how in his disarmed state he would contend with these intruders.

The answer to that question came as Derek, clad only in his breeches, bounded down the wide main staircase and hurtled past his partner, longsword drawn, though his first blow was struck by his bare foot. His kick lifted the lead attacker off the floor and launched him into his companions, and the three toppled to the floor.

"Get her clear!" Derek shouted.

Felix obeyed, grabbing the fallen woman, a matronly older lady, and dragging her toward the stairs. She had a savage wound across her forehead that bled liberally. Felix pawed at her neck for a pulse and found one, weak but regular.

Derek assumed a low guard. "Drop your weapons, fellas," he said to the trio as they disentangled themselves.

"Situation!" Erika shouted from somewhere upstairs.

"Three men, armed!"

"Could really use an extra hand here!" Felix added.

"I'm not leaving David unguarded!" Erika said.

"Yeah, well, screw you too."

"I got it, Felix," Derek said.

"I'd feel better if you'd just run 'em through already."

"I'm not going to kill a man unless I have to," Derek said in his infuriatingly chivalrous way.

The man with the axe regained his footing. He gave Derek a strange look, as though he were wholly indifferent to the events unfolding. "Wait, who are you?" he said in a drunken voice.

"I'll ask the questions, friend. Who sent you?"

"Wait, who are you?"

"What are you doing?" one of the axe man's companions said.

"Oh Gods no!" the other said with a lumbering step toward Derek.

"What are you doing?"

"Oh Gods no!"

"Wait, who are you?"

"Oh Gods no!"

"Can't be," Derek gasped.

The axe man raised his weapon, slowly and deliberately, granting Derek ample time to bring his fists, wrapped tightly around grip of his sword, up in a rising hammer-blow to his attacker's chin. Derek smashed the pommel into one swordsman's face and struck the other with an elbow to the temple. Neither of them made any effort to dodge the attacks. The second swordsman staggered a step then lunged forward with a wild overhead swing that carried his sword into the floor. Derek spun out of the way and, following his momentum, cut his foe's head free of his neck.

"What are you doing?" the remaining swordsman said, swiping at Derek. He deflected the blade and, with a quick flick, buried the tip of his sword in his foe's skull.

The axe man was undeterred by the loss of his comrades or of several front teeth; syrupy blood spilled over his bottom lip and oozed from a deep gash following the cleft of his chin. He charged at Derek like a man tumbling headfirst down a flight of stairs and swung. Derek caught his arm with one hand and drove the other, clenched hand into his face. Derek wrenched the axe away and backed his assailant into a wall, pinning him in place with a forearm across his throat. He did not struggle.

"Who are you?" Derek demanded. "Who sent you?"

"Wait, who are you?" the man said.

"What's your name?"

"Wait, who are you?"

"...What color are my eyes?"

"Wait, who are you?"

"Dammit," Derek said, followed by a soft prayer, followed by a swift decapitation.

---

"WHOA!" Felix cried. He knew Derek could be vicious in combat and utterly merciless when it came to dealing with Hruks, but he never once saw him strike down a helpless opponent. "Derek, what the hell?!"

"I did him a mercy," Derek said, and the remorseful note in his voice impelled Felix to believe him.

"What was wrong with him? He kept saying the same thing over and over."

"I noticed."

"Situation!" Erika called down.

"All clear," Derek said. "Follow my lead," he said to Felix.

Erika descended, David at her heels. He went as white as his guardian at the sight of the woman then a shade of green when he spied the bodies in the foyer. Erika knelt and examined the unconscious woman who she recognized from past official functions as Delphina Miggis, wife to Clarence Miggis. Erika removed the light shawl Mrs. Miggis wore about her shoulders and pressed it to her wound.

"Where's Mr. Miggis?" Erika said.

"Don't know," Derek said. "We only saw her. Well, her and them."

"Who were they?"

Derek shook his head. "Really didn't have time to chat them up."

"Does it matter?" Felix said. "I think we all know what these guys were here for."

"We'll bring Mrs. Miggis up and leave her with you," Derek said, "then we're going to search the house to make sure it's clear. Afterwards, we need to talk in private. David, get out of here, you shouldn't be seeing this."

David began to voice a protest, but speaking was enough to trigger his gag reflex. He vomited down the stairs with great force and volume.

"Man," Felix said, "the maids are going to hate us."

David, a few pounds lighter, returned to his room and slept under Erika's watchful eye while the men methodically checked every room, starting on the third floor and working downward. Their search did not reveal any further assailants but did succeed in locating Clarence Miggis, who was hiding in the pantry off of the kitchen.

"Are they gone?" Miggis squeaked, emerging from his fetal position.

"You cowardly bastard," Felix muttered.

Felix's unkind assessment of Mr. Miggis did not help matters any, yet Felix sincerely doubted his silence would have saved him and his companions from getting tossed out of the house.

"Hey, am I wrong?" he said. "The guy ran off and hid and left his wife to get chopped into stew meat. He's lucky all I did was call him a coward."

"Then why don't you go back and make that compelling argument to him," Erika said, "and maybe we won't have to spend the night ON THE STREET!"

"Hey, hey, easy," Derek said. "Listen, let's give Miggis a little time to cool off, then I'll go back and talk to him. Maybe I can convince him to let us back in."

"You trashed the man's house, Derek," Felix said.

"Protecting me," David said as if this was an extremely salient point.

"I only trashed his foyer," Derek said. "And I offered to pay for the clean-up. Blood doesn't stain that badly. Can you tell this shirt has had blood on it?"

"I don't think that'll make up for the fact he had no idea assassins might show up looking to hack Davey-boy into itty bitty chunks," Felix said.

"It was none of his business," Erika said.

"I think it should have been his business if it put him and his wife in danger," Derek said.

"I'm not paying you to think."

"No, you're paying us to put ourselves in the line of fire to protect David. We knew going into this there was a risk and we made an informed decision. Miggis didn't."

"I'm not paying you to be my conscience either."

"Nope," Derek said. "You get that as a free bonus with your purchase."

"Can we find someplace to stay? It's cold!" David whinged.

"Aw, it's not that cold out, Davey," Derek said, slapping David on the back.

"*David...*"

"If we can't find an inn, let's just rough it for the night. Find ourselves a nice out-of-the-way patch of grass and stretch out under the stars."

"You mean sleep in the woods like a bunch of savages?" David said, scandalized. "No thank you."

"Told you he could be polite," Derek said to Felix. "He said *no thank you.*"

"I owe you a drink," Felix said.

Alas, the two inns our itinerant quartet found were both closed. They succeeded in rousing one innkeeper, but he was disinclined to accept his normal rate plus a generous gratuity, so irate was he at being awoken at such an ungodly hour.

Accepting this defeat, they fumbled their way through the unfamiliar city and returned to Turner Goss's shop. It had once been a barn attached to farmland that over time, as Elesy grew and matured as a town, disappeared, consumed by the extravagant homes that comprised the bulk of the community. The barn stubbornly defied this gentrification and now stood as a silent testament to the town's rural roots while also providing a spacious home for Goss's business.

They hunkered down on a squat wooden porch stretching the length of the shop, saving their posteriors from the discomfort of the cold cobblestone road — not that this was up to David's high standards for personal comfort, a fact he shared with his companions in the form of a grating nasal whine.

"That's why it's called *roughing it*," an unsympathetic Felix said. "Shut up or get some sleep."

"You mean shut up *and* get some sleep," David said.

"I mean *or*. Either way I don't have to listen to you bitch."

"Are you going to let him talk to me like that?" David demanded of Erika.

"She's paying us to protect you, not like you."

"Man's got a point," Erika said.

"If my father heard you talking to me like that..."

"You know," Derek said, "none of us are going to get any sleep if we keep bickering. And we do have a long road ahead of us. Tell you what, I'll take first watch."

Derek rose and, mostly to put David at ease and make him think Erika was getting her money's worth, paced back and forth along an imaginary perimeter past which no assailant would pass.

"That's some mighty fine watching, m'friend," Felix said, settling into a comfortable enough position.

"Thank you."

Felix pulled his cloak around him and gazed upwards. The sky was clean and clear, a pure black blanket over the world, freckled with shining pinpoints. Unlike you, my learned friend, the people of Ne'lan know not what the stars truly are; astronomy has not developed to the extent necessary to reveal their nature. There were theories, of course, but Felix did not waste time on his own notions or pondering the ideas of others. He simply appreciated the stars for what they were: beautiful.

"It's a real nice night out," he said.

"Yeah," Derek said. "Sure is."

"You're idiots," David grumbled.

Erika pulled the hood of her cloak down over her face. "Shut up, David."

## EIGHT
## Making Friends and Influencing People, the Racewind Way

Felix found it curious how spring nights could be so comfortably warm up until the hour before the sun began to tint the horizon, when the chill would descend. He exhaled a cloud of mist and hugged his cloak tighter.

The remainder of the night had been uneventful. A constable wandered by once, cast a curious eye at the quartet, interrogated Felix at length about Erika, then moved on. The law here was appallingly trusting, and Felix thought, somewhat wistfully, oh, if only he'd discovered Elesy earlier in his storied and, more often than not, sordid career. Then perhaps he would not be here now, playing bodyguard for a spoiled brat on what amounted to a suicide mission.

Well, not for *him*. Technically, he'd been hired to get David to his destination, not to accompany him into the proverbial lion's den. The problem, he realized now, was that Derek might well volunteer to go that extra mile. Such an annoying habit, his propensity to always want to do the right thing. Talking him out of it would be a challenge — not insurmountable, but a challenge.

Felix was on the sixth draft of his argument when Derek signaled with a yawn and a stretch that he was awake.

"Whoo. Brisk," he said. "Hot cup of coffee would be great right now."

"Except all our stuff is locked up in the carriage," Felix said, "which is locked up in there."

"That was bright of us."

"Brilliant."

David was still sound asleep — of this, Felix was certain; a boy with so strong a sense of pride would not, in the interest of maintaining an illusion, allow a thick rope of saliva to dangle from his chin.

"You going to tell me what happened back at the house?"

"It's going to sound crazy," Derek said.

"Try me."

"I think they were zombies."

"Now normally," Felix said, "you could say the craziest thing and it'd sound totally plausible."

"Yeah?"

"You're a very credible person."

"Thank you."

"You're welcome. But yeah, that? That sounds crazy. Zombies are a myth."

"And what do the myths say about zombies?"

"That they're bodies of the dead reanimated by magic."

"That they're bodies of the *very recently* dead," Derek corrected. "Fresh corpses brought back to a semblance of life to serve the master that raised them. And, according to myth, one of the tell-tale signs that some-one's a zombie is that they only say one thing: the very last words they uttered before dying."

Felix thought back to the attack, and the assailants' baffling habit of repeating the same phrase *ad infinitum*

"He's right: they were zombies," Erika said, peeling back her hood. Her eyes were wide and bright; there was no telling how long she'd been awake and listening to them.

"The academies have denounced necromancy," Felix said, "not that I've ever heard of anyone ever successfully raising the dead."

"*Denounced* isn't the same as *outlawed*," Derek said, "and I don't think anyone practicing necromancy much cares for the law, do you? Especially...*him*."

"Yeah. But can he actually make zombies? And can he make them from Hesre? Doesn't seem likely he can reach across the continent to raise the dead."

"No one knows what he's truly capable of," Erika said, "but we have no reason to believe he can create undead long-distance."

"That's a relief."

"Except that means he has someone doing it for him," Derek said. "A minion."

"Minions, plural," Erika said. "An entire cult has risen up around him — fanatics who think he's going to bring about a twisted new world order and want in on the ground floor — necromancers, assassins, garden-variety lunatics, you name it. And they're everywhere, hiding in plain sight, pretending to be regular people."

Felix thought he detected a note of accusation.

"Wait a tic," he said.

"I uncovered two cultists in High Lord Ograine's household staff," Erika said, "so really, is it much of a stretch to think they might also try to pass themselves off as a pair of dimwitted adventurers looking for work?"

"Curses, you've uncovered our dastardly deception," Felix said. Erika was not amused by the jest, but Felix, suspecting the elf never laughed at anything, did not take it to heart.

"And yet, you hired us," Derek said, "so you must have trusted us."

"I didn't. Not entirely," Erika said. "It was a calculated risk."

"And now?"

"You haven't made a fool out of me."

"I think that might have qualified as a compliment," Felix said.

"Savor it. It's the only one you're getting."

Turner Goss arrived to open his shop a few hours after dawn. He invited the unexpected squatters in straightaway and took them to their repaired carriage. He had welded iron sleeves around the weakened spokes and wrapped thin iron bands around the wheel itself on either side of the damage. He'd also succeeded in prying free the arrowhead, and he'd patched the wound with a resin that perfectly matched the wood's rich russet hue.

"It's solid enough, lad," Goss said to Derek, assuming him to be the leader of the band; surely that responsibility could not rest with the scruffy rogue, the ghostface elf, or the scowling child. "But I'd advise getting a replacement as soon as you can, and in the meanwhile take it easy. Don't let the horses pull her above a trot. You don't have far to go, I trust?"

"We have a very long trip ahead of us," Erika said.

"It might hold," Goss said, still addressing Derek. "But don't bank on it."

Within the half-hour, Bravia and Titania were back in harness, no worse the wear for their night in Goss's stables. David, his back tight and angry, suspected they had the more restful night. Erika called for an immediate departure, but David's whining, compounded by Felix's whining, convinced her there was time enough to spare for a proper hot breakfast. They took their meal at the provocatively named Cock's Nook publick house, partaking of spicy sausage, eggs, and a dense dark wheat toast. David crabbed about his breakfast's middling quality, but Derek and Felix, who were used to subsisting on less extravagant fare, were just short of orgasmic. Erika was more in agreement with her adult compatriots, but being on the receiving end of icy stares from the patrons and waitstaff alike somewhat dampened her enthusiasm.

"Let it slide," Derek advised, picking up on Erika's mounting irritation.

"Easy for you to say," she said, stabbing at her eggs as if they too were regarding her with bold-faced contempt. "You wouldn't like it much if everywhere you went people stared at you like you were a freak."

"They don't think you're a freak," Felix said through a mouthful of toast, "they think you're planning to kill them."

"Because Clan Boktn are nothing but a bunch of

bloodthirsty killers. That's what you humans think, right?"

"Yeah, and frankly, you people don't do much to discourage the stereotype. I've met maybe a dozen Clan Boktn in my life, and every time they were working as a bodyguard or an assassin or a mercenary. How come I've never seen one of you people working as, I don't know, a librarian?"

"Lightfoot, if you say *you people* one more time —"

"What, you'll kill me? Yeah, that'd change my opinion double-quick. What are you laughing at?"

"If I didn't know better," Derek chuckled, "I'd swear you two were an old married couple."

"Sure sound like *my* parents," David said, and that remark, spoken to the table without a trace of humor, brought the conversation, such as it was, to an awkward end.

The uncomfortable silence lingered throughout the morning until they were within an hour of the Elesy/Aming border, along which sat the vast Lake Ochua, which was forty miles as measured from its most northwesterly shore to its most southeasterly. There were two points at which our travelers could cross: one was across a sturdy stonework bridge that was part of the Grand Avenue, the other a less well-maintained raised stone roadway stretching across the lake's narrowest and shallowest point — two miles wide, less than fifty feet deep. Erika's route took them to this second expanse.

At Derek's suggestion Erika pulled the carriage off the road so the horses could rest and take water at the shore of the crystal blue lake. The quartet took a beachside light lunch of dried meat and fruit — a humble menu that, once again, David could not resist commenting upon.

"This sucks," he said.

"So don't eat it," Felix said. "More jerky for us."

"We can't carry perishable food on the road," Erika said, hoping to appeal to whatever sense of reason the pampered adolescent might possess.

"I like it," Derek said. "What is it? It's not beef..."

"It is, actually. Marinated in brine and a combination of herbs then dried in a smokehouse over a low mesquite fire."

"My compliments to the chef."

"It's like shoe leather," David opined.

"Fine, gimme," Felix said, reaching for David's meal. David held it out of reach.

"Maybe if the stench coming off you slobs weren't so pungent my food wouldn't taste like — "

"Shoe leather, got it," Felix said.

"Welcome to the smell of life on the road, Davey," Derek said, polishing off his fourth strip of jerky and grabbing a handful of raisins for dessert.

The youth threw his meat down in disgust and rose. "You sleep on the ground and eat and smell like barnyard animals and you call it life? Are you actually happy living like this?"

"Happy enough. Not what I expected my life to be, got to admit," he said with the faintest note of regret, "but that's why I'm out here. I'm doing what I know how to do best and hoping it'll lead me to a better life."

David shook his head, a gesture of pity, albeit

not terribly sincere pity. *"Hoping* for a better life," he said with great gravity, "won't *bring* you a better life. You want a better life, Mr. Strongarm? Then go make one."

They allowed David to make his dramatic exit. It took him only as far as the carriage, but it sufficed.

"That was almost profound," Felix said.

"He does surprisingly well in his philosophy lessons," Erika said.

"A classical education, huh? Just how many private tutors does the little lord have?"

"You have a bad habit of saying things out loud you shouldn't. He's *not* a lord," Erika said. "He's a boy of no consequence, got it? He's not the son of High Lord Ograine; he's just some annoying punk kid, so treat him accordingly."

"I can work with that," Felix said.

The second leg of the day passed without incident and with a little more conversation than in the morning, most of this between Derek and Felix; despite Derek's many attempts to draw Erika into the discourse, she remained stubbornly taciturn.

They pulled up to a small inn a few miles over the Aming border. Erika told the men to stand guard while she inquired within as to vacancies and amenities.

"Give it up, man, she's not going to warm to us," Felix said.

"I don't know," Derek said, "I think she's loosening up a little. She didn't tell us to shut up once this afternoon."

"Oh, yeah, we sure melted that heart of ice."

"I admit, her social skills are, umm, lacking..."

The End of Aming Inn was a lovely old building. The wood had over the years settled and faded, giving the inn a slightly ramshackle character that danced along the Rubicon separating rustic charm from dilapidation. A large segmented picture window of dark green glass, which graced the downstairs dining area, was the original and had never needed a single pane replaced. It was the inn's only window that could make that claim — right up until the point a human body hurtled through it and landed at Derek's feet.

Spurred into action by the unmistakable sounds of a brawl, Derek and Felix stormed the inn and found two large men restraining Erika by the arms. A third was advancing on her, a fireplace poker in his grasp and raised high to deliver an incapacitating, perhaps lethal blow. In three leaping strides, Derek crossed the room, intercepted the latter thug's arm, and introduced his head to the floor. Felix appeared behind the men holding Erika as if materializing out of the air itself, and delivered a sharp rabbit punch to the nearest kidney. He dragged the man clear, and when he looked up again, the third assailant was on his knees, pop-eyed in horror as Erika choked the life from him.

"Whoa! Derek!"

Derek was moving even as Felix called out. He wrenched the elf's hands free and pulled her away with difficulty; her strength was considerably greater than her size suggested.

"Erika, stop it! STOP IT!"

"Get your Godsdamned hands off me!" She thrashed free of Derek's grasp. He jumped in front of her, presenting himself as a barrier.

"I said stop!" He tensed, bracing for another clash.

"That son of a bitch hit me!" Erika said, thrusting a damning finger at the man with the fireplace poker. "For no reason!"

"So what if I did? This is my inn!" the man said from the floor. "Who cares if I punched some ghostface elf?"

"First of all, don't call her that," Derek said, his voice level, "and second, she's with me, and I don't care for people attacking my friends."

"She's yours?" the innkeeper said with a skeptical chortle. "Friend, you look like you couldn't afford a half pint of watered-down beer much less her."

"Shut up!" Erika barked.

"Actually," David said as he marched into the inn, folding his arms in disapproval, "she belongs to me, and I assure you, sir, I *can* afford her."

"David!"

He raised his hand, calling for silence. "You're the innkeeper, you said?"

"I am."

"We'll leave, but I have no plans to offer reparations for the damage," David said magnanimously. "Let that be your punishment for assaulting High Lord Ograine's personal bodyguard."

The innkeeper studied David for a trace of humor but found none. He laughed nonetheless. "I know what High Lord Ograine looks like, boy, and you ain't him."

"He sure isn't!" Derek said, scooping the boy up and starting toward the door. "You know kids these days with their active imaginations. Felix, time to leave..."

"What about my inn?" the innkeeper demanded.

Felix looked around. "It's nice. Little drafty, though. Might want to fix the window."

The quartet beat a hasty departure before a bad situation could take a turn for the worse. Derek — who made a mental note to send the innkeeper some money to replace the window — doubted this was possible — but then again, this group did seem to have a knack for attracting trouble. Better safe than sorry.

Erika sat hunched upon the driver's box, the posture of a young child fuming over being sent to the corner to think about what she'd done. A small welt puffed under her left eye, the memento of the first poorly aimed sucker punch.

"How's the face?" Derek asked.

"Derek," she said softly, "you need to leave me alone for a while."

"Just making sure you're okay."

"I'm okay," she said, her voice barely above a whisper. "Leave me alone."

And so he did.

They did not encounter another inn until they were well in the middle of Aming, a city that had been built with no grander plan in mind; there were no organized districts wherein like-purposed structures consorted with like. Houses sat next to shops sat next to farms sat next to manors sat next to taverns sat next to churches sat next to gentlemen's clubs sat next to schools. From a distance, from atop the high hill the carriage crested upon its approach, the city skyline was erratic and jagged against the fiery red horizon, like a terrible flesh wound inflicted by a Hruk chisel. The inn they found looked respectable, even refined, despite being wedged in-between a large blacksmith's shop and what Felix identified as a brothel.

"And you would know this how?" Erika said, raising an eyebrow.

"The shingle," he said, pointing to a small sign — a red oval lacking any lettering or imagery — hanging above the door. "Legal one, too, else they wouldn't advertise like that."

"And you would know this how?" Erika repeated.

"Because I've had sex with women in brothels," Felix said. "*Duhr.*"

"I think I should ask about rooms," Derek said.

"And ask if they have hot baths!" David said from within the carriage.

"You heard him," Erika said.

Minutes later Derek returned with news that he had secured two rooms — one for the men, one for Erika and her charge — and the use of the private bath for two hours. "Half-hour each should do us nicely," he said. "You guys get settled. The innkeeper said there's a stable around back so I'll get the carriage tucked away."

Having had her fill of racial tension for the day, Erika pulled her hood up before entering. She nevertheless earned a few suspicious glances, but her eyes were fixed upon the floor and so she saw nothing. Upon reaching their rooms, the companions ordered dinner to be delivered to them, and by the time Derek had secured Bravia and Titania for the night, Felix was halfway through a thick steak and a bowl of mixed steamed vegetables glistening with fresh butter. A much larger steak and a baked potato awaited Derek.

"They brew their own beer here," Felix said, hoisting his tankard. "Good stuff."

"Nice. Aren't Erika and David joining us?"

Felix shook his head. "His lordship demanded a bath post-haste so he's eating in the tub, and where goes the brat..."

"Mm." Derek tucked into his meal without, Felix noted, his usual gusto.

"What's bugging you?"

"What do you think Erika's deal is?"

"Her deal? You mean why is she such a bitch?"

"No. Twice now someone's said something about buying her. I think she might be a..." He had trouble voicing so repugnant a thought. "I think she might be High Lord Ograine's slave."

Felix appeared unmoved by this distasteful possibility. "I've heard stories," he said, "that the Clan Boktn sells its dissidents into slavery to get rid of them."

"That's horrible!"

"To us, yeah, but in their society? That just might be how they handle their undesirables as opposed to, say, exiling them...or asking them in strong but polite terms to get lost, as the case may be."

"Doesn't make it right."

"Not saying it does, man," Felix said.

"And at least exiles retain their freedom to decide their own path," Derek said, bitterly. "No. No, it doesn't make sense. If Erika's a slave, why doesn't she just up and take off? She's not a *captive*."

"Maybe Ograine has something on her keeping

her in line. That's not outside the realm of possibility."

"That sounds sleazy."

"Oh, what, and our great and benevolent High Lord Ograine isn't capable of doing something underhanded?"

"Why would he have to?" Derek said, shocked at Felix's allegation. "He's the most powerful man in Asaches."

"So? That only means he has more to lose. The wardens have to fight to hold onto what's theirs, just like the rest of us, and I think every single one of them would throw their own mothers to the wolves if it suited their needs."

"You're appallingly cynical sometimes."

"And you're disturbingly naive about politics. Eat your steak before it gets cold."

The notion that Erika was living a life of slavery gnawed at Derek throughout his joyless dinner, and he could not bear to look her in the eye when she poked her head into the room and announced the bath was free. Felix availed himself of this pause to proclaim himself next in line.

Erika — her exhaustion evident in the dark circles under her dark eyes — rebuffed Derek's offer to watch David so she could grab a catnap. She shut herself in her room before Derek could press the matter further. Perhaps that was just as well, our conflicted hero thought as he lay upon his bed, unable to fully enjoy its comfort. Between them stood a wall high enough and thick enough to keep an invading Hruk army at bay for decades, and Derek believed he had in the past two days succeeded in chipping from this a stone or two; pushing too aggressively a line of questioning so personal — and potentially humiliating — might only rebuild the wall stronger than before. Slow and steady, he decided; erode the barrier, don't try and knock it down.

And with this, we draw the curtain on the first act of a drama still in its infancy, but we must turn briefly to another aspect of this unfolding tableau. This is what we narrators call...

## Interlude

Augus Greeley surveyed his handiwork with the critical and perennially unsatisfied eye of an artist with unattainable self-imposed standards. Every effort brought him closer to his admittedly nebulous vision of perfection, but oh, that journey was far from complete.

He sighed, his breath becoming mist in the cutting chill, and resigned himself to the product at hand, taking his satisfaction from the fact his lord would be less demanding. He stooped and, with a labored grunt, picked up from the floor a battered metal tub containing his night's work. He decided to clean up later, as usual, knowing on a subconscious level he would regret it, as usual. Cleanup was so much easier when the mess was fresh, but the contents of the tub were also fresh, and really, the need to finish his task before they spoiled was of greater import.

Greeley left the negligible comfort of the small fire he kept burning in an iron brazier and clumped up the spiral staircase, up to his lord's chamber, cursing the lack of a dumb waiter (as usual). The tub was so very heavy; his subject was — correction, *had been* a man of generous carriage, to state it charitably. He'd serve the master well and for longer than most, but *Gods* what a labor.

"Is it ready?" the lord of Hesre said. His voice was a desiccated rasp, and speaking expelled a faint cloud of dust — and dust it was, as he possessed neither breath nor warmth to clash with the frigid air.

Greeley conquered the last step and dropped the tub with a crash that reverberated like a bomb burst off the thick stone walls. His lord glared at him — no mean feat considering his eyeballs had an hour earlier fallen from their sockets. They were now two rotting, gelatinous globs on the floor. Greeley hated doing the eyes; he was not as adept in removing them as he was the flesh. The sharpened spoon made the job easier but not foolproof; mishaps sometimes occurred.

"My apologies, master," Greeley said, dragging the tub past a series of wooden tables abutting the walls, each of these burdened with books and loose papers, with glass and stone receptacles holding a staggering variety of esoteric and exotic distillations and extracts and concoctions — generations of research and experimentation, much of it failed. "He was a big 'un, he was. I'm surprised there's anyone left in the villages that well-fed. Well! I'm surprised there's anyone left in the villages, period, but people are stubborn, they are."

"People are fools," the master said.

"That as well, that as well," Greely said as he reached the throne. "All right, master, let's begin."

From the tub Greeley lifted the first carefully butchered sheet of flesh, no larger than the two outspread hands that cradled it. The blood, in the earliest stages of coagulation, had taken on a thick, pasty quality.

The master rose and sloughed off his robe, a frayed and tattered thing as old as its owner. After two hundred and two score and ten years the garment should have fallen apart many times over, yet it endured. Greeley often thought both robe and wearer were held together by sheer willpower alone — which was not out of the question.

What remained of the master's legs trembled dangerously so Greeley began there, with the feet. They were always the trickiest; they had so little flesh, even on a rotund man, and they tended to rot away the quickest. The legs were challenging for their thickness, but Greeley had succeeded in peeling them off the unwilling donor like a pair of woolen hose. He wrapped them around the master's emaciated stems. Almost immediately, the tremors ceased. Greeley stitched them in place with coarse twine. His needle, long and curved and wicked, easily pierced the wasted, leathery flesh beneath. The new flesh would fully bind to their new owner in time.

"Better," the master said. "Better."

Greeley rushed through his work on the pelvis area — never his favorite part, for handling the jiggling mass that was the buttocks was unsettling and offensive to his masculine sensibilities. The less said about the opposite side of this particular region of the human anatomy, the better.

It had taken Greeley several months to figure out the easiest method for piecing together the torso. He did the back in two long strips, tacking the top edges of each down along the upper trapezius muscles with wide basting stitches then sewing them together along the spine. The pectorals and abdominals were done in sections as well and finished off by binding them to the inner edges of the back pieces. He laid the flesh of the arms next, sewing them to the torso assembly and then binding them together along the seam running from the armpit down to the inner wrist. The process was, Greeley imagined, the same as for a tailor creating a custom-fitted jacket for a client.

"Ahhhhhh," the master sighed, the sound propelled by lungs that merely mimicked their original function. "Yeeessss..."

"Almost done, my lord," Greeley said as he tacked down a right-handed skin glove. The left followed.

Two inches of blood sat in the bottom of the tub, preserving the ultimate piece of the grisly puzzle. Greeley lifted it out with the greatest reverence and slipped it over the master's head like a balaclava.

"Turn around, please." Greeley stitched up the split that started at the crown and traveled down to the base of the neck, and tied the twine off in a crude knot. Once finished, he turned his master around again to fine-tune the placement of the flesh mask. He stepped back and took in his handiwork. The ears were even, the lips properly aligned with the mouth — very important, that last one. He'd allowed the face to set crookedly once, and the master spent the next several weeks speaking with an undignified slur, as if he'd consumed too much wine at a sitting.

"There," Greeley said. "Pretty as a picture. One last touch..."

He rinsed off the eyeballs in a bowl of water and popped them into the sockets. The master blinked slowly, reminding himself how to work the eyelids.

"Very good, thrall," he said. "My robe."

Greeley eased the fragile robe back onto its owner. "There you go. That should serve you well enough for a time."

"A time, *yessssss*," the master said, "but not time enough, no. No, never enough time. Never enough! Time is my friend and my foe — it taunts me! My time is borrowed, then stolen back, only that I may steal it back again! When? When will it end? It will not! No end! I will not end! I am endless! I am eternal!"

"I'll, er, just see myself out, shall I?" Greeley said, but his words were drown out by the master's increasingly furious tirade — typical behavior following a rejuvenation process as new life energy flowed into his crumbling body, inflicting upon him a mania that would, in a few hours, subside. Once calm returned to his mind, he would resume his research, and perhaps this time he would at last identify whatever went horribly wrong with the fateful spell he cast oh so long ago, the spell that granted him his hellish pseudo-immortality. He would solve the puzzle — yes he would, and he would reward his loyal servant with life immortal, and they would reign together over Asaches — nay, all of Ne'lan as new gods.

And though the master refused to acknowledge it, time was now his enemy more than ever, for each day brought the Reaper ever closer to their fabled final confrontation...

But for now, Greeley would retreat to the safety of his humble quarters in the bottommost level of the tower, and Habbatarr the Lich-king of Asaches would rant and rail in his high chamber atop his derelict castle, his voice echoing throughout the ruins and remains of the once-proud capital of western civilization — now a graveyard that not even the bravest, most foolish, or most insane of souls would dare to enter.

The Dead City of Hesre.

# Act Two
## In Which Our Heroes Bravely Venture Into a Dark and Unknown World

## NINE
## Struck in the Ass on the Way out the Door

"Eat up," Erika said, "because this is the last good breakfast we're going to see for a long time."

The quartet arose at dawn, roused by Erika, who showed a talent for detecting first light with a sensitivity and accuracy that would shame a prize cock — a fact Derek pointed out in those exact words. His turn of phrase undermined the compliment somewhat but succeeded in eliciting from David a prolonged snicker — the first sign that, somewhere under the veneer of youthful arrogance, a normal boy existed. They took a corner table in the inn's dining area and gorged on fine food and some of the best coffee Felix could remember ever tasting.

"Not necessarily," Derek said in response to Erika's declaration. "Hate to blow our own horns like this, but Felix and I are pretty good camp cooks. Leave the meals to us and you'll never go to bed hungry."

"What's your specialty?" David said. "Squirrel stew?"

"Don't knock squirrel stew," Felix said.

"You have to put the right spices in," Derek said.

"The meat itself can be a bit gamey —"

"On thin squirrels."

"Yeah, right, the thin squirrels aren't as good, but you get a nice fat one and the meat's real good..."

"You *are* joking, aren't you?" David said. "Good Gods, you're not. You people are barbarians."

"Ahh, you'll love it," Derek said. "Trust me, Davey, you take your first bite of squirrel and you'll wonder how you ever lived without it."

"Doubtful."

"We'll stock up on provisions before we leave town," Erika said, which was enough to placate David.

That satisfaction was not to last.

Derek once again took it upon himself to ready the horses and prepare the carriage for the day. The horses were feeling spunky this morning, as if eager to undertake the next phase of their mission despite the heightened prospect of danger that lay ahead. Derek took inspiration in this, and it was with a song on his lips that he mounted the driver's box and brought the carriage around. He approached the inn, and his good cheer flagged: two men — local constables, he guessed by their matching outfits and matching halberds — were engaged in an animated conversation with Erika and David while Felix stood to one side, playing the role of a simple spectator.

"Excuse me," Derek said, hopping down from the carriage. "Is there a problem?"

"None of your concern," one of the men said brusquely.

"It *is* my concern, sir, because these two people are my friends."

"Oh yeah? Well then," the constable said, facing

Derek, "perhaps you could explain why your *friend* assaulted four men at the End of Aming yesterday."

"I told you, you idiots," Erika said, "they attacked me!"

"And why should we believe you?"

"Why *shouldn't* you believe her?" Derek said.

The constable gave Derek a classic *What kind of stupid question is that?* scowl. "Look here, everyone knows these Clan Boktn types are nothing but trouble..."

"So of course she instigated it."

At this juncture the other constable, an older gent, intervened. "We have the owner and three men who all told the same story," he said, "that she walked into the inn and started a fight with no provocation. Who would you believe? Them or her?"

"I don't believe anyone starts a fight for absolutely no reason, especially when the odds aren't in their favor. Do you?" Derek said. The older constable pondered the question. "Sir, we're just passing through your town and all we want is to get back on the road. Let us go and we'll be out of your hair for good, I promise."

"Oh, he promises," the younger constable muttered.

"Sam," the older fellow said, waving his partner down. He studied Derek for a moment. "Straight out, then, lad. The lot of you, pack your carriage and leave, right now, and I won't press the issue."

"May we at least pick up some provisions?" Derek said. He caught the flash of resistance on the constable's face and added, "Please. Think of the boy's welfare."

"The *boy*?" David repeated indignantly.

"One stop," the constable said, "then out."

"Absolutely. Come on," Derek said. "Let's pack it up, people."

Derek followed his word to the letter. They stopped only once at a general store to purchase mostly jerked meat and dried fruit, enough to replenish what little they'd already consumed and a little extra for the long road ahead; some casks of water for the horses, should nature fail to provide; and several small tins of varied spices — the secret to eating well on the road for extended periods of time.

"Good-bye and good riddance," Erika said.

"It's your own fault, you know," Felix said.

"Excuse me?"

"I said," Felix said, louder this time, "it's your own fault."

Erika tossed the reins to Derek and turned around in her seat, giving Felix her undivided attention. "Explain to me how getting jumped by four assholes in a bar is my fault."

"You're kind of a bitch."

"Felix!" Derek said.

"Come on, don't tell me it didn't cross your mind that maybe she actually did say something to provoke them."

"I didn't say *anything*," Erika insisted. "And I'm not a bitch."

"*Ohhhh* yes you are. You're a bitchy woman from a race of bitchy people and you bring it all on yourselves."

Derek scanned the ground for a promising rock to hide under.

"You racist bastard!"

"It's not racism, it's a fact. You Clan Boktn elves give us no reason to trust you or even like you," Felix said. "Your people are cold, distant, belligerent, you avoid humans like we were diseased..."

"And why would we want anything to do with you? Humans have treated us like savages and freaks for generations!" Erika shot back. "We're sneered at, spit on, assaulted, insulted — people don't even do me the courtesy of waiting until my back is turned before calling me *ghostface*! Your people are just as bad as you think mine are!"

"So go back home and live with your own kind if we suck so much!"

Felix's riposte was not particularly artful, for he had exhausted the main thrust of his argument and was now merely hoping to claim the last word, and he was taken aback by his success; Erika had no retort of her own to offer. Her eyes narrowed into slits, and she turned away from the thief.

"Give me those." Erika snatched the reins from Derek. "Do you have something you want to say?" she snarled.

With a shrug, Derek said, quite earnestly, "I like you just fine."

The elf swallowed hard, and an inscrutable expression came upon her — and just as quickly fled, and she said no more for many long and uncomfortable hours.

Once clear of Aming, the party turned north. Erika's map indicated that she planned to take them up a secondary road and then hook west in the vicinity of

Fort Ven, a military outpost established by Constantine Ven, the High Lord of Asaches six generations past. The small keep fell to a Hruk assault when Derek's father was himself a lad, and though the invaders were subsequently driven out by a battalion of soldiers dispatched by (the now late) High Lord Angus Worther Ograine — David's grandfather — it was decided that the fort had outlived its usefulness, and so a regular human presence was never reestablished. The families of those soldiers who fell in the battle vociferously protested the sacrifice of men and women and resources in the name of personal honor, prompting the High Lord to abdicate to his son Malcolm in order to mollify the outraged masses. In the years that followed, various races — including but not limited to, ironically, Hruks — squatted in the remains until violently evicted by the next tenants. For that reason, Fort Ven was considered a highly dangerous locale and travelers steered clear of it — a fact Derek pointed out.

"Don't worry, we're not going to get that close to it," Erika assured him.

They stopped for lunch and to rest the horses. Erika chose to separate herself from David as much as she dared. She ate under the shade of a tree, its leaves the fresh bright green of early spring, while the menfolk stayed with the horses as they took water from two of the small casks.

"This afternoon might be rough," Felix said. He pointed toward the west where a line of gray peered menacingly over the horizon.

"Huh," Derek said. He stared briefly at the tree under which Erika ate then stooped and picked up a handful of loose dirt, which he tossed into the air. He watched the resulting cloud of dust drift a few inches as it fell and declared, "Four, five miles per hour..."

Felix finished the thought. "It'll be here within the hour."

"Yep."

"What will?" David said.

"Heavy rain, maybe a thunderstorm."

"Nah, just heavy rain, maybe not even that," Felix said. "The clouds are a light gray, so it's nothing too serious."

"You two made that all up," David said.

"No we didn't."

"Right. Throwing dirt in the air tells you how fast the wind is moving?"

"That and the movement of those branches," Derek said. "The leaves are rustling slightly. That's a light wind, moving between four and seven miles per hours. Old farmer's trick."

"Old *ranger's* trick," Felix said as if this was more impressive.

"People were farming before they were ranging."

"*Ranging?*"

"Rangering? Ranging? Whatever. Point is —"

"Oh, please, stop, this heady intellectual debate is so far over my head I can't keep up!" David said. "Do you two ever talk about anything *interesting*?"

"All the time."

"I have yet to hear it."

"That's because we talk about grown-up stuff that isn't suitable for a little boy," Felix said, punctuating his sentence with a patronizing pat on the head.

"Little b—?! How dare you, you impertinent...*peasant!*" a red-faced David squawked. "I'm the son of High Lord Malcolm Ograine, your lord and master, and the *man* prophesized to kill Habbatarr and forever purge his dark shadow from Asaches forevermore, and YOU WILL SHOW ME RESPECT, DAMMIT!"

Felix broke into slow, sarcastic applause. "That was *great*. Very impressive. I'm sure you'll have Habbatarr quaking in his boots. How do you plan to kill him, anyway? Whine at him until he throws himself off a cliff so he doesn't have to listen to you anymore?"

David sputtered and said something that Felix initially took as an angry curse — that is, until David jabbed a finger in his direction and a string of white-hot flame leapt from the tip. Fortunately for Felix, his feline reflexes were as sharp as ever, and he was able to twist out of the way in time.

The newly repaired front carriage wheel was not so lucky. There was a spontaneous and simultaneous burst of profanity from all four of the companions — one in elvish, which lent the curse an air of elegance — as the wheel caught fire with shocking intensity, like the heart of a raging forest fire rendered in miniature. The adults froze as their minds spun through their limited options, but David reacted immediately, stealing away from Titania her cask of water, which he overturned on the wheel, partially extinguishing it. The contents of Bravia's cask finished the job.

"What the hell was that?!"

"That was a Finger of Flame spell," David said distantly; he was impressed, if a little astounded, by his own performance.

"I meant what the hell were you doing trying to fry me, you little psychopath? That could have been me!" Felix said, indicating the smoldering carriage wheel.

"You moved," David offered lamely.

"Let's call this one no harm no foul," Derek said, placing a hand on Felix's shoulder — not so much to comfort his friend, but to make it all the easier to hold him back should he decide to harm and foul young David.

Which he did not, I am pleased to say. Felix exercised sound judgment in instead opting to storm off to fume in private for a spell (pun very much intended).

With his fingernail Derek scraped off the wheel a surface layer of crumbly soot. The wood beneath was darker, scorched deep.

"Whoo. That's not good," he said. "See this discoloration?"

"I see it," Erika said. "I know what it means."

"This can't be fixed. We need to replace this wheel or the carriage won't make it to Fort Ven, much less Hesre."

"Where?"

"We can make it back to Aming by nightfall..."

"Which means we'll lose a day, and then how long will we be stuck there while we're waiting for new wheel to be made? No. We have to push on."

Derek asked for the map. He unfurled it on the ground and studied the route Erika had traced out in red ink. "There's a village at Udon," Derek said, tapping at the black dot that sat precisely halfway between Aming and Fort Ven. "We can adjust our route slightly so we pass through. We won't lose any time, and if we're lucky they'll have a wheelwright."

"If not?"

"Then we have to be ready to ditch this carriage and some supplies along with it and take the horses the rest of the way."

"Absolutely not!" David interjected. "Riding on the back of one of these filthy beasts? You must be — "

"David, get in the carriage," Erika said. "Let us figure this out."

"Racewind, I will not — "

"I don't give a shit what you will or won't do!" Erika exploded. David shrank. "We wouldn't have this problem if you weren't so Godsdamned careless, so shut the hell up and get in the fucking carriage!"

David's disappearance was so quick and so complete it caused Derek to wonder if the power of teleportation was also the lad's to command.

"*That* was awesome. Erika," Felix said, rejoining the group, "I take back most of the bad things I said about you."

"I'm so happy you two could find common ground in chewing out a child," Derek said.

"He may be a child, but he can't afford to behave like one," Erika said, "None of us can afford that."

The rain began falling within the hour as the men predicted, but it was not the drenching downpour they feared — more of a light spring rain that felt every bit as refreshing as their baths the night before. But the novelty soon enough wore off, and by the second hour, the guardians had had their fill of precipitation, thank you very much, and they agreed to take turns drying off inside the carriage with David — against his very insistent wishes.

Our protagonists arrived at Udon accompanied by a premature dusk brought about by the cloud cover, which had thinned but not yet broken. It was a small village of unremarkable character, comprised of several small shacks and a few larger buildings that might have been businesses of some description, but none of them bore any signage to clarify this point.

"Where is everyone?" Derek said.

Felix shivered beneath his sopping cloak. "Inside for the night if they're smart."

"Then why aren't there any lights on?"

"What do you call that?" Erika said.

At first neither Derek nor Felix saw anything, their inferior human eyes unable to penetrate the gloom. Then Felix spotted a flickering dot of illumination at the end of the town's main street, a long, straight road of well-packed dirt. It floated in the air like a low-hanging star — a simple streetlight, Felix speculated, an oil lamp hanging from a pole. As they drew closer Felix saw that his guess was in part correct: an oil-fueled lamp dangled in the open hayloft door of what Derek identified as a massive horse barn, large enough to house two dozen animals at least. A circular dirt courtyard spread out before it and in the center of that a large fire pit. Stones the size of a man's head ringed the pit, all of them blackened with soot from a bonfire — and a recent one, judging by the stink hanging thick in the air, a smell of burnt wood and oil and meat.

No; not *meat*...

"Weapons out," Erika said.

## TEN
## A Small Village with a Big Problem

Erika jumped down from the carriage and unsheathed wicked weapons developed by the Clan Boktn for maximum carnage. The sica was short for a sword and heavy like a machete, with a blade shaped like a boomerang and honed to a razor edge on both sides; the outer edge was for slashing, meant to cut deep and spill blood, while the inner edge — Erika's preference — was capable of removing extremities with horrifying ease. The dagger was the sword in half-scale.

"What is it?" Derek said.

She waved him silent and, in a low crouch, approached the edge of the pit. She poked through the thick stratum of ash with the tip of her dagger and found within blackened splinters — but not of wood.

"Hey," Felix said. "People."

Two people, precisely — a man guiding a much older woman, both of them hustling as quickly as the elder of the pair allowed. Felix called out to them but did not receive a cordial response.

"Out of our way, you young fool!" the man shouted, and without sparing the group a second glance, he made a beeline for the barn. The villager frantically slapped a hand on the wide barn door and pled to be let in, he was sorry he was late, his mother is old and slow, please for the love of the Gods let them in! The door cracked open, and a man dressed in armor less glamorous than Derek's shooed them inside.

"Don't just stand there!" he shouted to the adventurers. "Get in here! Hurry!"

There was a note of terror in his summons that compelled Erika to comply, and she gestured for Derek to bring the carriage in behind her.

The horse barn was devoid of horses, Bravia and Titania notwithstanding. Its original purpose had long ago been abandoned so the structure could be converted into a town meeting hall, the hayloft now serving as a balcony — and, at present, an elevated guard post. This was a fortunate turn, for currently the building hosted with minimal room to spare the entirety of Udon's populace, every man, woman, and child. They sat on long, rough-hewn wooden benches and huddled together for warmth and comfort, and some had claimed small plots of ground to establish sleeping areas — not that anyone had slept recently, as evidenced by the exhaustion writ plain on their drawn, fearful faces. Déjà vu hit Derek so hard it made his stomach lurch: they were hunkering down and digging in; something terrible was coming.

The guard — what else could he be? — slid the door closed and reset a series of six iron pins in their latches while another man, likewise poorly armored and armed with a battered sword that had lost its tip, set about wedging heavy wooden beams between the door and the ground.

"This would seem to be an unlucky day for travelers," said a stout bearded man, a dwarf standing a pinch over five feet — tall for his race — with a bright face and twinkling eyes that were out of place under the circumstances, but he gave the distinct impression that he was always this way. "Though far unluckier for you, I think, had you not arrived until after nightfall. Oh, my apologies. Russe Orbom, at your service, my friends. I am the governor of this unhappy town."

"What are you bracing for?" Derek said. "Hruks?"

"Ah, a man who gets right to the point. I respect that," Orbom said, clapping Derek on the arm since he could not reach the warrior's shoulder. "No, my lad, Hruks would be a welcome delight compared to what we're contending with — and while I regret having to ask this of you, I can see you are a man-at-arms, and we have great need of any man of martial skill."

"We're just passing through," Erika said.

"Not tonight you're not, my dear, if you value your safety."

"What is it?" Derek said.

Orbom spread his arms and gathered Derek, Erika, and Felix into a small knot, like an aged storyteller drawing close a young audience around a campfire, and said softly:

"Ghouls."

The first of the fell creatures appeared a little over a week ago, Orbom informed them. It was alone, which in and of itself was unusual, considering that ghouls tended to stay in packs as they hunted — but stranger still was that it was not spotted in the cemetery at the edge of town, where one might reasonably expect to find it. No, this one wandered into the village proper and attacked a woman as she was returning home with some fresh milk for her newborn. She survived the attack itself thanks to the timely intervention of the town pub's regular clientele, who responded to the woman's screams and drove the thing off, but she died not quite two days later of a raging infection.

In that time Udon experienced another visitation, from a pair of ghouls, and soon the incursions became a nightly affair in which more than a dozen of the monsters participated. By then the villagers realized they were only making matters worse by observing their traditional funeral arrangements — burial — since that provided the marauders with easily obtained sustenance — and plenty of it, for over the course of that week sixteen unfortunate residents met tragic ends. Over the governor's objections — for he was a man who held tradition dear, especially when it came to honoring the dearly departed —  the villagers dug a crude crematorium outside of their meeting hall, into which they could drag their dead and reduce them to inedible ash. They also decided to abandon their homes before sundown each day and barricade themselves in their meeting hall, where they could fortify the structure and set a rotating schedule of guards and, quite literally, watch each other's backs.

"I personally dispatched a messenger to Cocor seeking aid from Lord Dennen, who I know maintains a sizable militia," Orbom said, "but that was three days ago, and we've received no reply."

"I appreciate your situation," Erika said, "but if you're asking us to go out there and clear out your town —"

"No! No, dear lady, I'd ask nothing of the sort. I've had to discourage my people from going on foolhardy seek-and-destroy missions several times. I certainly wouldn't ask guests in my town to risk their lives against those creatures."

"Sounds good to me," Felix said.

"Then what do you want from us?" Erika said.

"Only that you lend an extra set of eyes to the nightly watch," Orbom said, "and, Gods forbid, your swords should any of the creatures penetrate the hall."

"Done," Derek said.

"Excellent," Orbom said. "Then I believe we are as prepared for the worst as we can be. As poor as our luck has been as of late, I think the Gods are smiling on us tonight, because they have brought us three protectors *and* a healer. Come! Let me introduce you to her."

"Should we let our monster out of his cage?" Felix said.

"I beg your pardon?"

"Not literally."

"I'll get him," Erika said.

Orbom led Derek and Felix through the crowd, greeting everyone he passed warmly and by name, receiving a subdued but appreciative greeting in return, until they reached a woman who had claimed her own meager patch of real estate. She sat on the ground, cross-legged and lost in her own thoughts beneath a white hooded cloak.

"Excuse me, miss," Orbom said. "I wish to introduce you to some fellow travelers who have, like yourself, been brought to us by fate. I thought you would appreciate that."

"Absolutely," said the elf as she rose. She doffed

her hood and, in doing so, filled Felix's head with impure thoughts. She was taller than Felix by several inches; slender like most elves; and her flawless, youthful face was fixed in a permanent gentle smile, as though she were recalling a pleasant childhood memory. Her garb, a rich shade of ivory, suggested the robes of a holy order — if said holy order worshipped a god of exotic dance.

"Gentlemen, may I present to you Winifred Graceword of the Clan Lyth and a sister-in-service to the goddess Felicity. Sister Winifred, may I present to you — why, bless me, I never learned your names."

"Derek Strongarm."

"Felix Lightfoot," Felix said, turning on the charm, "adventurer for hire."

Winifred bowed slightly. "Greetings to you both," she said lyrically. "With the grace of the Goddess, may none of our skills be called upon this evening."

"Hear hear! I'd love nothing better than a nice, quiet, uneventful night of sitting around, talking, getting to know one another..."

"Singing songs," David said, "telling ghost stories, beating rocks together to make fun noises — all that simple-minded rustic garbage you people do."

"And this little charmer is someone you're welcome to kick in the groin if the mood strikes you."

"Try it," Erika said, sneering openly at Winifred. "*Please* try it."

"Greetings to you, sister of the Clan Boktn," Winifred said cordially, adding something in elvish which, to the ears of those humans close enough to hear it, sounded friendly enough.

"Yeah, whatever."

"Man," Felix said to Erika, "you don't get along with *anyone*, do you?"

"I don't like anyone."

"Oh, well, when you put it that way..."

Derek accompanied Governor Orbom on a tour of the hall to learn about its modest impromptu fortifications and its small complement of brave but unskilled protectors. They were mostly local tradesmen, men who could fend for themselves in a tavern brawl but had no formal training in how to use their weapons, an assortment of beat-up hand-me-down swords and a precious few newer arms, the latter forged by a resident journeyman blacksmith.

To Erika's ire, Felix took it upon himself to establish the party's encampment alongside Winifred's, who did not mind the company...or the less-than-comfortable conditions, the dreary mood penetrating every corner of the hall, the strong possibility of meeting a grisly demise at the filthy claws of a band of hungry ghouls — Winifred was impossibly imperturbable and never stopped smiling, a trait that inflamed Felix's lust for the comely elf and exacerbated Erika's contempt for the same.

"I'm going to get David some dinner," Erika said. "He's hungry."

"No I'm not."

"Yes you are," she said, dragging David away by the arm.

"Don't take it personally," Felix said. "She hates everyone."

"It's deep within her nature," Winifred said.

"The Clan Boktn have long been an aggressive people, which they believe is a sign of strength, but it's also driven many wedges between them and other races they might otherwise call friends."

"Elven clans too?"

"Oh, yes. The other clans regard the Clan Boktn as the lowest of the low," Winifred said, somehow making this assessment sound like the sweetest accolade. "If the clans agree with the Clan Boktn on anything, it's that it's best we leave the Clan Boktn alone."

"You don't seem too bothered by her."

"Hatred and anger are poisonous to the soul. The Sisters of Felicity believe there is beauty in all things. We nurture serenity within ourselves by finding and appreciating that beauty, and if we can't find the beauty in something, then we find and appreciate its purpose in the world."

"Sounds tough."

"Not at all, once you learn to view the world differently."

"C'mon. I mean, I'm not knocking your religion," Felix said, masking his deep-rooted disdain for all things spiritual, lest he queer any chances of a romantic interlude, "but not *everything* has beauty or purpose. This," he said, waving his hand at the crush of cowering townspeople. "What's beautiful about this?"

Winifred took in the hall and said without pause, "I see a community that's come together in the face of shared adversity to protect one another. Any personal differences, any rivalries, any petty disputes are for now forgotten, and any one of them would without hesitation lay down their lives for another. I see humanity at its best — and that, friend Felix, is beautiful."

"Wow. You're good."

Orbom concluded his tour at the foot of a staircase leading up to the hayloft-cum-elevated guard post. "As you can see, lad, our fortifications are not elaborate, but they have served us well thus far."

"Except you're worried the ghouls will figure out a way past them," Derek said.

"Hm. Is my anxiety so transparent?"

"It's a reasonable concern," Derek said, though he was not speaking from first-hand experience. Ghouls were an uncommon threat in Asaches, but as a (former) member of his hometown militia, he was educated about many of the possible threats he might face in defense of his people. He was taught that ghouls were among that rarest of species: the undead — though in his later travels he learned that this point was heavily disputed among academics, with some believing the creatures to be living beings and others believing them true undead, thus making their taste for carrion a bizarre sort of cannibalism. He also learned that they were dreadfully clever. Given sufficient time, they could puzzle their way past basic barricades such as barred doors, shuttered windows — all the things separating the villagers of Udon from a most gruesome death.

"Yet I am lost for other options short of abandoning the town," Orbom said miserably, "and I am loathe to do that. I suppose that makes me quite the fool, prizing a plot of earth so highly."

"Not at all, sir," Derek said. "You're fighting for your home. Nothing foolish about that."

Orbom patted Derek on the arm. "Good man."

"Lord Governor!" a guard cried out.

Derek followed Orbom up the stairs. The guard stepped away from the open loft door to allow the men a clear view of the street below, which was swarming with ghouls — far more than the dozen or so from the previous night. No, they numbered thrice that, at the very least. Moonlight peered through the tattered cloud cover, providing Derek with as much of a clear look at the monsters as he cared for. They were naked things, covered in pallid, warty flesh. Maybe at some distant point in history they were human, but now — with their elongated arms upon which they knuckle-walked like great apes, heads absent of details such as ears and lips, and mouths bristling with jagged teeth — they bore only the most passing of resemblances to man. Black pits for eyes stared up at the men, and a hiss drifted up from the roiling mass.

"My Gods," Derek said.

"We've not killed any of them, nor tried," Orbom said. "I don't know if those things have any concept of revenge, but I was in no hurry whatsoever to make that discovery."

"Just as well; they're tough to kill."

Orbom noted their behavior had changed from past nights. Previously they mindlessly clawed and pounded on the doors and shutters, as would any hungry beast seeking to access food secured within a sealed container, but tonight they were pushing and pulling at the main door experimentally, their feeble brains analyzing its function as best they could. Frustration would get the better of one every so often, and it would beat a fist on the door, then resume its curious fondling.

"What are those three doing?" Derek said. Orbom followed his pointing finger and saw a trio of ghouls, broken off from the pack, pawing at the door of a small, windowless shack of a home several yards down the main street.

"Oh no," Orbom gasped. "Oh, no no no — FARGUS!"

"What," Derek said, "what is it?"

"It's...oh, I pray I'm wrong...the boy, his parents, they were killed two nights ago..."

A man built like a scarecrow and topped with a mop of stringy black hair scrambled up the stairs. "Sir?"

There was no trace of joviality in Orbom's visage when he addressed Fargus, his aide, only a simmering fury Derek decided he never wanted to experience for himself. "Did you grab Daniel Fetch before coming here?"

"Daniel —? Oh...oh," Fargus said.

"Damn you, man! I told you to take care of the boy!"

"M-maybe he remembered to come on his own?"

"DANIEL!" Orbom shouted down into the hall. "Daniel Fetch! Has anyone seen Daniel Fetch?!" The villagers looked to each other, looked around, mumbled and murmured, and at last offered a collective shrug.

"Felix!" Derek shouted. "We have a situation! Grab your weapons! And get that coil of rope out of my pack!"

Knowing better than to waste time asking questions, Felix did as bade and, a curious Winifred at his heels, joined Derek in the hayloft, rope over one shoulder, longbow and quiver over the other.

"What's wrong?"

"There's a boy trapped in that house," Derek said.

"Aw, are you going to do what I think —? No, of course you are."

"As soon as the coast is clear," Derek said, tying the rope off into a secure lariat, "get the kid out and get him to safety."

"Let me get the child," Winifred said.

"No way," Felix said.

"Let her help," Derek said. "Besides, I need someone to lay down cover fire."

"So get Erika's ass up here!"

"Erika's ass is up here," Erika said, David close behind. "What the hell do you think you're doing?"

"There's a kid trapped in his house..."

Erika peered out. "No. You are *not* going out there."

"But there's a —"

"I said no!" Erika grasped a handful of Derek's shirt and pulled him down to her eye level. This required considerable stooping on Derek's part. "I hired you to do a job and I will not allow you to risk your life unless it's to protect *David*. As long you work for me, you follow my orders. Got it?"

Derek nodded gravely.

"Then I quit."

And he jumped.

## ELEVEN
## Even the Dead May Die

Ghouls have few redeeming qualities. They are repellant in appearance and worse in behavior; the phrase *six feet under* has meaning on Ne'lan as it does in your world, for that is how deeply those cultures that inter their dead in the earth must sink a body to prevent it from becoming a meal for the foul scavengers. If desperate enough for food, ghouls have no reservations about preying on the living, as the beleaguered people of Udon now know too well.

Among their few positive traits? They provide a serviceable cushion for a large man jumping from a second-story hay loft.

Derek's crash landing bowled several of the creatures over and disoriented the rest, giving him the precious seconds he needed to leap clear. Derek drew his sword in mid-air and removed a ghoul's head with a single motion — which was as effective as removing a handful of water from a lake, but it was a positive start.

"COME ON! COME GET ME!"

Fresh meat was staring them in their faces, and they could not resist. Derek fled down the main street.

The pack followed, loping and lurching, teeth gnashing in hungry anticipation. The trio investigating the Fetch home lashed out at Derek as he passed. One lost an arm at the elbow. Undeterred by this inconvenience, it joined its scabrous brethren in the chase, as did one of its immediate companions, but the third remained and returned its attention to the Fetch household.

"You better keep running, you crazy..." Felix muttered as he nocked an arrow and took aim. "HEY!"

The ghoul turned toward the sound. Felix's arrow found home in the meat of its upper chest — several inches below the intended target of its head. It barely flinched.

"Dammit!"

"Gods, you're a lousy shot," Erika said.

"Are you going to help or are you going to criticize?"

Erika, not wanting to waste her own arrows, took one from Felix's quiver. She placed it in the ghoul's eye socket without taking so much as a heartbeat to aim. It staggered several steps before falling, as though its brain was not quick enough to realize it had been destroyed.

"You're going to lord that one over me for the rest of the trip, aren't you?"

"Hell yes I am. You got your opening," she said to Winifred, "so move your skinny ass before they come back."

Felix and Orbom lowered the rope and anchored it while Winifred shimmied down. In the moonlit night, Winifred's white vestments glowed spectrally, and as she raced down the street, Felix thought her the loveliest ghost-elf he'd ever encountered.

Winifred tested the door and found it secure. "Hello?" she said, rapping gently. "Young man? Please open the door. I'm here to take you back to the hall so we can protect you."

"...Is it safe?" replied a small voice.

"It is, I promise, but we must go quickly before the ghouls return." She heard a scraping, the sound of a wooden bar being lifted from its brackets, and the door swung open to reveal a round, pale face. The fear left the young boy's eyes at the sight of his rescuer's warm smile. "Are you ready to go?"

The boy nodded and took Winifred's hand.

"Hurry up," Felix said. "Hurry up."

His anxiety was for naught, for Winifred led the boy back to the hall without incident or encounter. Orbom and Felix hoisted him to safety. They were lowering the rope back down when the situation abruptly changed for the worst: a lone ghoul loped into the courtyard and, upon spying the elf, charged.

"Winifred!" Felix cried out.

Neither Felix nor Erika could prepare their bows in time. The ghoul closed the gap with a few leaping bounds, its mouth wide — wide enough that Winifred's foot fit inside neatly. The force of her kick popped the monster's jaw loose at its anchor points, and it staggered back in a daze, its mandible swinging freely like a grotesque pendulum.

"I would like to come up now," Winifred said.

"You heard the lady," Orbom said. "Heave-ho."

"Hurry," Erika said, her head cocked.

"If Derek gets eaten," David said thoughtfully, "we should hire her."

"Shut up, David," Felix said.

"I'm just saying. Father always says one should plan for contingencies. I'm thinking ahead."

"You're pissing me off is what you're doing, you little bastard."

"Hey! You need remember who you're talking to, mister! I'm still the heir to the lordship of Asaches, and you better — "

"David!" Erika snapped. "For Gods' sake, shut your damn mouth!"

"What? What?" Fargus said. "You're *him*? You're...you're the Reaper?" he said in an awed whisper.

"What of it?"

"Ha! Ha ha! Well well well, isn't this fortunate?"

"Fortunate?"

David was unexpectedly treated to an utterly unfamiliar sensation: that of weightlessness as two hands launched him out of the loft and into space. This had barely registered when the ground brought the experience to a cruel end, sending a white-hot jolt of pain screaming up his arm and into his chest, thoroughly choking off any scream he might have otherwise released.

"Death to The Reaper! Death to the foes of Lord Habbatarr!" Fargus shouted. He threw his fists into the air in triumph. Erika threw her fist into Fargus's face with equal verve. He staggered and pitched backwards, falling from the loft and almost landing on two gentlemen passing the time with a game of cards.

"FELIX!"

"That was Derek," Felix said. "Ohhhh, *shit*..."

The thing that was truly unnerving Derek, beyond the thought of tripping on something in the gloom and becoming a living supper for the ghouls literally nipping at his heels, was that his pursuers were so bloody quiet. No growling or howling or hungry snarls, nothing but — no pun intended, I assure you — dead silence. Even the thump of their extremities striking the ground was lost in the relative din of Derek's panting — his only clue as to how long he'd been running; he could run at a smart pace for five or six minutes before breathing became difficult. He hoped that was more than enough time for the others to rescue the villager boy.

He had no sense of where he was anymore, and the town's architecture was so plain and unremarkable he doubted he'd recognize any building he'd already passed. Blessed with the dubious wisdom that comes with hindsight, Derek thought that he could have planned this one out much better.

Two quick right turns guided by nothing more than blind instinct brought Derek onto a long, straight street, at the end of which he spied a faint glow. It grew brighter, marginally, as he drew closer.

*I hope they remembered to keep the rope out for me,* he thought. "FELIX!"

The village's impromptu crematorium came into view. There was a ghoul there, its attention shifting back and forth between Derek and something on the ground.

Some*one* on the ground.

Derek brought his sword around in a high arc that bisected the awaiting ghoul's head. Once in the courtyard proper, under the stingy light of the high oil lamp, Derek could identify the body on the ground, and he could tell David was still alive — in great pain but alive. Derek was determined to keep it that way. He skidded to a halt and turned, realized that there would be no time to get David out of harm's way before the crashing tidal wave of carrion eaters washed over them, and exercised the only option available to him: he charged the ghouls, swinging madly. The first stroke deprived two of the things of their heads, but that left many, many more in possession of theirs. They surrounded him in a teeming swarm of snapping teeth and clutching hands.

Erika, Felix, and Winifred plunged into the mass, learning what Derek already knew: that a pack of ghouls provided a surprisingly excellent cushion.

"I can't take you anywhere!" Felix said as he joined his friend's side, hacking, slashing, and stabbing anything that looked like it wanted to eat him — which, technically, included Erika, but Felix gave her an exemption as she was dispatching ghouls with ferocity and efficiency. Her blades were the perfect tools for this grisly job, hewing limbs and necks in ever-mounting numbers.

While she wasn't striking down their assailants with any permanence, Winifred was doing her part by keeping at bay whatever ghouls slipped by the companions, deflecting them from David with a flurry of perfectly placed kicks and punches, driving them back into the three-person meat grinder for summary execution. Felix caught a glimpse of the lithe elf's long legs flashing through the air and was for a moment lost in the magnificence of it. It was more than enough of a hesitation for one of the vile beasts to capitalize on. Its teeth punched through the thin leather bracer on Felix's bow arm and pierced the skin beneath. His howl of pain was lost amidst the cacophony of combat, as was his scream of rage as he drove his saber up through the soft underside of the ghoul's jaw and deep into its brainpan.

Driven by hunger and having no sense of self-preservation, the ghouls pressed their attack with unwavering fervor even as their numbers dwindled, dwindled...

From above, Russe Orbom, a man who had until a week ago lived his life without ever seeing another living creature die by violence, felt his stomach spasm and heave at the ghastly tableau splashed before him. The ground — what could be seen of it through the crazy quilt of limbs and bodies and heads — was stained an unnatural blackish green from the noxious ichor that coursed through the ghouls' veins in place of blood. Three of those responsible for the slaughter were likewise spattered with gore. Winifred, untainted and pristine in defiance of all reason, knelt over David, whose right arm had acquired two extra angles.

"He's passed out," she reported. "We need to get him inside."

"You guys mind," Felix panted, "if I...take a pass on helping...with that? I'm feeling a little..."

The ghouls once again proved their worth as a splendid cushion as Felix, blood spurting rhythmically from his inner forearm, joined David in the void of unconsciousness.

"But it was a manly faint, right?"

"Very manly," Derek said.

Felix propped himself into a more solid sitting

position with his good arm. The bad arm had been wrapped tightly in several layers of white cloth — Winifred's work, Derek informed his partner, and that gave Felix an all-over warm feeling — which was in fact a rising fever.

The meeting hall was all but empty, the villagers having returned to what they could once again rightfully call the safety of their own homes, save for a few who had volunteered for ghoul disposal duty and were tossing bits and pieces into the fire pit for later immolation.

Orbom stood over the adventurers, lines of grave concern carved deep in his face. "How are you feeling, lad?" he asked.

"Hung over?" Felix said, wanting for a better descriptor.

"You lost quite a bit of blood," Winifred said, returning from her other patient. "The bite punctured one of the large veins in your wrist."

"How's David?" Derek said.

"I set his arm in a splint and gave him a tincture that will alleviate his pain. I have some for you as well, Felix, if you need it."

Felix became aware that Winifred's outer vestments had lost a great deal of their length and she was exposing what would, in some circles, be considered a scandalous amount of bare leg.

"You got half-naked for me?" Felix said. "Aw, that's so sweet."

"He's no doubt a little out of sorts," Orbom offered as an apology on Felix's behalf.

"No, he's usually like that," Derek said. "So that's a good sign."

Winifred knelt at Felix's side and gingerly took his arm. "A ghoul's bite is highly septic," she said, "so we must assume the wound is infected. My magic can keep it at bay for a while..."

"You're gorgeous, you kick ass, *and* you do magic?" Felix said, beaming. "I am so in love with you."

"*Ahh*, I think what he means to say —" Orbom began.

"Normal behavior," Derek said.

"I'm adept at simple healing magic," Winifred said, "but to purge the infection completely we need to take you to my temple."

"Otherwise?" Derek said.

"It'll ravage his body, killing him slowly and painfully." That her smile never ebbed did not make this news more palatable.

"Remember all that when Racewind gives us the *we're on a schedule we have a mission* speech," Felix said.

"I quit, remember?" Derek said. "If we have to go without her, so be it."

Felix smiled crookedly at Winifred. "Ditching Racewind for you is a definite trade-up. Wait. Where *is* the bitch queen?"

"She's, um...having a little chat with my former assistant," Orbom said.

Fargus could not see, could not move, could not breathe — at first, that is; when he gave up trying to breathe through the pulpy mass that used to be his nose, he fared better in that effort. He wondered if there was something amiss with his eyes as well. They were open — he knew this — but all was black.

"The first thing you're going to tell me," said

someone, her voice soft and measured yet hard as iron, "is whether anyone else in Udon is part of this."

"Part of what?" Fargus said. He tested his arms, but they defied him. He became vaguely aware of something wrapped tightly around his wrists as well as his ankles and neck — he was bound fast in a standing position. Rough, ragged tree bark scraped against his exposed skin.

"Don't jerk me around, Fargus. This is *not* the night to screw with me. Now: do you have any coconspirators in Udon?"

"Lord Habbatarr has eyes in every village. His reach extends across Asaches. His loyal servants — "

Erika snapped a fist high into Fargus's ribs. He uttered a coughing yelp as the breath leapt from his lungs.

"I said I wasn't in the mood. I know Habbatarr has followers everywhere. I asked you if there were any others *here*."

"I alone serve Lord Habbatarr," Fargus wheezed, "and that's all I'll tell you."

"You think so?"

Fargus's eyes adjusted to the dark well enough to let him see he was in the woods, which he already suspected. Fingers of moonlight poked through the thick forest canopy. His interrogator, the ghostface elf, drifted through one of them, appearing then disappearing like a graveyard specter.

"My name is Erika Racewind. I am of the Clan Boktn. You know what my race does for fun? We invent new ways to hurt people. If I wanted to," she said, her disembodied voice circling around behind Fargus, "I could keep you alive for days. *If* I wanted to."

"I'm not telling you anything, so go ahead and kill me," Fargus said with a manic titter. "I don't fear death. Lord Habbatarr will grant me life eternal for my service, and when he learns that I killed the Reaper —"

"He's not dead."

"..."

"Did you hear me? He survived your pathetic assassination attempt."

"You're lying."

"You're still alive, aren't you?" Erika let this sink in. "Now, I don't have a lot of experience with evil masterminds, but I do know that they don't tend to reward minions who fail them. My theory? When I kill you, you're going to stay dead."

"I...I won't betray my lord," Fargus stammered. "He may yet reward my loyalty."

"All right then." Erika pulled her dagger. "Let's help you earn that reward."

It was a few hours before dawn when Erika returned, a look of serenity on her face that Derek found inexplicably chilling.

"Where's Fargus?" he said.

Erika peeked into the carriage. David was curled up on the floor beneath a coarse wool blanket, asleep or passed out, but either way he was someplace where the pain could not touch him. Felix was in a similar state on the meeting hall floor. Winifred sat beside him, her fingertips resting lightly on his arm, her lips moving almost imperceptibly as she whispered her incantation.

"How's he doing?"

"Where's Fargus?" Derek repeated.

"Hell, I'd guess."

Derek scowled disapprovingly.

"We have him to thank for the ghouls," Erika said. "Fargus was a novice necromancer. He cast some spell designed to attract them."

"What? Why?"

"He claims he was a field general assembling Habbatarr's foot soldiers for the coming war on the living."

"Then...he was taking orders from Habbatarr himself?"

"Hardly," Erika said. "He said he knew of other followers receiving orders out of Hesre and making similar preparations so he followed suit. He was operating completely on his own."

"Are you sure? He could have been withholding information to protect —"

"He wasn't withholding anything from me," Erika said with a sense of pride in a job well done. "Get our stuff together and prep the horses. We're out of here at first light."

"We?"

"You're still employed, if that's what you were wondering."

"I think that depends."

"On?"

"Whether you'll allow a side-trip to Winifred's temple. Felix's wound is infected and she can't heal it here."

"Okay."

"Winifred said it's a half-day's ride from here, north, so it wouldn't cause a major delay."

"Okay."

"And I think you owe me that much," Derek

said firmly. "I saved David's life tonight, and I know that's my job but —"

"Derek. I said *okay*."

"Okay?"

"Yes. We'll take care of Felix. We'll go to her temple first thing."

"Oh. Um. Thank you."

"You're welcome," Erika said. She returned to the carriage and climbed up to the driver's box, the ever-dutiful guard returning to her post.

"She's not such a bitch," Winifred said.

## TWELVE
## The Invisible Hand Places another Piece of the Puzzle

Governor Orbom, deeply mortified that a servant of Lord Habbatarr had so successfully infiltrated his village and nearly caused David's premature demise, insisted that the party — now numbering five — join him at his home for a farewell breakfast. Neither Felix, who was in the grip of alternating fever and chills, nor David, who was pleasantly high on Winifred's painkilling medicines, was all that hungry, but at Winifred's gentle insistence, they forced some food down in the name of maintaining their strength.

"You have to understand, sir," Derek said at one point in the meal, "that you can't breathe a word of David's identity to anyone. It's probably best you pretend he was never here."

"Maybe I'm not here now," David said dreamily. "*OooooOOOOooo...*"

"I've jeopardized your mission enough merely through my ignorance," Orbom said. "I shall certainly do nothing intentionally to make matters worse if this lad is indeed..." Orbom leaned over the table and mouthed the words *the Reaper*.

"The *what*? The Reaper?" David said too loudly for anyone's comfort. "What about me?"

"Yes, folks, that's the kid who has the fate as Asaches in his hands," Felix said. "We're so screwed."

"Shut up, Lightfoot."

"You shut up."

"You shut up."

"This is going to be a long day," Derek sighed.

Their appetites sated, the companions returned to the road. Felix insisted he was fit enough for rear guard duty, but Winifred nonetheless offered to act as a second set of eyes. He did not mind the assistance (or the company).

Their course, as good fortune had it, needed but slight modification from the original, for instead of turning westward before approaching Fort Ven, they now intended to continue north until they reached *Temple* Ven.

"The order claimed it last spring," Winifred explained. "We knew the castle had no rightful owner, and we were in need of a home of our own..."

"Did you have any problems moving in?" Derek asked. "I know a lot of unsavory types use the fort as a hideout."

"It was empty when we arrived, but we have had to convince a few would-be evictors that they would do well to leave us in peace."

"And by *convince* you mean dish out a holy ass-kicking," Felix said.

"Distasteful, I know, but sometimes necessary."

"So all the sisters know how to do that stuff?"

"Oh yes. We spend many hours a week perfecting our skill in the art of Man'Mori."

"Cool."

"You spend *hours* a week practicing?" Derek said. "Sounds like my militia training."

"Aside from our studies in healing magic and tending to our crops and livestock, we have few responsibilities so we pass the time with Man'Mori, lovemaking, music...of course the fort needs maintenance —"

"Whoa whoa whoa whoa," Felix said. "Lovemaking."

"Mm-hm."

"I thought holy orders discouraged that kind of thing."

"Some do. Ours encourages it. There's little in this world more beautiful than intimacy between two people, don't you think?"

"No argument here, but, uh...it's an all-female order."

"Yes."

"What, then?" Felix said. "You just invite some men over every so often and...?"

"The order does not allow intimacy between the sisters and outsiders on temple grounds," Winifred said, very matter-of-factly. Despite himself, Derek was now fully engrossed in this thread of the conversation.

"You don't say. Wow," Felix said, his head filling with imagery of a pleasingly erotic nature. No, I will not describe it. "That's...wow. I guess, uh, that whole arrangement must have been, you know, awkward the first time you, uh, you know..."

"Why would it be?" Winifred said. "Love for us knows not the bounds of gender. That is the nature of elves. Didn't you know that?"

"No. I did *not* know that," Felix said, fixing his gaze on Erika. "Honey, you just got a *lot* more interesting."

"Keep your eyes on the road," Erika grumbled.

By midday Felix's body temperature fluctuations settled on the fever end of the spectrum, forcing him into the carriage. David lodged no complaints about sharing his quarters, further proof of the power of Winifred's analgesic concoction. Felix's turn for the worse kept their lunchtime respite brief.

"He's sleeping," Winifred said after checking on her patient.

"Is that good?" Derek said.

"In the short-term. He's conserving his strength to fight off the infection, but after time he'll be unable to wake up..."

"I got it," Derek said abruptly. "I got it."

"Don't worry, Derek. We'll arrive at Temple Ven long before Felix is in any real danger."

And, by the grace of the Gods, Winifred's words rang true: late in the afternoon, the companions arrived on the grounds of the former Fort Ven. The original outer curtain, once a towering wall of solid stone ringing the castle a mile out in all directions, had all along its perimeter crumbled and fell, the result of repeated attacks and decades of brutal weather and exacerbated by a protracted period of neglect. The inner curtain was mostly intact, its continuity interrupted by two separate, massive fissures — damage inflicted long ago by a mighty siege engine. As they approached, Derek could detect in the smaller of the breaches evidence of recent repair work; debris from the original wall had been re-cycled for that purpose, put back in place and set with fresh mortar that popped white against the dreary gray stone. In-between these defenses lay a no-man's land in transition: large patches of dense scrubland had been cleared in a series of tidy rectangles to expose the soil beneath, which had been tilled and prepared for springtime planting. The keep itself had held up well, all things considered; it suffered but mild degradation along the battlements and its corner towers, giving the structure as a whole a slightly out-of-focus quality.

The drivers dismounted outside the inner gate-house and let Winifred lead the carriage in on foot. The inner ward was now an exercise yard for the sisters, and the companions' entrance brought to an end one-on-one sparring matches in progress between several acolytes. The sisters converged on Winifred, exchang-ing embraces and pleasantries in elvish. Derek caught his own name amidst the stream of otherwise alien vo-cabulary, at which point the elves in unison offered him a slight bow. Winifred introduced Erika, who received a polite nod. She did not return the nicety. Derek heard Felix's name, then David's, and then the elves proceed-ed past him to the carriage to assist a bleary-eyed Felix. He blinked the sleep from his eyes and looked around, taking in the historic if faded grandeur of ancient Fort Ven — and then taking in the fort's occupants.

"Ladies. Love what you've done with the place," he said.

A gentle hand roused Derek from the light sleep into which he had fallen — how long ago? When he sat down on the carriage's running board, right after the sisters spirited Felix and David inside, it was still daylight, but it now appeared to be the trailing edge of dusk — or the leading edge of dawn the next day, for all he knew.

The woman standing before him was as striking as any of the sisterhood — older, by several years, but age on an elf did not bring with it the same deterioration it visited upon humans, only a subtle maturity and complexity that one could spend hours analyzing. Beholding an older elf was not unlike sampling a finely aged wine.

"Greetings to you, Derek Strongarm. I am Matron Delsina," she said in a rich, husky voice. "Welcome to the Temple Ven."

"Thank you, Matron Delsina. I'm so sorry to impose on you like this..."

"It's no imposition, none at all. It's quite pleasant to have someone show up on our doorstep who isn't interested in claiming the temple for themselves. And I must thank you as well, for returning our sister to us safe and sound." She looped her arm around Derek's and guided him toward the temple entrance. "Winifred told me about your encounter in Udon."

"She hardly needed us, Matron. We were the lucky ones for meeting her, truth be told. She helped us save a young villager and David."

"Did she now?" Matron Delsina said. "Hmm. She neglected to mention that."

Matron Delsina escorted Derek into the keep's great hall where, during its life in wartime, troops would stage before they were dispatched. His bootsteps echoed coldly off the walls, which were devoid of the usual gargantuan tapestries used to mute the pervasive chill inherent in all-stone construction. Matron Delsina, in her flowing ivory robes, was like a phantom shadowing his every move, silent and ethereal. The ceiling was high but flat instead of arched, as was typical for this breed of small castle; there were rooms overhead.

"Your companions are in the chapel," Matron Delsina said. "Their wounds are not serious. A few hours under the sisters' care and all will be well."

Overcome with relief, Derek grasped Matron Delsina's hands and kissed them. "Thank you, Matron. Thank you so much. If there's anything I can do to repay you..."

"Your gratitude is sufficient. Repayment is unnecessary."

"I'm going to repay you anyway," Derek said. "Maybe not right away, but I promise you it'll happen. You did right by me; I'll do right by you."

Matron Delsina beamed up at him. "How curious."

"What is?"

"That an elf of the Clan Boktn should travel with so gentle and generous soul."

Derek chuckled, and his cheeks flashed pink. "I'm afraid I'm not that gentle, Matron. Not always. And Erika's not as bad as everyone thinks. When she's not trying so hard to keep up the hardened warrior façade she's —"

"Façade? Oh, lad..." Matron Delsina patted him on the shoulder the same way his grandmother used to whenever he unknowingly said something foolish. "Might I offer a word of advice? Don't believe for a moment there is anything there other than a ruthless killer. She will not soften, now or ever."

"But — wha— why not?" *What happened to finding the beauty in everything?* he wondered.

"She is M'ribela. It's not the way she was trained," she said as though this was an obvious point. Upon seeing the confusion on Derek's face, she said, "You're unfamiliar with Clan Boktn's culture."

"I guess so because I have no clue what you're talking about."

"In the Clan Boktn, it's traditional that families have no more than three children," Matron Delsina began. "Should a fourth be born, the eldest is given up to the clan."

"Given up?" Derek said, already distressed at the direction this was heading.

"Disowned, in a sense. The child becomes a ward of the clan to be trained as an elite soldier: a M'ribela, which would translate loosely to English as 'War Ghost.' As part of their training they're taught to shed all emotional connections to others."

"Even their families?"

"Ah, the family is the first to go," Matron Delsina said with a note of pity. "The family holds a private ceremony akin to a symbolic funeral, signifying that from that moment on, the child is dead to them. Erika could be in the same room with her parents and they would act as though she wasn't there at all."

"Oh my Gods," Derek said, a rage rising within him. "That's — Gods, that's appalling! How can anyone do that to their own child? It's...it's inhuman!"

"And they are not human. That is their way," Matron Delsina said, "and it is not for you or anyone to judge the right or wrong of it."

Derek tripped over his tongue several times in impotent frustration then spit out, "David — he made some crack about paying for her."

"She's not a slave, if that's what you're wondering. Slaves generally aren't allowed to wander about unfettered."

"If she's not a slave..."

Matron Delsina let out a long, soft sigh that told Derek he was definitely not going to like what he was about to hear.

"She's an exile," she said. "The Clan Boktn holds its soldiers, particularly the M'ribela, to the highest of disciplinary standards. Those who fail to live up to those standards? Their services as soldiers, body-guards, assassins, et cetera, are placed on the open market."

"How is that not slavery?" Derek said, his hands curling into fists.

"Rarely are their services purchased for a life-time," Matron Delsina said, "and if so, it's with their consent. No, they're usually hired for a period of time — sometimes several years — then, once their contract has been fulfilled, they're released from service and they're free to find their own path."

"As long as that path doesn't lead back to their clan or their family."

Matron Delsina nodded. "As I said: that is their way."

"Their way sucks."

Matron Delsina led Derek to a basement ante-chamber. He found Erika staring spitefully at a closed set of double doors — the chapel, Derek assumed.

"You may wait here," the matron said before departing.

"I didn't want to wake you up," Erika said. "You needed the sleep."

"I got plenty of sleep last night."

"No you didn't. You were awake all night, watching over Felix."

"And you know this how?"

"I was awake all night watching over David."

Derek decided to nudge her. "You care about that kid, huh?" She looked at him as though he'd sprouted a second and third head under each arm.

"He's an infuriating little shit," she said, not at all affectionately. "If he weren't High Lord Ograine's son I would have slapped the spit out of his mouth a thousand times over. I watch over him because it's my duty. That's it. What's that look for?"

"Hm? Oh. I, uh, I just think it's kind of sad that you've known that kid for, how long? And you don't feel anything for him?"

"I was there when he was born," Erika said. "And no, I don't. Why do you care?"

"I don't know. Just do."

Erika shook her head.

The doors swung open on groaning hinges. The room beyond was dimly lit and covered by a carpet of wispy, musky smoke that wafted into the antechamber like morning fog. Two acolytes emerged, each with an arm around David, who had been stripped of his clothes and was now clad in a loose robe of heavy ivory cotton. He saw his protectors, smiled drunkenly, and waved with his restored arm as though signaling a distant ship, to make absolutely sure they saw it. The sisters took him upstairs as Felix, also robed, stepped into the open, escorted by Winifred and one of her sisters, their arms intertwined. He looked like a hedonistic playboy heading out for a fancy dinner and a night of theater with his finest companions.

"Derek," he said, smirking. "Erika."

"Hey, buddy," Derek said. "How're you feeling?"

"I just spent two hours lying naked on a really comfy bed while gorgeous elven women put their hands all over me."

"So...good, then?"

"This?" he said, holding up his arm, where the faintest of scars remained: an arc of reddish spots suggesting a row of crooked teeth. "Totally worth it."

As a deposit on his promised repayment, Derek commandeered the temple's crude kitchen and well-stocked pantry to create for the sisters a dense beef and lamb stew, a variation on an old family standby. What it lacked in aesthetically pleasing qualities — it too closely resembled the slop he used to feed the pigs — it made up for in flavor and gut-busting satisfaction.

Felix and David, redressed and fit for mixed company, squeezed in at the long wooden banquet table where the sisters took their meals together. Neither complained about the cramped conditions. The sisters drove the conversation with inquiries about their visitors' journey thus far. Erika reined in her companions' responses with strategically placed throat clearings, but David, driven by that most natural impulse among men — the need to impress lovely young ladies — was too wily to be restrained so.

"My father's High Lord Ograine," he blurted out, an answer to a question no one asked. "I'm the first-born. I get everything when my father passes. Well, my brother Alexander gets some, but I get most of it. Because I'm first-born."

This did not have the effect David desired; he had hoped for a dulcet concert of *Oohs* and *Aahhs* and *Do you have anyone back home*s but was met instead with dead silence that turned into guarded whispers.

"The Reaper," Matron Delsina said.

"That's me," David said.

Erika stabbed the table with her fork. "Do I have to nail your mouth shut?"

"How amazing, that fate should deliver you to us," Matron Delsina said, causing David to go rigid; the last time someone said something similar, he found himself involuntarily airborne. "We can guide you to the weapons you need to defeat Habbatarr the lich-lord."

"What weapons?" David said. "There's no mention of weapons in the prophecy."

At this point you are no doubt wondering if the nature of David's mission shall ever be revealed to you or if our *dramatis personae* shall continue to tease and tantalize with their off-hand references. Let me pull back the curtain from this mystery that you might better know that which drives our heroes.

The prophecy, one of many drafted by long-dead mystics from an age gone by, pertains to *the Decaying King, he who will reach out with a million distant hands and devour the world with a million undying mouths.* This dire event is believed by modern scholars to foretell the ultimate expression of Habbatarr's contempt for the world of the living, a contempt born of the madness that claimed the lich-lord soon after his figurative re-birth, and is fated to occur on the last day of the Decaying King's two hundred-fiftieth year — unless, that is, the savior of Ne'lan, the Reaper, intervenes on the world's behalf. It is said that only he possesses the great magic necessary to strike down the lich-lord; that many, many brave men and women have failed in their attempts to preemptively bring about the prophecy's more favorable conclusion stands as compelling evidence in support of this theory. It is foretold that the Reaper — the first son of the lord of all Asaches, born fifteen years before Habbatarr launches his final assault — *will enter the Decaying King's towering tomb in the Dead City, armed only with his strength and his stealth and his heart and his hate, and the Reaper shall deliver the Decaying King into the arms of the Gods*, thus forever lifting his foul and ever-darkening shadow from Asaches.

"Your strength," Matron Delsina said, "your stealth, your heart, and your hate. These are your tools in your battle with Habbatarr. These are the Might of The Shattering Hand."

Erika sat bolt-upright.

"We know where her tomb is. We can show you the way, and we can tell you what we know of the Lost City of Wihend."

"If it's a lost city," Felix said to Derek, "how do they know where it is?"

"Lost as in lost forever to our people," Matron Delsina said. Felix flushed; he'd forgotten how keen elven ears were. "When Artemisia Renn the Shattering Hand fractured the One Tribe centuries ago, creating the clans, she decreed that, as long as we were unable to live together as one, no clan could claim the city as their home. No elf has lived there since, nor to my knowledge stepped foot within the city."

Matron Delsina turned toward Erika. She said nothing, but there was an accusation in the matron's gaze.

## THIRTEEN
## Telling Stories around the Campfire

Morning came too soon.

The sisters had provided the company with some deceptively comfortable wood-frame cots, and David was loathe to pry himself out; another day brought with it several hours in his rolling prison with naught but two dimwits and the bitchy elf for sporadic and undesirable company. The accommodations at Temple Ven were not up to his extravagant tastes, but the acolytes did provide for some exquisite scenery.

The decision to stay put was taken away from him when Derek, the marginally less offensive of the oafs in David's estimation, entered the empty storeroom Matron Delsina offered for use as semi-private quarters — alas, well away from where the lovely sisters slept — and whipped off his blanket, exposing him to the sharp morning air.

"Wakey-wakey!" Derek crowed. "C'mon, sleepyhead, up and at 'em."

"Gods, I hate you!"

"Ohh, sounds like *someone* isn't a morning person. A good breakfast will fix you up."

"I don't want breakfast," David snipped. "I want my blanket back. Gimme."

"All right," Derek said, complying. "I'll let the sisters know you don't want to eat with them."

David was dressed and in the meal hall five minutes later.

Breakfast was doubly enjoyable for the lack of David's guardians, who had eaten and were preparing the carriage, and for the amount of attention paid him by the sisters, who were quite fascinated with David's quest.

"How long have you been studying magic?" a raven-haired elf by the name of Lucette inquired — with, David fancied, a come-hither smile.

"I've been training since I was five," David said, offering for the sake of a good impression a slight lie. True, he had received his introduction to the mystic arts at the tender age of five and received steady instruction ever since, but his lessons had ever been very basic. He could cast the Finger of Flame with ease; he could summon a dense, vision-obscuring fog; he could cause a light rain to fall from his supine palm; with some effort he could conjure an invisible globe of force that acted as a shield against physical attacks; and once he managed to very briefly negate the force of gravity to float four inches off the ground. He never came close to learning anything particularly destructive, or even useful in his estimation, but his father did not see cause for concern. The prophecy said Habbatarr would fall by the Reaper's magic. He reasoned that as long as he possessed even fundamental magical aptitude he would prevail.

Nevertheless, David took no small amount of

comfort in the prospect of acquiring the Might of the Shattering Hand, a set of armor worn by Artemisia Renn — the last woman to rule the elves as a single people — said to be imbued with ancient magic. Matron Delsina said the armor's arms, legs, and chestplate — the strength, the stealth, and the heart respectively — were enhanced to protect the wearer, while a gauntlet — the hate — magnified the wearer's inherent power. David definitely liked that last part.

With breakfast drawn out as far as it could be, David resigned himself to another day on the road. He said his goodbyes to the sisters — he did not receive the farewell kisses he'd hoped for — and trudged down to the great hall much like a man on his way to his own funeral. The Big Doofus and the Small Jackass, as he had taken to calling them privately, were there, reviewing Erika's map with Matron Delsina and Winifred. Erika greeted David with a deep frown.

"I know, I'm late," David said. "We have a schedule, I have a destiny, great responsibility, fate of the world, blah blah blah."

"Nice to see you taking this seriously," Erika said.

"Yeah, whatever," David said, climbing into his hardwood cell and slamming the door.

"Man. You'd think a kid who spent part of his night getting groped by gorgeous elven women would be in a better mood," Felix said.

"You'd think," Matron Delsina said. "Before you all depart, I have one last gift for you, to assist you on your journey."

"Matron Delsina, you've done so much for us already," Derek began, but the matron silenced him with a gesture.

"What I do now is as much for the good of the world as it is for you," she said. "I've asked Winifred to accompany you, to act as a guide to Wihend and to administer aid should you need it, which I pray you don't."

Felix, needless to say, was delighted at this news; Erika, less so. Derek sensed the opposition rising within her and stopped it with a shake of his head.

"We need to get going," Erika said. "We're looking at a two, three-day trip, and there's not much civilization between here and Wihend."

"A number of small villages," Matron Delsina said, "but no large cities. You'd be wise to conserve your supplies as best as you can."

Derek thanked Matron Delsina again, mostly to cover Erika's complaint that conservation would be unnecessary were there one less mouth to feed, then climbed aboard the Moste Grande.

"Gods be with you all," Matron Delsina said to him, "and if you wish to consider any debt to us paid in full? Return our sister to us."

He said he would. He didn't think he sounded all that convincing. If his vow did lack conviction, Matron Delsina was kind enough to let it pass without comment.

Their day passed without incident and without seeing another living soul — a condition they expected to persist as they trundled ever more westward, away from the more densely populated regions of Asaches. They were heading now into the untamed lands, where human settlements were sparse and small; where

Hruks roamed in gangs, in packs, in armies; where larger species of drake and smaller species of dragon dwelt in hidden caves, isolated from other races; where one of the Great Colossi, the oldest and grandest of all mysteries, held its eternal vigil, silent and still.

By the end of the travel day, just after sunset, the dirt road had become a vague path that required full daylight and Erika's sharp elven eyes to follow. Just as well, Derek said, because traveling through such territory at night was not safe.

"Here," Derek said, tugging the reins to signal a stop. "Perfect place to camp."

"It's wide open," Erika said, scanning in all directions for a hint of a tree line and finding none. "Do you know how vulnerable we'd be here?"

"Do you know how hard it'd be for anything larger than a field mouse to sneak up on us?"

"No fire, then. Attackers could use a campfire fire to target an arrow strike."

"Or they could wait until morning and ransack our bodies after we've frozen to death," Felix said. "It's not so warm out yet we can go without a fire."

"We could always cuddle together under some blankets, share our body heat," Winifred suggested.

"We could make do without a fire."

"We'll start a fire," Erika said.

"Man..."

The chill came as Felix predicted, settling on their makeshift camp before Derek had returned with some firewood; there was no usable fuel to be found near their camp, so Derek was forced to unhitch Titania and backtrack along their route toward the last patch of woodlands they'd crossed. Felix used the time productively, digging and ringing with stones a shallow pit for the fire. Upon Derek's return the men got to work. Derek stabbed a branch into the center of the pit and placed at the base a small ball of wood shavings bound together with pitch, around which he laid twigs snapped from the larger branches. Against the central column they leaned several smaller branches, erecting a cone. This they surrounded with thicker limbs arranged log cabin-style.

"It's lovely," David said, "but you're supposed to be making a fire, not playing amateur architects."

"We *are* building a fire," Derek said, "but you can't just dump a pile of wood on the ground and light it. See, the inner cones are arranged to allow the fire to grow fast, and the outer pile — "

"I don't care!" David keened. "Light the damn fire! I'm freezing!"

"You light it, you whiny punk," Felix said. "You have the magic finger."

"You want me to squander my talents lighting a campfire?"

"No no no," Derek said. "We'd *never* ask you to do that. We'll take care of it." He took from his pack his chunks of flint and steel and lazily smacked the two together, eliciting faint sparks. "May take a while."

A talent is not squandered, David rationalized, if it is utilized in the interest of self-preservation.

His need to feel his fingers again now addressed, David impressed upon his guardians the necessity of preparing dinner to quell the gnawing in his belly. He was, to his amazement, actually disappointed when Derek and Felix made no mention of their ballyhooed squirrel stew and instead passed around a tin filled with thin strips of jerked meat. He forced two pieces down before declaring the evening's repast wretched and unfit for human consumption. Comparisons to an array of materials not widely considered edible followed.

"Find the beauty in *him*," Felix challenged Winifred.

"He is emotionally honest," she said. "He is true to his feelings and truthful when expressing them, and in a world where lies and deceit abet evil, unvarnished truth is our greatest weapon."

"Gods *damn*, you're good."

"At least someone here recognizes my virtues," David said airily.

"*Virtue*, singular," Felix corrected. "And being one hundred percent honest one hundred percent of the time isn't necessarily a good thing."

"For once, I'm with him," Erika said. "Lies are necessary sometimes."

"Lies are poison to the soul," Winifred said. "No good can ever come from deception."

"Deception is keeping David safe."

"Safe? Is that what you call two sneak attacks?" Felix said.

"Lord Randolph David Ograine is still the most famous boy in Asaches — prophecy notwithstanding," Erika countered, "and Habbatarr has minions everywhere. We're running a gauntlet all the way to Hesre as it is, and it'd only be worse if we advertised David's presence."

"Like if he were — oh, I don't know, rolling across the country in a carriage bearing the Ograine family crest."

"Not my decision," Erika said, smoldering.

"Don't look at me," David said. "My father insisted on that carriage. It's the sturdiest transport he owns. And it was the nicest-looking, until *someone* hacked off the crest with an axe."

"Adze," Derek said.

"To maintain the deception," Erika said, hoping to silence David and Winifred with a single rebuttal.

"I have to agree with Erika on this one. I'm usually all in favor of honesty," Derek said, "but there are people out there who want to kill David, and the best way to protect him is to hide who he is."

"There are many more people who want David to succeed in his quest," Winifred said, "and they would lay down their own lives to safeguard him from the few who would do him harm. But they can't offer aid if they don't know the young man in their midst is their savior. Your shield of lies is no match for the mighty sword that is the truth."

"Lovely sentiment, but since I'm in charge of this expedition, keep your sword of truth in its sheathe," Erika said, "because if you expose David, I will take your head off at the neck. Truthfully."

"You can try," Winifred said, her smile unwavering. Derek stepped in before Erika decided to put that boast to the test.

"I don't think Winifred would intentionally put David in harm's way," he said. "I mean, just because she's honest doesn't mean —"

"That I'm stupid," Winifred said. "It's my world too, and I'd very much like to keep living in it."

For the most fleeting of moments, Winifred's expression slipped. So minute was the change that only Felix, sitting right next to her upon the ground, detected it.

"Something wrong?" he said.

She shook her head. "I was thinking about my mother. When we met in Udon, I was returning to the temple from her funeral in Lyth."

"Oh."

"I'm sorry," Derek offered.

"She'd lived a very long, full life. She marked her two hundred-fiftieth year this past winter."

Felix did the math; Winifred's mother would have been the equivalent of a human woman in her early eighties — which led him to realize Winifred, who appeared as a girl in her later teens, was in fact in the vicinity of her late forties and thus more than twenty years his senior. It made him feel like less of a dirty old man.

"I was fortunate," Winifred said. "I received word of her failing health in time to return home and be there with her at the end. Her entire family was there, right down to the most distant of my cousins. My brother Terrance joked that there was no possibility of death finding her in such a crowd..."

"That sounds like a nice way to go," Derek said.

"If there is such a thing," Felix said.

Winifred took his hand. "There is."

Felix could not help but believe her.

He somehow doubted he could ever be so blessed.

Erika nominated herself for the first watch of the evening. Felix gladly allowed her the honor and curled up under a wool blanket as close to the fire as he dared get; he'd more than once in his journeys awoken to find that an ember had leapt onto him and set him ablaze. He nodded off directly — and thus was, alas, oblivious to Winifred sliding under his blanket that they might pool their body heat as a powerful defense against the bone-numbing cold that settled upon their camp like a giant, stifling hand of ice pressing down from on high. David eschewed the heat of the fire for the solitude of his carriage, leaving Derek and Erika huddled before the hearty campfire.

"Two hundred fifty years," Derek said.

"It's a long life for an elf," Erika said.

"Hm? Oh, no. I wasn't talking about Winifred's mother," Derek said, and for a moment he wondered how old Erika was. She looked no older than he, which would mean she was no younger than sixty. "I was thinking about Habbatarr."

"What about him?"

"He's been holed up in Hesre for two hundred fifty years. Doing what?" Erika shrugged in response. "Exactly. The prophecy says two hundred fifty years from the day he became a lich, he'll destroy the world. Why now? Why not last year, or ten years ago, or a hundred years ago?"

"I don't know, and I honestly don't care because it's completely irrelevant to our mission."

"Is it? We're assuming we're under a deadline to stop Habbatarr from doing something he could have done literally thousands of times over already..."

"Habbatarr's a lunatic, Derek," Erika said. "You can't explain the actions of a lunatic."

"Maybe not, but...I'm just saying."

"What you should be doing is getting some sleep for your watch."

"In a bit. I'm not tired," Derek said, and this was true; he felt awake, keenly so, despite the long day and the late hour. Perhaps it was the cold.

No words passed between the protectors for several minutes, which turned into nearly two hours without either of them realizing how much of the night had crept away. The sounds of nature in their rawest of forms — a stiff gust whistling across the grass, the hoot of an owl, or the howl of a fox — intruded on their vigil from time to time, and they would cock their heads and listen through the crackle of flames for any signs the noises were more than innocuous.

"Derek."

"Hm?"

"If you don't stop looking at me like I'm a whipped puppy I'm going to poke your eyes out."

She would, too, he reckoned. "I'm sorry," he said — too meaningfully, as it turned out, for Erika's lips twisted into a vexed pout.

"What did David tell you?"

"David? No, he didn't say anything." She was about to chide him for lying when he added, "It was Matron Delsina. She told me about the M'ribela."

Erika nodded once, slowly, as if confirming to herself it would be acceptable to express her displeasure with Matron Delsina in a violent physical manner. "It's none of your business," she said.

"I know."

"Good. I'm not a slave, if that's what you've been thinking," she said defensively. "I serve High Lord Ograine willingly."

"Okay."

"He pays me very well."

"That's good."

"And he's always treated me with complete respect."

"I'm sure he does."

"If he didn't, believe me, contract or no, I wouldn't tolerate it for — "

"I believe you," Derek said. "I don't think you're lying to shut me up. If you say everything's fine then I believe you."

"...You better."

"I do."

"All right."

Figuring he already had his metaphorical foot deep inside the metaphorical door, Derek asked, "How long have you been with High Lord Ograine?"

"He hired me when he learned his wife was pregnant with David," she said, and she seemed on the cusp of saying more, but checked herself at the last.

Derek guesstimated that Erika had been the elven equivalent of a sixteen-year-old when she was contracted. How young had she been, then, when pressed into service with the M'ribela?

"How much longer is your contract?"

"Until the end of this assignment," she said, giving no indication one way or the other how she felt about this.

"Really?"

She nodded. "High Lord Ograine knew this would be a particularly dangerous mission, so he's promised to terminate my contract if and when I return."

"Wow. I mean...wow," Derek said. "That's huge."

"Mm. I guess."

"What'll you do then?"

"I plan to remain his bodyguard, if he wants me," Erika said.

"Oh."

"What?"

"I don't know. I thought if you didn't have to stay with High Lord Ograine you might go back home or something," he said, realizing too late that may have been a very wrong thing to say.

"That's not an option," she said, making it clear that the conversation was, for the nonce, well and truly finished.

## FOURTEEN
## The Children of Artemisia Renn Return Home

In the interest of efficiency, I shall spare you the dry and sundry details of the next morning, which was as routine a morning as our heroes could rightfully ask for: sleepers were roused, a crude but tasty breakfast was prepared and eaten, David complained, Felix threatened to do him a mischief — same-old same-old, though with the added wrinkle of Felix waking up to find pressed against his body a young woman whose company he did not pay for. That was something of a novelty.

So too shall I skip over the bulk of the day, which again was unremarkable, save for the uncomfortable silence that hung between Derek and Erika — a silence Felix soon picked up on since Derek normally tried, if not succeeded, to engage the taciturn elf in the smallest of small talk. Something had happened to sour what was, admittedly, not the most amiable of relationships to begin with, but Felix felt no compulsion to learn what that something was — and he was even less interested in playing a role in repairing the rift. This was a business arrangement and nothing more, he reasoned, and making friends with the boss was never a sound business move.

Soon after lunch, when the adventurers returned to the road, the last feeble traces of a marked road vanished, and they were left with naught but the sun above by which to navigate. Derek called for a stop. The party — sans David, who had lapsed into a deep post-lunch doze — spread the map out on the roof of the carriage to assess their situation.

"We left Temple Ven, here," Derek said, pointing to a tiny illustration of a castle. He'd crossed out the word FORT and replaced it with TEMPLE. "We've been on a northwest-by-west track..."

Felix shielded his eyes and gazed up, muttering to himself about the time of day and the time of year. "Yeah, northwest-by-west, on the button."

"Excellent. And we've been traveling at a steady pace...I'd say we're here-ish," Derek said, laying a fingertip on a large patch of blank parchment. He then pointed to a formerly blank patch where Matron Delsina had drawn a circle the size of a gold half-coin, which she'd labeled WIHEND. "And there's where we're heading. Assuming nothing holds us up, we should be there by this time tomorrow."

"According to Matron Delsina, there's a gatehouse at the eastern city limits, about here," Winifred said, pointing to a spot to the right of Matron Delsina's mark. "On the other side of this forest."

"Yeah, the forest," Derek said. "That could be a problem. There's no way around it, and for all we know, no way to get the carriage through it."

"There had to have been a road through at some point," Erika said.

"But if the city's been abandoned for centuries, it's probably grown over."

"Then we take the carriage as far into the forest as we can, abandon it if necessary, and take the horses if we can."

"If we can't?"

"We abandon them too," Erika said ruefully but not out of sentiment. Without the horses their pace would plummet to a crawl; they would never reach Hesre in time on foot.

"Then we make damn sure we get them through," Derek said.

"Yes we do," Erika said.

By mid-afternoon, the party had reached the outskirts of the great forest once known by the One Tribe as the Green Mother. It was their aboriginal hunting ground, replete with animals and sprawling patches of edible vegetation that, when harvested in quantity in the summer and fall, provided the elves with ample stores of food for the lean and unforgiving winter months yet left behind enough to feed the creatures and beings that called the trees their home. Its elvish name had been lost to the ages, and it was now known by the unimaginative appellation the Great Northern Forest.

Derek led the way on foot, hacking away at confounding undergrowth with a machete he carried for such occasions; he respected his sword too much to use it as anything but a weapon. While a clear road had not reappeared as hoped, they found a shallow gully running through the woods that, with pruning, allowed the carriage relatively unhindered passage. Winifred speculated they had found the bed of Wihend's ancient east road.

As they ventured ever deeper, the illusion that dusk had fallen prematurely intensified; the canopy was stingy with the sunlight, which denied Felix an orientation point by which to confirm they were still traveling in the right direction. His habit of procrastinating was returning to deliver a swift kick in the rear; had he been more diligent in replacing the compass he'd lost last summer, the loss of the sun would not be an issue.

In a moment of remarkable coincidence and bad timing, Erika said, "Hey, Lightfoot. We still heading in the right direction?"

"That," he said, "is an excellent question."

"You don't know?"

"I'm a little out of my element here. Deep-woods orientation isn't a specialty. Can't *you* tell if we're going the right way?"

"And why would I know? Because I'm an elf?"

"Well, yeah."

"What the hell would I know about the forest? I've lived in cities my entire life," Erika said. "Just because I'm an elf doesn't mean I'm some sort of natural-born ranger who can track people in the wild or hunt game or navigate through the Godsdamned woods. That's nothing but a stupid, baseless stereotype."

"I can tell which way we're going," Winifred said.

"You're not helping!"

"See that sunbeam?" Winifred said, pointing out a fat beam of warm yellow light pouring through the dense forest ceiling. "We know it's afternoon so, judging by the angle of the sunlight, we're traveling in a general westerly direction."

"There you go," Felix said.

Fingers of sunlight guided their way for the next few hours until the sun sank too low to be of use, forcing the companions to make an early camp. Felix slipped off, promising to return with fresh meat — and on this he was as good as his word, returning shortly with two fat rabbits.

"Uhh, how are we going to eat those?" David said, eyeing the dead coneys suspiciously. "They still have fur. And heads."

Felix whipped out a large hunting knife. "Easily taken care of."

David's appetite vanished long before Felix got around to stripping out the entrails.

It failed to return by morning, and even the smell of coffee brewing in a dented tin pot made his stomach twist.

"You sure you're not hungry?" Derek said. "We have bacon."

"Where in the world did you get —?" David began, only to then notice Felix's shirt sleeves were rolled up and his arms were stained red to the elbow.

"Technically we're only having pork," Felix said. "It's not bacon until we cure and smoke it."

"Yeah, you're right," Derek said. "Maple syrup is great for curing bacon. We're far enough north, you know, we could maybe find a maple tree, draw some sap, boil it down..."

"Or we could not," Erika crabbed. "We have a lot of ground to cover before we reach Wihend."

"And then we must find Artemisia Renn's tomb

within the city," Winifred added, earning her one of Erika's trademark glares.

"*Find the tomb?*" she said. "You don't know where it is?"

"No. Why would I? No one knows where it is anymore."

"Matron Delsina said you'd guide us to the tomb!"

"She said I'd guide you to the *city*," Winifred said.

"That's what I remember," Felix said.

"No one asked you! Why didn't you tell me this earlier?" Erika demanded of Winifred, who responded:

"You didn't ask me."

"You've got to be kidding me," Erika fumed. "Do you know how much time we could lose searching an *entire city* for *one tomb*?!"

"Maybe we should worry about finding the tomb once we get there," Derek suggested.

"Here's another idea: screw this whole thing," Felix said. "Let's forget about finding a tomb in a lost city in the middle of a huge friggin' forest for the sake of recovering allegedly magical armor that may not even be there. For all we know it's been stolen or rusted away or —"

"We're not leaving without the armor," David said, crossing his arms to show everyone that he was dead serious and planned to stand his ground on this point. *I have spoken*, his pose said.

"Why not? Because it's all part of the *prophecy?*" Felix said, making a twiddly-fingered *booga-booga* gesture. "Kid, let me clue you in on something: prophecies are complete horseshit."

"No they're not!" David said.

"Yeah they are. You know what prophecies are, really? They're the incoherent ravings of a bunch of ancient self-styled sages who spent all their time getting stupid off of whatever hallucinogenic mushrooms they could get their hands on."

"That's not true! They're real!"

"Real horseshit, you mean," Felix said, ignoring Derek's gentle suggestion that maybe he should back away from this line of conversation. "Prophecies are so vague you could interpret any one of them a hundred different ways. You were ready to march into Hesre with nothing but your awe-inspiring flaming finger because that's what one person told you the prophecy meant, now you want us to turn over every rock in Wihend looking for an old suit of armor because someone else told you *that's* what the prophecy meant. You're being led around by the nose by people who all think they know what the hell a bunch of drug-addled pseudo-mystics were talking about."

"I AM NOT!" David exploded, his face a red mask of rage. "This is my destiny! This is my purpose — my *only* purpose! My whole damn life has been about killing Habbatarr and saving the world and nothing else so don't tell me prophecies are horseshit," he squealed, tears pouring down his cheeks, "because that means my whole life has been a complete waste and *I'm just going to Hesre to DIE!*"

The carriage afforded David the opportunity to make a dramatic exit, complete with slamming door. It also hid his breakdown from his guardians' eyes and muffled his wrenching sobs. Mostly.

"Honesty," Erika said to Winifred. "Sure is beautiful."

The sun grew brighter as the tree cover grew thinner, signaling the travelers' emergence from the Great North Forest. Erika checked her map. By her best guess, they had traversed a point where the forest pinched in like the tube connecting the bulbs of an hourglass — the narrowest point along the eastern edge of the forest, which ringed Matron Delsina's mark like a natural curtain wall for a castle of inconceivable size. It did not feel like coincidence that this was where the marked road ended and a literal path of least resistance began.

Erika brought the carriage to a stop as Derek paused atop the crest of a gentle slope. He seemed to be fixated by something that, from her current vantage point, she could not see.

"We're here," he called over his shoulder.

His companions leapt down and sprinted up the hill, where they met with mild disappointment; before them lay not the fabled Lost City of Wihend but what was once a stately barbican anchoring a low, sloped curtain wall that stretched off in either direction as far as they could see. Thick, verdant vines slithered up the stonework and into a jagged gash on the fourth level, exposing a great bronze bell that dangled precariously from crisscrossing wooden beams. It was as if the earth itself had reached up with dozens of green fingers and was in the process of reclaiming its stolen elements.

"The gatehouse," Winifred said.

"Kind of run-down," Felix remarked.

"What did you expect?" Erika said. "No one's been here for centuries."

"That's not no one," Derek said.

Indeed, the Hruk who wandered out of the gatehouse chewing on the shank of some unidentifiable animal — freshly killed, as evidenced by the blood smeared across its face — was not no one, but a potentially very dangerous someone since, as explained previously, Hruks are not solitary beings.

Derek estimated that a hundred yards or so separated him from the gatehouse — too great a distance to cover before the Hruk could sound an alarm to any as-yet unseen companions. As he turned to appeal to his bow-wielding companions, Erika nocked an arrow. The arrowhead was a wicked thing, a fine example of the Clan Boktn's artistry in crafting weapons fearsome and cruel. Halfway down each of its four flanges was a small barb, and its fletching was delicately curved to promote rapid spinning. These features turned the projectile into a flying corkscrew that bit deep and made its extraction more destructive than its entry. Erika loosed her arrow. It found home in the soft flesh of the Hruk's throat. It instinctively grabbed the arrow and pulled, removing the shaft and with it a considerable chunk of meat. Blood ejaculated from the wound, and the Hruk collapsed.

"Cover us," Derek said.

The men exchanged a quick series of hand signals before charging in. Derek moved straight toward the gatehouse, Felix arced off to one side. Derek reached the gatehouse and assumed a ready position adjacent to the entrance, a wide, tall archway that could have accommodated two Moste Grandes rolling side-by-side. The thief clambered up the craggy curtain wall with spiderlike ease. He paused near the top and peered over. He then threw his partner another series of hand signals. Derek nodded, and he dashed in as Felix slipped over the wall

A minute passed. Two.

The elves heard a faint and distant clamor of guttural shouts that turned into cries of panic and squeals of pain. They raced toward the gatehouse, and a Hruk sprinted out to meet them, Derek in hot pursuit. Erika loosed in mid-stride an arrow that pierced the Hruk's sternum. It staggered and stumbled but did not fall until Derek's sword chopped through its spine as though it were a young sapling. Derek ran the point through its carcass thrice, piercing its heart and each lung in succession.

"Oh my," Winifred said.

"Yeah," Erika said. "Derek..."

He turned his back toward the women and started toward the gatehouse. Felix appeared there, his sabers painted blackish-red. "All clear," he reported.

"I'll make sure," Derek said as he passed.

"Ain't going to get any deader, man."

"I'll make sure."

"Four down," Felix told Erika. "Looks like it might have been a hunting party."

"Is something wrong with Derek?" Winifred said.

"He has a thing against Hruks. Nothing you need to worry about."

"If it's anything that could endanger the mission," Erika began.

"I said it's nothing to worry about, and it's none of your business anyway," Felix said. "Bring the carriage through."

And she did, and thus she and Winifred became the first elves to set foot on their ancestral land in half a millennium. Winifred's eyes glistened with joyful tears, but Erika? The achievement did not move her in the least, and with this her resentment toward her sister elf grew.

The western face of the gatehouse was intact despite its age and neglect; a large, square hole in the fourth floor wall was not, as Erika had first assumed, more damage but was part of the design: an integral horn to amplify the bell within and direct its sound — an early warning system. She'd seen its like before, many years ago, on the outskirts of City Boktn. The safe side of the curtain wall had at points along its length, carved directly into the stone, stairways leading to platforms large enough for a single person to stand, high enough for an archer to shoot over the edge at attackers as they crested the final rise before the barricade.

A separate guardhouse sat several yards beyond the main fortifications, a low stone structure now missing its thatched roof. Derek, his expression hard and grim, emerged from the guardhouse wiping Hruk blood from his sword with a rag.

"They've been using this place as a slaughterhouse for a long time," Derek said.

"They've been living here?" Erika said, but Derek shook his head right away.

"No. They're filthy things but they don't kill their meat where they live."

"Then they're living nearby."

"Yep."

"Three guesses where," Felix said.

Anticipation is a capricious thing. At times it inspires impossible dreams that reality cannot hope to match and leads ultimately to disappointment — sometimes mild, sometimes crushing.

Then there are times when the reality is so magnificent that no earthly imagination could conceive a fraction of it. It could not conceive of a city that was not a city in the traditionally accepted sense — a composition of individual structures large, larger, and larger still, connected to one another by the elaborate veinwork of main streets, secondary roads, footpaths, and alleys. It could not conceive of a looming, sprawling megalopolis that looked as if some titan of myth had stacked hundreds upon hundreds of castles one atop the other until they touched the heavens, their keeps and towers and turrets melding and merging into a single great mass of monotonous stone gray dotted by explosions of green from now-overgrown wards and courtyards. What our heroes beheld in all its prehistoric glory and incomprehensible scope was the product of centuries of labor by dwarven miners and masons working from, contrary to appearances, painstakingly conceived and meticulously detailed plans drafted by elven elders whose rhyme and reason were as lost to the ages as Wihend itself. Our adventurers — and yes, even jaded David — could but marvel in mute awe.

"It's glorious," Winifred managed, her voice cracking. "Absolutely glorious. The Lost City of Wihend, and we're the first of our people to lay eyes upon it in centuries. Erika Racewind, this...this is the most momentous day in our lives, in the modern history of our race. This day shall remain with us until our passing from this world. We are forever changed."

"Let go of my hand," Erika said.

"No. We're sharing this moment whether you like it or not."

"...Okay, enough sharing, we need to — no — oh, for — don't *hug* me."

"Glorious," Winifred said, weeping.

"You can hug me," David said.

"Back of the line, kid," Felix said.

"Enough, already." Erika peeled Winifred off. "Minds on business. We need to find the tomb."

"Easier said than done," Felix said. "I mean, Gods, this place is...we could spend the rest of our lives exploring it."

"We don't have the rest of our lives. There has to be a logic to the layout, we just need to figure out what it is."

"How do elves dispose of their dead?" Derek asked. "Burial? Entombment?"

"Burial is traditional," Winifred said. "It symbolizes a return to the earth from whence we all came."

"Not for the Clan Boktn," Erika said. "Most are burned in a funeral pyre. Honored warriors are entombed. Elven legend says that on the day of the Final Sunrise, our warriors will rise up to defend the living against the returning Dark Gods and escort the survivors into the Final Sunset."

"Hm," Derek said. "One of those options leaves us screwed, so let's pretend Artemisia Renn is either buried or entombed. These courtyards or whatever they are," he said, pointing out one of the green patches at random, "could be graveyards. If she's in one of those —"

"No," Erika and Winifred said in unison.

"When I say we bury our dead," Winifred said, "I mean *in the earth.*"

"And we entomb our dead in underground catacombs," Erika said.

"Two votes for going down," Felix said, smiling. "You know what this means, don't you, partner?"

"Dungeon dive!" the men said with the giddy verve of two little boys embarking on a fine day of mischief.

"I am *not* going into a dungeon," David said.

"No, you're going into a catacomb," Derek said. "It's just an expression."

"He's not going in with us," Erika said. "It's far too dangerous."

"No it's not," Felix said.

"Says who?"

"Says whoever said the kid's going to kill Habbatarr. The prophecy says David will *enter the Decaying King's towering tomb in the Dead City*, right? That's what it says? So if he's destined to face Habbatarr, if that's absolutely going to happen, no question, then — following prophecy logic — nothing fatal will happen to him before that."

"Really?" David said, finding the prospect of immortality, albeit temporary and contextual, quite appealing.

"Kid, we could drag you to the top of the tallest tower in the city and throw your ass off and you'd — hey!"

Erika grasped Felix by the neck as though scruffing a cat and pulled him aside. "What the hell are you playing at?"

"I'm not playing at anything," he said with mock innocence, "I'm stating a fact. If the prophecy says David makes it to Hesre —"

"But you don't believe in the prophecy."

"But they do. David does. You do. So what does it matter if I — wait. You *don't* believe in the prophecy, do you?"

"What I believe is irrelevant," Erika said.

"Ohhhhhh, what you believe is *extremely* relevant. We've got to do *something* with him, and since David's your baggage, that makes it your call. Now, you either believe in the prophecy and it doesn't matter whether you leave him up here or bring him with us, or you don't believe in the prophecy and...well."

"You're a bastard."

Felix smirked. "Coming from you, that's a high compliment."

"We're moving out," Erika announced. "All of us. David, you're in the carriage and you don't come out until I let you out. Everyone else, weapons ready. If Derek's right, this city could be crawling with Hruks, and Gods know what else. If it moves, kill it. Quietly."

"What are we looking for?" Derek said.

"Anything that resembles a chapel or a small church," Winifred said. "Before burial, the dead are carried through a *caelo'i* — a gateway that separates the land of the living from the land of the dead, literally and symbolically. Most of the clans observe this practice, so one could assume it started here."

"Sounds reasonable," Derek said.

"And we've got nothing better to go on," Felix added.

"Let me make sure I'm following this," David

said. "We're going to wander around an ancient city that's probably crawling with things that want to kill us, hoping we'll stumble across the entrance to an underground graveyard so we can wander around some more, all on the off-chance we'll find magic armor I need to kill a powerful lich."

"Yep," Derek said cheerfully. "And that's why they call it adventuring."

# FIFTEEN
## Into the Cold Earth, Where the Dead Dwell

It took some coaxing on Derek's part to get Bravia and Titania to enter Wihend. The horses stopped short of the southern gatehouse, where rusted remnants of an iron portcullis hung like jagged teeth, stamping their hooves and sputtering and pulling against their reins.

The roads were wide and smooth, designed to accommodate several lanes of carriage traffic, and these sprouted gentle inclines to allow horses and vehicles to access, without undue strain, the upper levels of the city. Pedestrians once traveled along narrow raised sidewalks that ran parallel to the roads, ascending and descending on wide stairways. All around them the companions saw innumerable vantage points, high and low, from which a foe could spring an ambush. Any moment now, a volley of arrows could tear through them, launched from a window in a high tower or from a dark alley or by whatever might be skulking in what appeared to be a basic sewer system: an intermittent series of iron gratings dotted the ground-level road. Erika was suitably impressed by the ancients' sense of innovation.

"Wait," she said, an idea blooming. "These are drainage grates."

"Yeah," Derek said, "to prevent flooding."

"But they wouldn't direct the water *into* the ground where the dead are," Erika said, "they'd divert it *away* from the catacombs. If we assume the grates are only on the lowest ground to catch rainwater as it sluiced down from the higher elevations..."

"We look for low-lying areas where there are no grates."

"Exactly."

With this information in mind, they proceeded along the ground-level main street on an easterly course; tradition held that the final march into hallowed ground should follow the track of the sun, sunrise to sunset — elves then, as now, cherished symbolism — and thus the caelo'i would have an eastern exposure. Derek kept the horses at an amble to minimize the ringing of iron shoes against hard stone. This leisurely pace allowed the companions to partake of the austere grandeur of ancient Wihend — its clean and simple lines, which yet retained a certain elegance for the lack of the telltale details of conventional construction. Derek, in his militia days, when he entertained halfhearted notions of joining one of the grand armies, studied castle design and construction techniques, and he realized that the stonework on every wall, every keep, every tower was mirror-smooth and seamless. This city, he sensed, did not rise up brick-by-brick, and in this Derek Strongarm was correct; the entire city, unbeknownst to our heroes — but, of course, beknownst to your humble narrator — was once a skyscraping, majestic mountain, and from this the dwarves chiseled and chipped Wihend free like an army of sculptors releasing from a block of marble the statue hidden within. This unmatched artistry had survived the centuries admirably, grudgingly succumbing to only the slightest of the inevitable ravages of time. Sheets of moss crept across the masonry. Erosion dulled the city's once crisp, sharp edges. Wild cockatrices claimed as a grazing area an old courtyard, complete with wooden picket fence and a large coop.

"What the hell?" Felix said.

The cockatrice — should you find the name unfamiliar — is a birdlike creature boasting the size of a fat tom turkey and the general characteristics of a gamecock — had that gamecock been born of a tryst between the ugliest of farmhouse chickens and a rattlesnake. Despite popular belief, the cockatrice's touch was incapable of turning flesh into stone — a ludicrous notion! How then could it feed? — but there is a sort of truth behind this myth: the cockatrice's hooked beak secretes a natural toxin that induces in its victims nearly instant paralysis and, as a side effect, a sickly gray pallor. The cockatrice is widely considered a perversion of nature and of no value to civilized man. Not all races share this opinion...

"Is someone raising them?" Winifred said. "Like chickens?"

"Yep," Derek said. "Sure looks that way."

"People eat cockatrice?"

"*People* don't."

In that moment every dry leaf skittering across the street became a shuffling footstep, every shadow in every alleyway hid a skulking assailant waiting for the perfect moment to pounce.

"We're safe for now," Derek said, taking his cue from his equine escorts; Bravia and Titania clopped past the cockatrice pen without so much as a nervous stutter-step.

"That won't last long," Felix said. "Not too late to turn around. We could put this place miles behind us before dark."

"No," David said, predictably. "We have to find the Might of the Shattering Hand."

"I'd like to restate for the record that prophecies are horseshit."

"Noted and ignored," Erika said.

Hope of discovering the tomb of Artemisia Renn before nightfall came and went, and came again and went again over the course of the afternoon, which turned to twilight too soon for the adventurers' comfort. They encountered three likely candidates in the form of high arched doorways secured by ponderous wooden doors bound by iron bands. Two of them proved to be simply churches, one in service to the God Prospero, the other to the Goddess Felicity. Winifred positively beamed at this latter discovery. The other chamber? Its original purpose remained a mystery, but it was not a caelo'i, that much Derek could tell from his very brief glance inside. As for its present purpose, I shall say but this: Derek had smelled compost heaps more pleasingly fragrant.

The party discovered a third church a little after sunset, at which point Erika made the difficult decision to call off the search until morning. The church — dedicated, Winifred noted, to the God Ward, the protector

— became their shelter for the night. The double doors had no locks or latches or means of laying a crossbar, but the doors opened inwards, which meant they could be braced from within. From each door hung an iron ring large enough for a man to stick his head through. They pushed the doors shut, plunging the church into perfect darkness. Derek took a spare coil of rope from the carriage and bound the rings to one another, sealing them in.

"I think we're good," he said.

"Not quite," Felix said.

"Where are you?" Derek called out to the disembodied voice, which seemed to be coming from somewhere overhead. Erika and Winifred spotted the thief peering down from a balcony that stretched the width of the church.

"There's a side entrance up here," Felix reported. "Leads to what looks like a small courtyard. Can't tell if that leads anywhere."

"I think everywhere leads to everywhere in this city," Erika said. "We need to seal it up."

"No, not yet." Felix shrugged off his longbow and quiver. "I'm going to keep nosing around, see if I can find our cowl-eye."

"Caelo'i."

"Yeah, that."

"It's a good idea," Derek said. "Anything we can do to save time tomorrow..."

"But if he gets caught," Erika said.

"Felix doesn't get caught."

"All right," Erika said. "You're on your own, Lightfoot. Stay out of sight, don't engage the enemy, and you make damn sure you do not get caught, because we won't — "

"You heard the man," Felix said. "I don't get caught."

And with that, he was gone.

The courtyard outside the church's upper level — which could as accurately be called the roof of the adjacent building — was accessible by multiple staircases and walkways. One of them led back down to the street; the others led up to other courtyards and into other structures. Erika was correct: the entire city was interlinked; enemies could pour in from multiple directions. While they would only have two access points to defend, attackers in sufficient numbers could wear them down within minutes and turn the church into an abattoir.

Felix was pleased with himself; he'd picked up some very useful information from hanging around Derek. Not terribly optimistic information in this instance, but useful.

A waning half-moon, hanging low in the sky, was as good as a willing accomplice, giving Felix an orientation point and just enough light to work by. He darted from shadow to shadow, from doorway to pathway to staircase, a flitting blur that might be mistaken by anyone not paying close attention for a trick of the light or a rat skittering between overgrown courtyards. Felix felt within his breast a sense of exhilaration so long dormant as to be nearly alien — the unique thrill known only to the stalkers in darkness, the secret masters of the world, the silent kings as they process through their silent kingdom. Working as a bodyguard, a courier, a bounty hunter, a dungeon diver — these paid the proverbial bills (barely) and added to life an air of danger and adventure (barely), but this — this was when Felix felt truly alive. More addictive than any opiate it was, and Gods, how he missed it.

As he paused atop an arched roof to get his bearings, Felix was jolted from his euphoria by a noise, the first real sound he'd heard since entering Wihend: the raucous tumult of revelry — and it was coming from directly below. The street was tinted orange from the dancing glow of a large fire. Leaning over the edge of the roof, Felix could make out the unmistakable snarls and howls of Hruks in the midst of an evening Bacchanal of meat and alcohol and — yes, there was most definitely some carnal grunting in the mix. Felix certainly did not want to witness that particular horror, but he had to know how large the enemy force was. He searched around for another entrance or a window to peek through, but the structure upon which he was perched, strangely, had none.

The hard way it was, then.

Felix took the coil of rope from his pack then cinched the pack up tight. He turned it upside-down, gave it a good shake. The contents shifted but nothing rattled, nothing fell out.

The roof extended over the street and came to a point, and around this Felix tied one end of his rope. He snaked the rope around one leg in a manner taught to him by Lars of the Gentle Fingers — and then came the scary part. Felix crawled out onto the jutting lip, slipped over the edge, and lowered himself head-first, like a spider sliding down its web — though Felix suspected spiders were more comfortable in this precarious position than he was. It had been a long, long time since he last employed this trick, and his arms began to burn and tremble right away.

He inched down, down...

"Ohhh, shit," Felix whispered.

There were dozens inside, sitting on the floor around a bonfire feasting, carousing, making baby Hruks — or, at the very least, going through the nause-ating motions thereof (and Gods help him, Felix could not distinguish the males from the females). But the scope of the Hruk intrusion was not what elicited Fe-lix's oath, nor was it the overwhelming gut instinct that the Hruks had claimed as their encampment the caelo'i — his evidence of this a bas relief image carved into the threshold directly beneath him, depicting two elves bowed toward one another as if in prayer. It was the first visible artwork of any kind Felix had seen in the city, exquisite in its detail and craftsmanship, but he hadn't the time to admire it at length, for he had a more pressing matter to address, and it was this matter that prompted the profanity: the peak from which he now dangled had shifted, sending an ominous vibration down the rope. The roof was about to fail.

Felix held his breath and pondered his next move. Up, away from the Hruks, was his preferred di-rection, but life as a habitual skeptic filled him with doubt as to whether the roof would accommodate the stress of frantic climbing. Sliding down would be smoother, quicker, and would put the lie to his boast of never getting caught.

*Unless*, he thought, *I outrun the sons-of-bitches.*

"If she tries to hold my hand one more time," Erika said.

Derek chuckled. "Trying to share a meaningful experience with you," he said. "How dare she."

"This isn't a meaningful experience," Erika said, pacing the edge of the courtyard. "I'm in a derelict city to play grave robber."

"As part of a quest to destroy the greatest evil Asaches has ever known," Derek said, "but that's beside my point. This is your ancestral home."

"I don't have a home, Derek," Erika said. "And if I did, this wouldn't be it."

"Where would it be, then?" Erika shrugged. "C'mon, where do you want to live after you retire?"

"Retire?" Erika said with what sounded vaguely like a laugh. "People like us don't retire. That's not a luxury our kind enjoys."

"Our kind?"

"Warriors. We don't get to die peaceful deaths. We don't get to die of old age. We die in violence, and the best we can hope for is to go down swinging in service to a just cause. If you think you're going to someday be a fat old man surrounded by grandchildren, you're fooling yourself. What are you smiling at?"

"Nothing," he said, but in truth he was tickled that Erika regarded him as a fellow warrior — and a peer is one step away from a friend in his book. "You know what? I'm taking that as a challenge. I'll make a bet with you: in, let's say, five years, five years from this day, I'll be sitting on the porch of my own farm and my sword will be hanging above my mantle collecting dust."

Erika raised an eyebrow. "What're the stakes?"

"If I win, you have to retire too. No matter where you are or what you're doing, you put your weapons away and settle down. Do whatever you want after that, as long as it's not fighting."

"And if I win?"

"Well, if you win," Derek said, "that would mean I'm dead, and it's kind of hard to pay off a bet when your ashes have been scattered to the wind. Would you be happy with the satisfaction of being right?"

"No," Erika said. "I wouldn't."

"More incentive for me to win."

"What's that sound?"

Derek cupped a hand over his ear. "I don't — no, there it is. Ohhh..."

"What?"

"Go tell the others we're going to have company."

"Hruks?"

"Yep. I'd know that sound anywhere," Derek said, unsheathing his sword. "There."

"Down!" They dropped flat, trusting the Hruks' poor night vision would help mask their presence. The roiling wave howled and snarled its way down the street below, threatening to engulf anything in its path — which did not, Erika noted, include a certain wayward thief.

"I don't see the idiot," she said.

"Screw you too," Felix panted.

Erika caught her startled yelp before it escaped. "Where the hell did you come from?"

"Originally? The mean streets of Roury. Most recently? Your caelo'i thing. You're welcome."

"I thought you said you never got caught."

"I'm here, aren't I?" Felix loved semantics.

"Yeah, and look what you brought with you," Erika said, nodding toward the Hruk horde. "Great job."

"I lost them five minutes ago, they have no idea I'm here," Felix said — and indeed the Hruks, upon closer inspection, were searching, not chasing.

"He's right: they aren't even looking our way," Derek observed. "They should pass us by as long as we don't call any attention to ourselves."

You see where this is going, of course...

"HEY! Stop stargazing and come fix dinner! I'm starving!"

David's strident nasal twang echoed and rang off the ubiquitous stonework, creating the brief auditory illusion that a race of whiny adolescent boys had re-populated Wihend. Alas for our heroes, it was obvious even to the dull-witted Hruks that the sound had a sole source, and that source was somewhere nearby. The mob scattered, and a trio of them found the stairs leading to rooftop.

"Go! Go!" Derek said, prompting but not leading the retreat into the church. Hoping against hope, he met the Hruks as they reached the courtyard, relieving the first and second of their heads with alacrity, but the third called out to his companions before Derek could silence him.

"Derek!" Erika shouted. "Get in here, now!"

The next wave of Hruks bottlenecked in the narrow stairway, giving Derek time enough to rejoin his friends. Erika slammed the door shut.

"We need to brace it!" Derek said.

"We don't have anything!" Felix said.

The ground-level doors throbbed as the first

wave of flesh crashed against them. The hempen rope, for the moment, held.

"What do we do?" David squeaked. "What do we do?!"

"In the carriage!" Derek said, and David's feet obeyed, carrying him across the balcony, down the spiral staircase, and into the Moste Grande. "Winifred, take the reins, we're getting out of here!"

Winifred knew better than to question Derek at the moment, trusting that he had a plan and that it was brilliant. The first Hruk burst through the balcony entrance, opening the proverbial floodgates. Derek met the brute with a rising strike that split it up the center navel to neck.

"Here we go!" Erika said, and a second Hruk fell to her slashing blades. Derek dropped the third, Erika the fourth.

"Let's go!" Winifred said, swinging the carriage into position. Bravia and Titania stomped and reared — not out of fear, the courageous beasts, but in anticipation of their pending flight. Felix vaulted over the balcony and landed squarely on the carriage roof. The front doors lurched. The rope groaned. A Hruk chisel slid through the gap and sawed at the binding.

"The woman said let's go!" Felix said. Erika eviscerated one last Hruk before joining the thief atop the Moste Grande. "Derek!"

"Not yet!" he replied, mowing down the Hruks as they streamed in one at a time; in true Hruk fashion, their attempt at a bright idea, that of entering single-file to avoid clogging in the doorway, was backfiring spectacularly.

Their other rare moment of brilliance also paid

dividends for the companions: the rope split, and a wall of Hruks three bodies deep collapsed into the church, like a wave breaking upon the shore.

"NOW!" Derek shouted in midair.

Winifred snapped the reins. The horses charged, stomping over the prone Hruks and storming past their upright brothers, who possessed enough sense to get out of the animals' way lest they also be ground into a gory paste beneath their earthshaking stride.

"Left!" Felix said as chisels rained down upon the passing carriage. The Hruks gave chase but quickly fell behind, unable to match Bravia and Titania's full gallop.

"How far is it?" Winifred said.

"Don't know, I was traveling the back roads," Felix said. "Look for the church with a rope dangling from the roof."

"You mean that one?" Winifred said as they overshot their destination by several yards.

"Yes! Turn around!"

Disasters are often the result of a confluence of individually minor events, and such was the case here. Winifred, a virgin carriage driver, pulled too hard on the reins, causing obedient Bravia and Titania to veer hard to port. The strain proved too great for the compromised wheel; the repairs, while sufficient to mitigate the normal stress of travel, failed catastrophically, and the wheel shattered. The topside riders were flung to the unforgiving ground as the carriage crashed onto its side, as though the hand of an angry God had lashed out from on high and slapped it over, taking the horses with it.

Derek got to his feet too quickly and promptly

careened into a nearby wall, the world spinning madly. "Check in!" he said, an old militia habit returning to him. "Check in!"

"Shit!"

"Ow..."

"Son of a bitch!"

Three out of four accounted for.

"Up! Get up! Felix, Erika, cut the horses loose!"

"Leave the horses! We don't have time!" Erika said, and what little time they had was slipping away; the Hruks, only moments ago an unpleasant memory, were catching up.

"No! We don't leave them behind!"

"Derek, dammit —!"

Derek fixed her with a look. "How fast can we make it to Hesre on foot?"

Erika and Felix hacked at the thick leather straps as Derek climbed onto the overturned carriage. He pulled the door open to find David lying half-buried in supplies. "David! Come on, we have to go! Take my hand! Come on!"

David reached up blindly, guided only by Derek's beseeching voice. Within seconds David was out and on the ground. In that same time Erika and Felix had sliced through the last of the tangled web of harnesses and grasped the horses' bridles.

"Into the church, quick!"

The church's erstwhile tenants had vacated in their entirety, giving the party one less thing to worry about, albeit temporarily. Erika and Winifred slammed shut the outer doors.

"There's no way to secure these!" Erika said, but Derek was a step ahead of her. He pulled open the inner double doors and beckoned for the elves to join him at the edge a black portal leading down into an ancient elven netherworld. If Erika needed any convincing that plunging headlong into this great unknown was their only option, she received her incentive in the form of approaching Hruks howling for the taste of elf-flesh.

That terrible cacophony followed the party as they raced into the darkness, but the Hruks themselves did not. Erika dared to glance over her shoulder, expecting to see the brutes coming at her like the hordes of Hell, but instead saw the doors closing on them.

"Everyone, wait! Stop!" she said.

"Uhhhh...not that I'm complaining," Felix said, "but why aren't they following us?"

"They're afraid," Derek said.

"Since when?" Erika said.

"They're afraid of where the dead rest," Derek clarified. "Elven legend says your dead will rise to defend your people? Hruks believe the dead will rise up to seek revenge for all the sins others committed against them in life — and Hruks have sinned a *lot*. They wouldn't set foot in a graveyard if you doused yourself in gravy."

"Don't mention gravy," David said. "I never got any dinner."

"Yeah, and whose fault is that?" Felix said.

"I have some jerky, but first thing's first," Derek said, feeling around in his pack for a travel torch. It flickered and sputtered at first, as though the darkness was fighting back.

The torchlight revealed an arched stone corridor, high-ceilinged and wide enough for the men, elves, boy, and horses to stand shoulder-to-shoulder with room to spare. Derek turned toward Erika to solicit an opinion on their next course of action, and he realized that he was looking up at her.

"This corridor's on a slope," Erika said before Derek could voice the same observation. "I think we're in the right place."

"I bloody well hope so," David said. "We lost the carriage getting here."

"The carriage isn't important."

"And what about all the supplies we left behind *in* the carriage? Hm? Are those not important either?"

"Well, shit," Felix muttered.

"Can't do anything about it now," Erika said, snatching the torch from Derek's hand. "Nothing to do but what we came here to do. Let's move."

Within the corridor's confines, Bravia and Titania's hoofbeats were as thunderclaps echoing through a high mountain pass. The party traveled down, down, ever deeper down.

The air felt as cold as a late fall day and smelled old, like a disused basement, but dry and not at all musty. Derek snapped his fingers, testing the echo to gauge how large a space they were in.

Erika spotted an iron torch set into a sconce. Its fuel was simple but ingenious: a plug of wood into which a wick had been set and sealed in place with beeswax. It was not meant to burn for long, an hour at most, but age had not compromised its flammability. The light from this torch revealed another farther along with wall, and that revealed a third — Erika ignited six before reaching a corner, and the last was illuminating in more than the literal sense.

To call it a mere carving would be insulting; it

was a lifelike portrait in stone. The subject was a male elf clad in full battle armor that had been rendered in painstaking detail, down to the last ring of chainmail peeking out between the gaps in his plate. His hands were crossed in front of his chest over the handle of a longsword, which was oriented blade-down — a sign that he'd died that rarest of deaths for warriors. Indeed, upon closer examination, Erika could discern delicate age lines around the elf's eyes and mouth; he had died an old man. There was writing encircling his head like a halo — elvish, definitely, but an unfamiliar dialect.

"Winifred. Get over here," Erika said, but her entire entourage responded. Winifred crossed her hands over her chest, mirroring the image on the wall.

"What is it?" David said.

"A sarcophagus," Winifred said.

"A very old style," Erika added. "The body is placed inside an alcove, which is then sealed by a stone slab," she said, tracing her finger along lines invisible to the human eyes in the room, sketching the outline of the aforementioned slab.

"This image is of the person entombed within. And this," Winifred said, pointing to the halo of writing, "is his name. It appears to be an older form of elvish."

"It looks like it might be a combination of Boktnese and Lythian."

"But this character is unique to Clan Alrive's alphabet."

"Unless the guy's name is Artemisia Renn, who cares?" David said, and for once his carping served a useful purpose: it reminded his protectors they had a specific task at hand.

"If all the sarcophaguses —" Derek said.

"Sarcophagi," Felix said.

"Sarcophagi. If all the sarcophagi have these images on them, that'll speed up our search. We just look for the ones with women on them."

"Artemisia Renn wouldn't have been placed in a sarcophagus like this," Erika said. "She'd be in a place of high honor. Trust me; she'll be easy to spot."

"All right. Tether the horses here, grab some torches, and let's get to it."

With the education that comes only with hindsight, that most humbling of teachers, Derek knew now that a quick in-and-out was an unrealistic expectation. The catacomb was not a single underground vault but many — level upon level of Wihend's noble dead, penetrating the cold earth two, five, eight floors deep and counting. Each level was identical: two parallel walls of sarcophagi entombing men and woman alike, the majority of whom had fallen in battle. Each level was connected by a ramp large enough to accommodate a full funeral procession, so the appropriate sense of reverent ceremony could be maintained throughout the deceased's final sojourn. The ramps descended in one direction for two levels, reversed course, descended the other way for two levels, reversed direction, so on.

With each successive descent Erika's concern they were on a fool's errand grew. She feared reaching the bottom only to learn that this was not Artemisia Renn's final resting place, that she'd chosen a different tomb, someplace hidden, or was in a different catacomb altogether — or worse still, was nowhere. It hadn't occurred to her until this moment: if Artemisia Renn the

Shattering Hand dissolved the One Tribe and banished her people from Wihend, who would have carried her to her grave — assuming she had remained here at all?

No one.

"There's nothing here," Erika said aloud.

"Was thinking that myself," Felix said. "You notice that, Derek?"

"Yeah. It's weird."

"It makes perfect sense, unfortunately," Erika said.

"Mm, maybe. I know it's been sealed up, but I've been on enough dungeon dives to know things have a way of getting into completely sealed areas."

"What are you talking about?"

"Spiders. There're always spiders."

"And bats," Felix said.

"And rats."

"Yeah, rats galore."

"I think we're having two different conversations," Erika said.

"Uhh...when you say spiders," David said, "you're talking really tiny ones, right?"

"I wish," Felix said. "I've seen them as big as your head." David raised his torch a little higher to scare away anything that might be lurking on the ceiling. "But there's not so much as a cobweb in this place. No webs, no bat or rat shit on the floor..."

"Don't complain," Erika said.

"Not complaining, I'm pointing out something that might be important. Either this place is airtight and there's absolutely no way so much as an ant could get in — which I doubt, because those doors up topside sure didn't look sealed to me..."

"Or?"

"Or there's something down here scaring everything else away."

"You don't think...?" Derek said.

"That's exactly what I think."

"Gods, I hope not."

"I'm with you, man."

"Now what are you on about?" Erika said.

Derek and Felix exchanged grave looks. "If I tell you to do something," he said to the others, "do it, immediately, no questions. And that goes double for you," he said to David with a sharpness he'd never before used with the lad, as deserving of it as he might have been.

"I'll go on ahead," Felix said, and Erika was disinclined to argue; she would not admit it to them, but she was the novice here, Derek and Felix the experts. "Ten minute runs."

"Right."

Felix tossed his torch to Derek. "I'm off."

"Be careful."

"Hey, man, I want to live to collect my gold for this job."

"You mean the gold that was in the carriage?" David said.

Felix sneered. "Thanks for the motivation," he said, and then he melted into the darkness, a shadow returning home.

"Now what?"

"We wait," Derek said. "This is a ten-minute advance scout pattern. He goes out five minutes, checks things out, comes back. If it's safe, we move on. If it's not, we figure out how to deal with whatever problem lies ahead or withdraw if we can't."

"And if he doesn't come back?" Erika said.

Derek said, heavily, "We get the hell out of here."

"We leave him behind?" Winifred said.

"That's standard operating procedure. If he doesn't come back it means he's run into major trouble. If we go after him, we'd only be following him in blind and probably getting into the same trouble. Sort of defeats the purpose."

"You'd leave him behind."

Derek shrugged with his eyebrows.

"Like hell. You wouldn't leave him behind in a million years," Erika said. Derek eyebrow-shrugged again.

They waited.

Nine minutes and fifty seconds later, Felix returned. "Next three levels are clear, and it looks like there's more to go beyond that."

And there was. Felix struck out and returned three more times, searching three levels per sweep, but his report on the twentieth level was less than promising. "We need to be careful."

"Dammit," Derek said. He drew his sword, Felix his sabers. "We move slowly and quietly."

And so they did, and when they reached the bottom of the final ramp, their fading torchlight revealed a yawning crevice in the floor — narrow enough to jump over but wide enough to fall through should a leap fall short. There was something about this gash in the stonework that struck Erika as wrong. She thought it did not look like the result of natural forces — more like a wound that had burst from within.

"Derek," she whispered, "what am I looking at?"

"Remember my story about how Felix and I met? Remember the things that killed everyone in our party?" He nodded toward the crevice. "I don't know if they have a name, but we call them Underdwellers. They're big, ugly, nasty, tough, and scary as all hell."

"What happens if one of these Underdwellers — ?"

"Pray, for starters," Felix said.

"We drop our torches in a pile, freeze, and don't make a sound," Derek said, addressing the more practical issues. "Our theory is they respond to heat and movement. The fire from the torches should blind them to our body heat, so as long as we don't move and stay quiet they should pass us by."

"*Should*," David said. "As in, you don't know for sure?"

"That's why it's a theory, kid," Felix said.

Felix kept a wary eye on the crack once they cleared it, leaving the search to his companions.

They did not need the extra set of eyes. The object of their quest was there, in the back of this chamber, unhidden and unguarded, as though it were waiting lo these many centuries for their arrival.

Erika's doubts as to the Might of the Shattering Hand's reality were banished, if somewhat cruelly: the armor was displayed upon the remains of who could be none other than Artemisia Renn. The body sat upon a stone throne like a queen holding court; she had, after splintering her people and expelling them from their only home, passed through the caelo'i; closed its doors behind her; and made a solemn, lonely march into her own tomb, where she calmly waited for death to claim her. Here in the dark and in the chill of the deep earth, her body had gone undisturbed by scavengers — two-legged or four — and was preserved to a remarkable degree; her flesh appeared as shriveled leather, drawn tightly to display the contours of the skeleton beneath. A tarnished gold circlet, a modest symbol of her office, sat upon her head, ringing a mane of long white hair.

Winifred knelt before the dead elf-queen and bowed her head. Erika joined her, and in unison they said in their respective native tongues, *"Mother of us all, your daughters have returned. May your grace bless us that we may reunite your children in the House of Renn."*

"Knew it," Winifred said.

"Shut up," Erika said.

"I hope that was an apology," Derek said, "because I don't know if we're getting the armor off without causing some damage."

"Give me some light," Felix said.

"You better be better at this than you were at staying undetected," Erika said.

Felix knelt before the corpse of Artemisia Renn. The stealth, which he'd assumed would be boots, were a pair of heavy leather greaves embossed with elvish runes. These were secured in the standard fashion, with straps that looped around the now-emaciated calves. These he removed easily. He passed them to Derek to secure in his pack and got to work on the strength, a leather mantle that anchored a pair of spaudlers. These too came off without undue wear and tear upon the late elf-queen. The heart was a sturdy breastplate fastened by heavy straps at the shoulders and at seams running down the sides. Felix had to take extra care while wriggling the backplate out from behind the remains, but he kept his winning streak alive.

"This one's going to be a problem," Felix said, examining the final component of the Might of the Shattering Hand: the hate, an impressive piece of the leatherworker's craft adorning the right hand and forearm. The solid gauntlet was not going to be the issue; the glove, comprised of a series of small leather plates riveted together to provide articulation, was curled into a loose fist. Felix tested the fingers and found them frozen.

"This isn't coming off," he said.

"Make it come off," Erika said.

"I can't. The fingers are locked. If I take the gauntlet I'm taking the hand with it, and snarling at me isn't going to change anything."

"But I need it!" David said, his volume rising far above comfortable levels. "I need *all* the armor, the prophecy said so!"

"Quiet!" Derek said. "Quiet..."

And it was quiet...at first.

"What was that?" Winifred said.

"A bat," Erika said because what else in the catacombs might squeal like that?

"Shit," Felix said. "Shit shit shit!"

"Torches in a pile! Now!" Derek said, tossing his to the floor. "Ladies, I'm really very sorry for this."

Before either elf could ask why he had offered his regrets, Derek grasped the hate of Artemisia Renn and removed it — along with the forearm it sheathed — and stuffed it in his pack. The elves' stunned expressions told him he'd be offering fruitless apologies for the rest of the journey — assuming they survived the next few minutes, that is.

Derek grasped his sword and ordered his companions to freeze and for the love of the Gods do not move do not make a sound do not *breathe*.

The squeaks — a staccato series of shrill yips, each burst followed by a brief silence — grew louder. Closer.

Three fingers, thick and pallid, slithered over the lip of the crevice. An arm as long as Erika was tall unfolded from the gash and braced against the floor. A second arm followed, and the thing wriggled out of the fissure as though Hell's womb was giving birth to the most repulsive demon-child — a spindly thing with joints that recognized more than one axis and elongated digits well-suited for grasping the rocky surfaces across which it scurried. It spied the flames and crawled toward them on all fours. It bent low and studied the waning torchlight with large, milky orbs that dominated its head. These saucer-like eyes, combined with a tiny puckered mouth, lent the creature a comically astonished appearance, yet the sight of it caused an unpleasant warmth to spill down David's leg.

The Underdweller craned its head and swept the room, its gaze passing over each of the adventurers without pause, first one way then the other, then back again, and on this third pass, it stopped in front of David. Its nostrils, a pair of vertical slits set between its eyes, flared and took in air. It bowed low, seeming to prostrate itself before David as if in worship, sniffed deeply, and rose up, bringing its prognathous face level with the petrified lad's head. A proboscis, glistening with mucous, pushed through the tight sphincter of its mouth and, not unlike an elephant's trunk, reached for David.

"Erika..." he whimpered.

Its dying screech rang throughout the catacomb's lower levels and reached deep into the earth. Erika braced a foot against its skull and pried her sword free.

Derek scooped up the brightest of the torches. "Run," he said. "Run!"

They had reached level sixteen when David staggered and collapsed against a wall, gasping for breath. He wheezed at his guardians, his hands clutching his chest as though he was trying to physically force his lungs to work.

"They're coming," Winifred said.

"Gods," Erika said; it sounded as if every bat in the world had been loosed in the bowels of the catacomb and were now surging up to meet them. "Derek..."

"Way ahead of you," said Derek, who slung David over his shoulder like a rucksack.

The twitters became a dissonant chorus of squeaks by level thirteen, a cacophony of keening barks by level nine, an earsplitting riot of shrieks by level four. Felix, his lungs burning, his legs threatening to quit him as protest against such punishment, fumbled his pack off of his shoulders and felt around for their possible salvation.

"David!" he said, flinging a glass flask of lamp oil behind him without a glance. "Hit it!"

Fortunately, David's bewilderment was extremely short-lived. The bottle shattered, coating the ramp, providing David with a target he could not miss despite the vigorous jostling that came with his role as Derek's baggage. Flame leapt from his outstretched finger. The corridor lit up as brilliantly as daylight. The adults wisely chose not to look back, but David had little choice — and had he not already purged his bladder, he would have done so now down Derek's chest, for the flames revealed a writhing, screaming mass of contorted limbs and perpetually shocked expressions and sightless eyes reflecting the pyre that separated them from their fleeing meal.

Bravia and Titania sensed something was amiss; the normally unflappable mares strained violently against their tethers, bucking and whinnying and stomping. Derek, after divesting himself of David, freed Bravia and had to drop his weight to anchor her as she reared up on her hind legs.

"Small problem," Felix said. "There's still a small army of Hruks loitering topside."

"I'll take care of that," Derek said, the din of pursuit again increasing in volume. "Just get ready to get the hell out of here."

The double doors, the penultimate barrier standing between the companions and freedom, were shut tight, and a shove told Derek there was something on the other side holding them closed — nothing too heavy by the feel of it, but after his twenty-story uphill marathon, a pebble would have been as good as a boulder. He leaned against the doors, hoping against hope his weight alone would do the job — and the Gods granted him his wish. The Hruks had merely thrown a few armfuls of debris in front of the doors, reasoning that anything dead that might try to escape would lack the strength of limb to overcome their barricade, and then returned to their revelries as though nothing had happened. Needless to say, the encamped

Hruks were quite astonished to see Derek, red-faced and wild-eyed, spill out into the caelo'i.

Too exhausted in body to fight them, too exhausted in mind to come up with a clever ploy for circumnavigating the mob, Derek resorted to the time-honored tactic of throwing his arms up and screaming like a madman. This produced not one but two beneficial effects. His friends, thinking his cry the all-clear signal, spurred their steeds into motion. His Hrukish foes, short on smarts and long on superstition, took the grimy, sweaty, pale, wild-eyed Derek Strongarm as a vengeful revenant and, instead of attacking him, proceeded to swirl in place like a swarm of confused hornets. Bravia and Titania's thunderous arrival parted the masses, giving the great beasts a clear path to freedom. Derek leapt onto Titania's bare back and wrapped his arms around Erika's waist, sandwiching David in-between, and the horses galloped away as the true horrors of the tomb — a legion of very hungry, very angry Underdwellers — erupted into the caelo'i.

The Hruks' screams chased the adventurers as they raced through the moonlit city; back through the southern gates; into the forest; and away, so very far away from the Lost City of Wihend.

## Interlude

"Master?" Augus Greeley said. "I bring news."

Habbatarr, lord of the undead, gave his thrall a brief sidelong glance before returning to his labors, flipping through one of the many, many volumes of his accumulated knowledge, looking for...something. He knew he was looking for something, but what that something was had slipped his mind. That happened frequently.

"Well," Greeley said. "I suppose I'm actually bringing a lack of news. I've received word from Clarence Miggis. He's failed you, I fear."

"Eh? Who?" Habbatarr asked.

"Miggis. Your man in Elesy."

Habbatarr turned his stolen eyes on his minion. "My man? *Pfah.* A fool who fancies himself my servant, you mean."

"A man who supports your cause, my lord."

"MY CAUSE?! *This* is my cause, thrall!" Habbatarr thundered, lifting up and slamming down his book. "Reclaiming my lost life is my only cause! I care not for these weak-minded fools who claim servitude to me! They are useless! Less than useless!"

"My lord, if I may be so bold as to remind you," Greeley stammered. He took a measure of comfort in that his lord's wrath was not intended for him — but only the smallest measure, mind you, since masters of evil were, as a rule, inclined to channel their anger toward whoever might be at hand. "These disciples are not without their value. They have been tireless in their efforts to slay the Reaper before he — "

Habbatarr flinched at the mere mention of his fabled foe. "Tireless," he said, "but not successful..."

"Sadly true, my lord, but worry not. They will stop the Reaper long before he reaches Hesre," Greeley lied; his confidence in the cultists was fast fading for want of a single report of success. "And if not them, well...the castle is not without its own defenses, should it come to that..."

Habbatarr had stopped listening. He paced about his inner sanctum, alternately examining his current flesh sheathe for early signs of decay and staring off into space. He gestured as might a master orator making an important point then shook his head as though dismissing a weak argument.

"As you are of course concerned with greater priorities, my lord, I'd be most willing to continue monitoring the situation, if you wish it."

Habbatarr nodded, grunted, waved dismissively, and then turned his mind to poring over a stack of notes written in his own hand — that is to say, notes written in a hand that became his but once belonged to another. It vexed him that his own transcriptions were oftentimes illegible, but the flesh that sustained him throughout the centuries came with many costs — foremost among them the shadow-memories he acquired from the original owners. Their ghostly voices whispered in his head constantly, and Habbatarr would sometimes feel wistful for places he had never been, pine for loves he'd never known, catch himself humming unfamiliar tunes for which he did not know the lyrics. Most of his notes, detailing decades upon decades of research into his self-inflicted condition and what might be done to stabilize it — perhaps even reverse it and return him to true life — contained unrelated passages dictated to him from beyond: portions of shopping lists and clips of love letters and repeating lines of the alphabet rendered in crude block lettering intermingled with arcane formulae and incantations. Habbatarr blamed these uninvited distractions for his failure to undo that cursed spell, but in moments of clarity, he wondered if the failure was entirely his own — or if there was any remediation to be had at all.

Sensing an opportune moment to slip away, Greeley did so and descended into Castle Relok, pondering his next move. His decision — made, as with all his decisions, without his master's express knowledge or explicit consent — to cast a wide net had so far failed, and miserably...

The library in the western corner of the castle was a pitiful shade of its former self, little more than an alphabetized collection of rotting silverfish colonies. Greeley found on a dusty shelf a map of Asaches — older than he by a generation, but it should suffice. He located the Reaper's point of origin in Oson and then Elesy — the one location through which he knew the Reaper had passed (unscathed, damn that fool Miggis) — then traced a line point-to-point. He continued the line that he might divine their course from Elesy, and determined the next destination of note would be the Grand Avenue. Greeley's intellect, keen in certain realms, failed him here; he debated with himself whether taking the Grand Avenue was clever or foolish but was unable to reach a satisfying conclusion. There were countless unmarked shadow roads the Reaper could take — hidden from prying eyes but slower going, and time was increasingly a factor. He pressed his face to the map and looked for a viable alternate route the Reaper might —

"The Traders' North Highway," Greeley said out loud, tapping his finger on the northern corollary for the Grand Avenue, a route that served the same purpose as its larger cousin but saw less traffic, what with the hamlets along that road so few and far between.

*But which one?* he pondered. Where should he tighten the noose? A wrong guess could mean the Reaper slipping through.

He shifted his gaze westward and experienced an epiphany: no matter which road the Reaper took to cross Asaches, he would eventually have to pass through a handful of hamlets at the edge of Habbatarr's growing domain to reach Hesre itself — Helure Falls, Aley, Reeild, Bersre...

Greeley transcribed the same message many times over on small squares of parchment, which he took to the high east tower — the rookery, quite literally, for here is where his messengers nested. They squawked and screeched at Greeley as he entered — the crows did not care much for him, nor he for they — and slapped their wings against his face while he bound the notes to their legs. He pitched more than a dozen out the window, trusting that the feathered idiots remembered their destinations well enough.

They did indeed, and within two days of their release, the ebon messengers had reached as far east as Erig Forest — about halfway between Hesre and where we now find our weary adventurers...

## Act Three
### In Which Truths are Revealed and Destinies are Realized and None of it is Terribly Pleasant

## SIXTEEN
## The First Day of the Rest of
## Randolph David Ograine's Life

Growing up on a farm had attuned Derek to the dawn on a profound instinctual level, and rare was the day he slept well beyond the sun's rising. Today was such a day; he awoke around mid-morning and found that he, indeed all his companions, had fallen asleep precisely where they'd sat down the night before, when the horses could no longer run, after they had put who knows how many miles behind them. His friends looked disturbingly like they had dropped dead on the side of the road.

Derek's stomach growled. The first thing he removed from his pack was Artemisia Renn's arm, and his appetite wavered. He set it aside with a delicacy denied in its removal and found a meager ration of jerky — barely enough for himself, let alone the others. He nudged Felix awake and asked for the contents of his pack, which produced another few strips of dried beef.

"This sucks," Felix said, thinking about how much food they'd left behind with the Moste Grande.

"Guess I'm going hunting."

"Good luck," Derek said. He let the others sleep, thinking it the best way to keep their hunger at bay until Felix's return. At this juncture, he decided, any boon, no matter how small, would be welcome, for the next leg of their journey would most certainly be the most difficult for the loss of their carriage and the supplies therein. He conducted a mental inventory. The tally was greatly discouraging: a half-dozen casks of water, feed for the horses, most of their jerky and dried fruit, the small canvas tent that had served Derek and Felix well on many a wet night, their blankets and bedrolls...

Erika, upon her awakening some minutes later, added to the list of damages a small chest of gold stashed under David's seat — six thousand pieces of gold, give or take, much of that intended for Derek and Felix.

"I see," Derek said. "What do you have for money on you?"

"Not enough to replace what we lost," Erika said. "You?"

"A dozen goldies or so, a few silvers. Don't suppose you could parlay any connections into a few favors."

"I don't think High Lord Ograine has any decent connections this far out. We shouldn't count on it."

Derek nodded. "We'll make it work," he said. "We have the horses. We can hunt for food. Our big concern will be finding fresh water. Do you still have the map?"

By way of a small blessing, Erika did indeed have the map in her pack. Derek tapped on a thin blue line running north-to-south. "There's the Uly River. If we head west we'll reach it after nightfall, then we can follow the Uly south until we hit the Traders' North Highway, then take that straight through to Hesre. I know it would expose us more than sticking to the back roads like you want, but time's really a factor now and you're not paying attention to a thing I'm saying."

She was not. Derek followed her gaze and felt a hot flash of shame.

"Erika...Erika, I'm so, so sorry I, um...desecrated your queen."

Erika Racewind blinked. Inhaled. Exhaled. "You did what you had to do," she said distantly. "Can't hold that against you. Besides," she added with half-hearted shrug, "she's not *my* queen."

Squirrels, spit-roasted over a small fire, were the first, last, and only course on the breakfast menu. Felix informed his companions that the forest was replete with animals, which told him there was a source of fresh water somewhere nearby, and so they agreed to search for this source after their morning meal.

"We'll spread out," Erika said, "take a different direction, go out fifteen minutes, then return to camp whether we find anything or not."

"I've done my work for the morning," Felix declared, reclining against a tree. "Your turn. I'll watch the brat."

"Brat?" David said.

"That's what I said, brat."

"You know, I'd appreciate it if you could show me a little respect."

"I bet you would."

"Oh, you be nice," Winifred said.

Felix smiled crookedly. "For you."

"Stay safe while we're gone."

"Back at you."

David ignored protocol and did not wait until Winifred was out of earshot before remarking, "You don't have a chance in Hell with her."

"Oh, well, if *you* say so..."

"She is a woman of intelligence, grace, and class," David said as if delivering a scholarly dissertation, "and you are one step above a street urchin. A small step."

"And yet, the last female breast I had in my mouth wasn't my mommy's."

What first spilled from David's mouth could have passed to an unknowledgeable ear as fluent Hrukish. Then the profanity flowed — no nouns, no verbs, not so much as an article — followed by vague threats, followed by very specific threats to Felix's physical well-being, to be carried out by the many and sundry underlings at his beck and call, starting with Erika Racewind and working all the way down to his father's personal bootblack.

It was at this point that Felix silenced the boy by grabbing him by the throat and slamming him to the ground.

"Your mouth is a very dangerous thing," Felix said into the lad's ear. "It caused us a lot of unnecessary trouble last night. Almost got us killed. Repeatedly. Plus, I'm getting real sick of listening to you. Now — correct me if I'm wrong — the prophecy didn't mention anything about your need to *speak* when you go after Habbatarr. So give me one reason why I shouldn't slice your tongue out and feed it to you."

"*Aakkkkkkhhhh...*"

"Right. Sorry," Felix said, easing his grip. "Again?"

"I need to say the incantations," David rasped, "or I can't cast my spells."

"Huh. Good reason." He let David up. "But you give us away one more time..." Felix drew a finger across his throat.

David curled into a tight ball and remained that way until Erika returned a half-hour later, on the nose. "Felix tried to kill me and threatened to cut my tongue out!" he blurted out, leaping to his feet.

"That true?" Erika said.

"Uh-huh," Felix said. Erika nodded and sat.

"Uh, hello?" David said. "This is the part where you kill him."

"I am in no mood for your shit, boy," Erika said. "Sit your ass down and shut it."

David stammered in pseudo-Hrukish.

"No luck finding water?" Felix said.

"None."

Winifred, however, had better news to report upon her return a few minutes later: she'd discovered several yards out a large pond of clear, clean water, and the surrounding woods were not so dense that they could not lead the horses there. Derek, after learning of this, volunteered for that duty.

"No, I'll take care of it," Erika said, taking the horses' reins. "The rest of you, take an inventory of our remaining supplies."

"Yes ma'am," Felix said, throwing her a sardonic salute. "Right. Let's see what's in the old — oh, yeah," he said as he turned his pack over and Artemisia

Renn's armor — and little else useful — fell out. He tossed the pieces at David. "Here you go. Now you'll look all snazzy and bad-ass when you light Habbatarr on fire with your finger, or whatever the hell you're prophesized to do to him."

"The leather is in amazing condition. Look at this," Derek said, taking up one of the greaves and showing it to Winifred. The quarter-inch thick leather possessed a rich sheen and was smooth to the touch, no cracking to be found anywhere on its surface, no signs that it had grown brittle. Even the straps were strong and supple. Aside from a few gouges and ragged grooves, unmistakable signs that this armor had seen use in wartime, it was as perfect — more so — as one could have rightfully expected. By all rights, it should have been as flaky and crumbly as parchment in an ancient tome. How could it have so completely defied the ages?

Magic. There was no other answer.

And thus did Derek Strongarm's world become a little more amazing.

"And it looks like it'll fit you pretty well," he said, turning the greave over in his hands. "May be a bit big for you now, but hey, you'll grow into it."

"I certainly hope not," David said, displaying the heart of Artemisia Renn to his protectors.

They had all of them quite forgotten that the armor had been constructed to fit a woman.

"Hey," David said, "where did Racewind get to?"

It was not until this moment that Derek became aware of Erika's inordinately lengthy absence. "She only went to water the horses..."

"She's fine," Felix said. "She's probably beating up a bear or something."

"I can see her doing that," Winifred said.

Derek could as well, but he nevertheless thought it best to find her in case she had not lost track of time whilst assaulting the native fauna, which was as plentiful as Felix had claimed. Derek's footsteps dislodged a chipmunk or fat rabbit every few yards. There seemed to be a squirrel in every tree, looking down on this rare human passing through their forest. The higher branches cradled nests small and large, from which drifted nature's finest music, carried upon air tinged with the sweet scent of honeysuckle. This land was so alive, more so than any he'd ever seen, and he dearly wished to sit a while and bask in its tranquil splendor.

Alas, he had a missing elf to find.

A wide, deep hoofprint in a muddy patch told him he was on the right track — so to speak. He continued along the vector Winifred indicated, with only the nigh noontime sun as his guide.

*Noon*, he realized. Half the day gone and they'd not moved a foot closer toward their destination. Erika would never allow that to happen. Never.

Derek broke into a run.

He found the pond at the base of a shallow depression, a bowl of earth cradling a body of sparkling water small enough to swim across, large enough to make it a chore. Trees rose up on all sides like the rim of a great emerald crown, hiding this little treasure from intrusive eyes — eyes that would have espied a naked elf as she broke the surface.

"OH!" Derek mashed his palms into his eyes.

"I'm sorry! I didn't mean —! Crap, I — Erika I'm — I didn't —"

"What the hell is your problem?"

"I-I didn't know you...you were...you know..."

"Naked?"

Derek nodded. "I'm so sorry. I am *soooooooo* sorry." He heard Erika leave the pond, heard water splash on the ground as it cascaded off her lithe alabaster form, her lean muscles, her high, firm — *No, Gods, don't think about them. Don't think about it, don't think about her naked, she'll know you're thinking about her and she'll kill you or worse rip your manhood off so STOP THINKING!*

"Oh, quit it," Erika said. "I'm naked. Big deal. You've seen a naked woman before."

"..."

"Are you serious? You've never seen a naked woman before."

"No. Yes. I mean...once," Derek said. "When I went skinny-dipping with some friends. Uh. Well, *they* went skinny-dipping, I went with them and...watched their clothes...so they wouldn't get...you know. Lost. Stolen."

He had to peek. Not to steal another glance at Erika's form *au naturale,* no no, but to confirm that he was indeed hearing what he thought he was hearing.

And he was: Erika was laughing. She was really laughing.

"Oh my Gods," she said breathlessly. A minute passed. "It's safe to look now."

Derek cautiously lifted a hand. Erika was back in her pants and shirt and was slipping into her hose.

"Interesting tattoos," he said, a lame and unsuccessful effort to steer his mind's eye away from Erika's body.

"They're a tradition among the M'ribela," Erika said. She pulled up her sleeves so Derek could see them, this time without any shapely distractions. The tattoos on her right arm — lines rendered in dark gray ink that traced the contours of her muscles, like outlines waiting to be colored in later — began at the shoulder and ended on the back of her hand. A similar design adorned her left wrist and hand, and Derek realized they matched the smaller tattoo bracketing her right eye. Ancient elven warriors, she explained, would tattoo the parts of their body which they wished to endow with the grace of the Gods — in Erika's case her sword arm, her off hand, and the eye that picked out targets for her dreaded flesh-rending arrows.

"Good thing you don't like to head-butt people," Derek said. This failed to earn him another laugh or even a hint of a smile. The moment had passed. "We should probably hit the road, don't you think? We've lost a lot of the day."

Erika nodded. "You're right," she said, but without the usual air of urgency.

Bravia and Titania were tethered to a tree on the line separating beach from forest. Derek unhitched them while Erika finished dressing, though she stopped before slipping back into her armor. Derek thought she looked naked without it, and that thought set his mind wandering — not necessarily unbidden — back along an impolite path.

"You're blushing again," Erika said. She chuckled and shook her head. "You are precious."

Erika hunkered down in front of the quintet's

collected belongings, and seeing them gathered into a pile small enough to fit into one pack drove home how destitute they'd become, all in the time it took for cruel fate to twist but once.

"It's going to be rough from here on out," Erika said.

"As opposed to the light-hearted romp this disaster has been so far?" David said.

"Now that you're going to be sleeping on the ground with the help instead of your cozy carriage, sure," Felix said, his sense of perspective heading off at the proverbial pass any further complaints.

Their net worth was now measured in a few torches; two sets of flint and steel; two flasks of lamp oil; two whetstones; a coil of rope; a woolen blanket that had been crudely repaired several times; the map; a small leather-bound journal (Derek's); a small wooden case containing charcoal pencils, a small bottle of ink, and a wooden pen with a steel nib (also Derek's); a leather pouch that held cloth bandages, herbal mixtures, and a variety of medicinal tinctures (Winifred's); and a leather case of assorted lockpicks (Felix's). Felix informed Erika the pooled hard cash amounted to forty-seven gold pieces and sixty-two silver. Then there was the food...

The jerky would last two days, maybe three if they were stingy with their rations, though that would be a negligible concern if the wildlife remained abundant. The greater cause for worry was their limited supply of potable water; they had four waterskins between them, and just one of the horses could drain those at a sitting and want for much more. The Uly would sustain them for as long as they followed it, but eventually they would have to track west toward Hesre. From that point they would, for a time, be able to rely on the villages and way stations dotting the Travelers' Highway, but when those ended they would be at the mercy of whatever streams and ponds nature saw fit to provide — and it appeared that Asaches would completely exhaust its mercy during the final two days of their expedition.

"There may be some small ponds that aren't on the map," Derek said, "or unmarked villages with wells."

"We can't assume that," Erika said. "We have to assume there's no good luck ahead."

"Done and done," Felix said.

Erika named Derek the pack mule, trusting that he among the company would be most effective in safeguarding their precious remaining belongings. She rode with him on Titania — bareback, which was a new experience for Derek — while David rode Bravia, sandwiched between Winifred at the reins and Felix at the rear. Neither David nor Felix especially cared for this configuration.

"I should have my own horse," David decided.

"One horse can't carry four people," Derek said.

"Why not? These things are enormous."

"They still get tired," Erika said. "Four people on one horse would tire out that horse more quickly that the other, which means we'd have to stop more often so it could rest."

"So they can haul a big carriage just fine, but can't carry four people at once," David said. "Is that right? I just want to make sure I'm following you."

"Put a cork in it, Davey," Felix said.

"My name is not *Davey*, dammit, it's David, and I'd love it if you called me — no, scratch that. My name is Randolph David Ograine, Prince Lord of Asaches, the Reaper, the Bane of Habbatarr, the guy who's going to save the entire friggin' world, and I demand you show me the respect due to me! From now on, you address me as Lord Ograine — all of you," he said, his eyes darting to each of his guardians in turn, "or you don't address me at all. Got it?"

"Don't address you at all," Felix said. "Got it."

"That's right, keep cracking wise..."

"Don't mind if I do."

"...because when I inform my father about how you've treated me..."

"Oh my Gods, are you actually threatening to tell your daddy on me?"

"Since my so-called bodyguard isn't doing her job..."

"Excuse me?" Erika said. "My job is to protect you until you get to Hesre, not kill everyone who pisses you off — not that I wouldn't enjoy it in Lightfoot's case..."

Titania jerked to a halt at Derek's command. "Erika," he said with a weary sigh, "your surly attitude is doing nothing to ease the tensions around here. Felix, stop provoking David and Erika. It entertains you but irritates everyone else. David, respect is a two-way street. You've treated us poorly from day one, even though we're risking our lives for you, but you expect us to take your abuse with good humor. You want us to treat you respectfully? You need to do the same."

"You don't think that maybe the respect should

flow my way first?" David said. "I *am* the most important person in the world."

"You're important today, sure, but what about after you've killed Habbatarr? What happens to you then?"

"Uh...I eventually become High Lord of Asaches and life is great. Duh."

"I don't remember 'and he lived happily ever after' being in the prophecy," Felix said.

"He's right," Derek said. "The course of your life is only guaranteed until you fulfill your destiny. After that, you're fair game. If there's one thing I've learned in life, it's that the Gods can take their favor away as fast as they can give it."

Derek jabbed his heels into Titania's flanks, and she compliantly eased into a gentle trot. "I'm sorry I snapped like that," he said for Erika's ears only. "I didn't mean to lose my temper."

"That was you losing your temper?" Erika said. "I think Winifred would throw a less dignified tantrum."

"I don't like to get angry. Anger causes problems." The rueful edge in his voice did not go unnoticed.

## SEVENTEEN
## A Moment's Respite at the Outskirts of Hell

The party made camp before midnight at the bank of the Uly River, a narrow but deep expanse that ambled south until it reached its terminus at Uly Lake. The party enjoyed the Uly's company for a few hours in the morning and spent the rest of their day covering the remaining distance to the Traders' North Highway. This portion of their journey was far from carefree, the knowledge of their paltry rations weighing heavily upon them, but it was quite uneventful — save for one moment of awe and wonder that I shall share with you now.

An hour south of the Uly River lay the Lawon Forest, a sprawl of forest primeval that made amends for its utter banality, as forests go, by boasting one of the great marvels of the world — a mystery older and greater than even lost Wihend. It rose from the impenetrable mass of stately conifers, towering over the trees as Derek might tower over the spring tulips in his mother's flower garden. The simple dirt road, carved into the landscape by generations of habitual travel rather than intentional design, observed a wide circuitous flow around the Lawon — but even the most well-trained eye would be challenged to accurately estimate the distance between the former and the latter, for the Great Colossus of Asaches confounded all sense of scale with its impossible size. From miles away, the Colossus appeared to our travelers as a man standing within arm's reach, his feet lost in tall grass.

It was shaped like a man in the general sense: there was a head, arms, legs, fingers, but it had neither visible neck nor clearly defined joints along its extremities. Its proportions were more dwarven than human, for it was squat and broad of build, but there was otherwise no way to know for certain what race the Colossus represented — if indeed it represented any known race on Ne'lan. These revealing details were absent; the Colossus appeared to be wearing head-to-toe armor of an unknown design — at least, this was the majority opinion of the few scholars who overcame their nameless dread to more closely study the Colossus. Opinions on the stone statue's method of construction, however, were sharply divided, and no one theory held any more authority over another. One hypothesis proposed that a titanic mountain once stood in that spot, and the Colossus's creators sculpted it from the top down over generations, perhaps centuries. As you have seen already, that concept is not outside the realm of possibility.

The Colossus that now inspired mute fascination in our heroes was one of six across the globe, each of the other five providing spectacle and speculation in each of Asaches' companion continents. That each of the stone titans was to the last detail identical fueled further debate over their origins. How could a single force be behind six epic undertakings separated by thousands of miles — and yet, how could the Colossi have been raised up in isolation from one another?

I of course know these answers, and many more, but I shall not reveal them here and now; that, as the saying goes, is a tale for another day.

Bravia and Titania, freed of the burdensome Moste Grande, made excellent time. The companions reached the Traders' North Highway before nightfall, and an hour after that, they arrived at Padevil, a tiny hamlet that existed only to provide basic provisions and services to travelers. Sadly, their fiscal resources were insufficient to cover room and board for the bipeds or quadrupeds.

This was not an uncommon problem according to the woman named Denise Swiftsword (née Shelbourne), a former adventurer-for-hire who retired to a quiet life as Padevil's constable. Travelers wanting for cash took to camping in a tent city at the edge of the village — a commune of traders, pilgrims, and adventurers that arose each night and vanished each day with the morning sun, only to rise up again the next night with all-new residents. The barter system was the prevailing economic model, though people in need of coin also resorted to the buying and selling of services both respectable and sordid — the latter of which Denise discouraged but did not outright abolish so long as such transactions were conducted discreetly.

"Not a bad little set-up at all," Felix said as he surveyed the area, a vast open field that provided the foundation for dozens of tents and lean-tos that looked more dropped at random than erected according to any plan. They were densest toward the rear of the field, where a backdrop of stout oaks provided generous natural cover. One area near the front, scoured clean of grass, hosted a cone of branches as tall as Derek — a bonfire awaiting ignition, around which gathered the tent city's residents to chat, trade, and bargain.

"Yeah," Derek said. "Looks pretty good."

"Best looking hobo shanty town I've ever seen," David said. "Don't worry, you'll fit right in," he added, making Derek keenly aware of the dense stratum of scruff shading his jawline

"Boy, you don't know a golden opportunity when you see it," Felix said. "You guys find a spot to set up for the night. I'm going to go conduct some business."

"Business?" David said. "I can only imagine what sort of lucrative business opportunities one might find among transients."

"They're only transients because they haven't gotten to where they're going," Derek said, "and instead of treating them with contempt, maybe you should go out and get to know them a little."

"And I'd want to do that why?"

Derek said in a firm but fatherly manner, "Because they're going to be your people one day. They're going to look up to you, and they'd like to know that you're not looking down on them."

"I was planning to wander around a bit," Winifred said. "Why don't you come with me, Lord Ograine?"

An invitation from a fetching woman who deigned to use his proper title proved an irresistible combination.

Derek found a patch of ground near the back

beneath the sheltering hand of a high branch thick with healthy spring leaves. It wouldn't keep them perfectly dry in the event of rain, but dry enough — and besides, the sky was empty of all but the evening stars. Their closest neighbors were a family traveling east from Helure Falls, one of the villages more recently fallen under Habbatarr's shadow. The father, a veterinarian by the name of Gerald Farr — livestock a specialty — said a few of his neighbors back home had disappeared over the past few months. He'd heard other towns closer to Hesre were experiencing similar disappearances, and Gerald was not a man who held his hometown so dear he'd let pointless pride keep him rooted at the cost of his family.

"I didn't want to wait until the ghouls started showing up," Gerald said, dropping his voice to a whisper on the word *ghouls*.

"Ghouls," Derek said. "A lot of them?"

"Well, like I said, I never saw any myself," Gerald said, "but I heard Aley was close to overrun with them. Aley's only a day's travel from Helure Falls, and that was too close for my comfort."

"I know it's hard leaving the only home you've ever known," Derek said, "but for what it's worth, I think you made the right choice. Your family is more important than anything else."

Gerald smiled and nodded. "Nice to know I'm not the only one who feels that way."

"You sound like someone speaking from experience," Erika said after Gerald returned to the task of setting up a tent for his kids. Derek gave her a look but said nothing. "As I recall, we had a deal: you got to tell me one thing about yourself every day. By my count, you're a few days in arrears."

"Uh-huh..." Derek said.

"So? What's the story?"

"You don't get to hear that one," Derek said.

"Why not?"

"Because you haven't earned it."

Erika considered this and then said, "You saw me naked."

"True," Derek said with a nod and a flushing of his cheeks, "but that isn't enough. Not for that."

"Trade you, then. You tell me, I tell you."

"Seriously?"

"Seriously."

And so he did. It was the first time Derek had related his story since he told Felix, which was six months after they formed their partnership.

And so she did. It was the first time Erika had related her story. Ever. None of what she said came as a surprise — Matron Delsina had not been inaccurate — but that it now came from Erika herself...

They agreed in the end that time may heal all wounds, but the scars? They were eternal.

Since first meeting Winifred, David suspected she was — as his father would put it when referring to his oddball cousin Vincent — *a little off*. Her optimism, her sunny outlook on the darkest of situations, the way she smiled *all the time* — surely the symptoms of madness, if only a benign madness, like the kind that gripped artists and playwrights. She seemed especially cheerful now walking among the rabble, slowing from time to time to steal a snatch of an insipid conversation or observe a few seconds of their mundane busywork.

"You're enjoying this," David said.

"Oh, very much," Winifred beamed. "This...this is life at its very best."

"You think? Looks to me like life sucks."

She turned her smile on David, and somehow he felt guilty to receive it; there was reproof in her eyes. "You don't understand."

"I...don't think I do, no."

"Tell me: what do you see here?"

David hesitated. "I, uh, I see...I see a bunch of people, I guess."

"That's all?"

"Yeah," he said with a shrug. "Just a bunch of people doing stuff." Winifred nodded: *continue,* the gesture said. "They're talking. They're setting up tents. Making dinner. There are some kids over there running around in circles. Now they're dizzy. Now that boy is throwing up. How is this life, exactly? I mean, no one's doing anything special. This is all just boring normal stuff people do every day."

"Exactly," Winifred said. "Right now you're surrounded by all the tiny moments that make up a life, happening all at once, in this one place. It's like you're seeing an entire soul in all its individual bits and pieces — every experience, every joy, every sorrow, every triumph and tragedy simultaneously. This is life. This is the world — the world you'll inherit one day. *This* is your true destiny, Randolph David Ograine. Not Hesre, not Habbatarr. *This.* And you should know them."

Beautiful or no, she was starting to wear on his nerves — perhaps because she was making him feel astoundingly stupid.

They reached the leading edge of the camp

where a portly man squatted over a small nest of excelsior, the tinder for the evening's bonfire. Around him several expectant men, women, and children rubbed their hands together and stomped their feet, the universally recognized ritual dance for warding off a pervasive evening chill.

"I think it would be kind of you to offer to help them," Winifred suggested.

"My father always says a good sovereign allows people to solve their own problems and steps in only when necessary," David said. "If you do everything for them, they either lose their independence or resent you for running their lives."

"Sage advice," Winifred said, "but you're not their sovereign right now; you're an ordinary young man. And he does need help."

David grunted, grumbled, and tapped the failing fire-starter on the shoulder. "Hey. You need some help with the fire?"

"I'm not havin' no luck, young sir," the man puffed. "If you can do any better, have at."

The man rose, groaning like an invalid rolling out of his sickbed, and stepped back. David cast his ever-reliable Finger of Flame. The crowd gasped in awe and fell back as the pyre erupted with a *whoomp*, throwing off a wave of heat that caused their exposed skin to tighten and prickle. Appreciative chatter and a smattering of impressed applause followed.

"Amazing," the portly man said, clapping David a bit too hard on the shoulder. "You studyin' to be a wizard, are you?"

"Obviously," David said. Winifred *ahem*ed softly. "I mean, obviously I'm still studying."

"What else can you do?" one little boy demanded. "Can you turn into a monster?"

"Can you fly?" a little girl chimed in.

"Can you turn my sister into a monster?"

"Can you make my brother disappear?"

"Uh, I, uh, I have that one spell down," David
explained to his young admirers, "a couple other simple ones, but I'm still working on the, you know, the
real show-stoppers."

"Show us!" the children cried, a few adult voices
insinuating themselves into the enthusiastic chorus.

"Never seen real magic before with me own
eyes," the portly man said by way of requesting a
demonstration.

"I don't want to be a show-off," David lied before proceeding to show off at length, neatly managing
to dazzle the crowd with creative variations of the same
basic spell. He created a pillar of fire, which he pre-
tended to balance on his finger; he sent an arc from the
index finger of his right hand over his head to land upon the corresponding digit of his left; he traced patterns
and dragged fiery contrails in the air, posing and gesturing dramatically like a stage illusionist. A stray fire-
ball splashed to the ground and without missing a beat,
David sprinkled rain from his overturned palm on the
rogue flame, and this the audience received with thunderous applause.

"Great sport! Great sport!" the portly man
crowed. "Oh my, young sir, if these aren't your show-
stoppers...why, I'd wager you'd be fair competition for
the Reaper himself!"

David was about to enlighten the fellow when
another called out from the throng, "Aw, the Reaper's

just a myth."

"Go on! You sayin' High Lord Ograine's eldest is a myth?"

"The boy's real enough, I'm not saying he's not," the dissenter said. "I'm saying the whole prophecy nonsense is...er...nonsense," he fumbled.

This gentleman's opinion was in the minority, as evidenced by the many jeers that met his statement. One woman angrily browbeat the skeptic, railing about Habbatarr's unholy minions encroaching on her village, driving out her family and friends, leaving them homeless and destitute, about how they'd invested their one precious remaining shred of hope of ever returning home in the Reaper, he who would destroy the lich-lord and forever purge his poison from the land. The woman, in tears by the end of her impassioned monologue, called the Reaper her hero, her savior, her salvation, and the salvation of all good souls in Asaches. He would deliver them from evil. He would send Habbatarr to Hell.

Every day of David's life, ever since he was old enough to understand what his father was saying to him and likely before that, High Lord Ograine would sit his boy down and tell him how important he was. He would one day end a terrible, timeless evil and bring a joy to the land unknown in this lifetime, and no man had ever known a higher calling. David believed him completely — why would his father lie to him about such a thing? — but he never truly grasped what it all meant until this moment, when young Randolph David Ograine found himself awash in the cheers of these men and women, perfect strangers all, giving voice to their inextinguishable hope.

They were cheering for him. For *him*.
And in this moment, he understood.

Back at our heroes' modest parcel of borrowed land, Erika was having a similar but less flattering experience: Gerald's two young sons were staring at her as openly and unselfconsciously as only children can gape at something new and curious.

"You're really white," one of the lads observed.

"Now, boys," Gerald said, breaking away from his discussion with Derek about the challenges of proper hoof care — a topic of interest to a very select audience, to be sure. "Don't bother the nice lady."

"No, it's okay," Derek said, hunkering down between the boys. "Her name's Erika Racewind and she's an elf of the Clan Boktn," he told them. "Have you ever met one before?"

The boys shook their heads.

"What do you think of her?"

"She looks mean," one of the boys said.

"Oh, she is...but only to bad people. If you're a nice person then she's nice." Erika forced a thin smile that did little to reinforce Derek's claim but guaranteed that neither child would misbehave until well after puberty.

"I guess we'll be safe from bad people tonight, eh, boys?" Gerald said cheerfully.

"Speaking of bad people," Erika said, pointing with her head.

"Got a present for us," Felix said, presenting to Derek and Erika a pile of wool blankets.

"Where did you get these?" Derek said, inspecting them. They were of a good heavy weight, perfect for keeping the cold at bay — and, Derek noted, brand new.

"The general store in town," Felix said. "Since we only had the one left I thought —"

"You stole these?" Erika said.

"I *bought* them."

"With what?"

"Our money."

"But I have —" Derek began. Felix tossed him the leather pouch in which they had deposited their shared wealth — the pouch Derek knew for a fact he had placed in his pack. It felt much heavier than before. "Ohhh, don't tell me you've been picking people's pockets."

Felix threw his arms up. "Thanks for the vote of confidence, man! Appreciate it! What do you people think I am?"

"A thief," his companions said as one.

"Hey, there's a time and a place for that stuff. The only money I stole was our own, and really, I didn't so much steal it as I borrowed it to make some shrewd investments."

"Translation?"

"I found a card game and made a killing."

"How badly did you cheat?" Derek said.

"Should I turn around so you can more easily twist the knife in my back? I didn't have to cheat. That's the beauty of it. People here can't play cards for shit. That particular lucre," Felix said, gesturing at the sack, "is squeaky-clean. Promise."

"Huh. Good work, pal."

Felix took a bow.

"How much?" Erika said.

"Maybe a shade under a hundred gold," Felix said, "which includes what we had before. Not enough that we can eat steak dinners every night of the week, but we can restock on some of the necessities before we hit the road."

Winifred and David returned in time to overhear this last part of the conversation. "Don't suppose that would be enough to buy a new carriage?" he said. "Or at least another horse?"

"Sorry, David, no splurging," Derek said. "This might have to last us the rest of the trip."

David opened his mouth to add yet another complaint to his lengthy list then dismissed it with a wave. He sat down at the base of their sheltering tree, his eyelids heavy.

"You all right?"

"Tired," David said.

"He was busy making new friends," Winifred said.

"Great," Felix said. "So the lynch mob will be here in, what, five, ten minutes?"

"I'm not being ironic. He was quite the charmer. And I think he took Derek's advice to heart."

"My advice?"

"About getting to know people better. I saw him reach out to these people, talk to them, learn about their fears and hopes and dreams, and I think he now truly understands and appreciates what drives them."

"Yeah? Good for you, David," Derek said. "That shows a lot of empathy and maturity on your part. I'm proud of you. Really."

"I learned something else, too," David said. "Remember you asked what I think will happen to me after I finish off Habbatarr? You said I was only important now but I might not be afterward?"

"I don't think that's exactly what I said..."

"Well, let me tell you something, Mister Derek Strongarm Blah-smith, or whatever you want to call yourself," David said, standing so he could better look Derek in the eye. "I just heard a bunch of people cheering for the Reaper — for *me* — because of what I'm going to do, and you know what that says to me? That once I kill Habbatarr, every single person in Asaches is going to love me *forever*! I could spend the rest of my life sitting on my ass not doing a Godsdamned thing and I'll *still* go down in history as the most important person that ever lived because I killed Habbatarr and saved the entire friggin' world! So...HA!"

David jabbed a finger at Derek to emphasize his anti-climactic crescendo then sat back down and almost immediately fell asleep, as though his diatribe had exhausted the very last of his day's energy.

"He sure told you," Felix said.

"I guess so," Derek said, but in truth he could not find the humor in David's outburst. This, clearly, was not the lesson Winifred had hoped to impart upon the young noble — but sometimes the hardest lessons, he lamented, can only be delivered by the cruelest of teachers.

## EIGHTEEN
## An Undead Fist Sheathed in a Velvet Glove

If I may be permitted to adapt an old axiom to my needs, there is before every terrible storm a period of calm, and in the days following our heroes' departure from Padevil, they experienced a profound calm. As they proceeded west along the Traders' North Highway, they encountered few travelers, and without exception the few they did pass were eastbound evacuees from towns within what they had come to call Habbatarr's Shadow. Their stories were eerily identical: ghoul incursions had become more commonplace in the preceding weeks, disappearances more frequent, and their local militias — typically a token line of civil defense comprised of a handful of able-bodied men and women — were ill-equipped to fend off such threats. In most cases they had left behind the bulk of their worldly possessions that they might travel more quickly, but more troublesome was the oft-repeated lament that they'd also left behind foolhardy neighbors who prized their land and material possessions more than their safety and had resisted all entreaties to join the exodus.

Before they left Padevil, the companions spent

their unexpected windfall on extra waterskins, jerky, and dried fruits in anticipation of decreasingly available game and fresh water. This proved a wise decision; with each mile the terrain seemed to drain of color, as though some divine artist was gradually exhausting his palette of more vivid hues and resorting to grays and sepias. The fauna completely vanished midway through day two — completely, if one does not count the odd rogue crow the adventurers spotted soaring high overhead or sitting on a desiccated tree branch, croaking at them as if in warning: *Turn back. Turn back while you can.*

They passed the last manned trading post late on day two, at the border of Reeild and Helure Falls. The proprietor's stock was woefully thin, his food stores empty. He offered to sell what little he had for coppers on the gold in the interest of hastening his departure; he too planned to head east and put as much distance between himself and Hesre as possible, but the businessman in him could not bear to simply abandon his merchandise. They purchased a lone sack of oats for the horses but passed on the rest.

Then came day three.

The Traders' North Highway passed directly through the hamlet of Aley, which announced its presence with a wooden sign mounted on a tall post. The sign had been bleached of all color, reduced to shades of gray, like the landscape, as to be almost illegible in the opening act of the evening. The first homes lay several yards past that, all windows dark, their doors ajar. A blacksmith's forge, not unlike the one Derek's father maintained back home, sat cold and empty, rust growing like moss upon an orphaned anvil. Across the road sat a long-disused farmers' market pavilion, a sloppy skirmish line of high tables beneath a long communal awning.

The phrase *ghost town* floated through the adventurers' minds like a foreboding cold wind.

"Look," Winifred said.

As they rode into the center of town, the companions spied the first and only sign of life in this sad, lonely hamlet, loitering on the front porch of the Forest's End Inn. At first he appeared as naught but a disembodied head hanging in the darkness, a round face with a wide and finely groomed mustache and a mismatching bird's nest beard, but as they drew closer, the elves could discern a black cloak enshrouding his body. The question of whether he was a dwarf or a seated human was answered when he stood to greet the travelers.

"Good evening," he said in a rich bass.

"Evening," Derek said. The party dismounted, their hindquarters groaning in relief. "Are you the innkeeper here?"

"Hm? Oh, no, no. I'm not from Aley. My name is Adolphus Drakemore," he said with a nod. "I'm a necromancer and loyal servant of Lord Habbatarr. I've been awaiting your arrival so I might ambush you."

"...Seriously?"

Adolphus rolled his eyes. "Of course I'm serious, you nit. Why else would I say such a thing?"

"Just wanted to make sure," Derek said — and this was true, because it would have been an inexcusable social faux pas to grab a fellow and hoist him off his feet in a threatening manner if he in fact posed no threat.

"Lad," Adolphus said, "did you not hear me when I mentioned the ambush?"

"Doesn't matter," Derek said. "What've you got? Zombies? Ghouls? Bring 'em on."

"Consider them brought."

He pointed over Derek's shoulder. Derek heard Erika's blades leave their sheathes.

Perhaps they had simply secreted themselves in the abandoned houses, waiting for some veiled command before making their presence known, but from our heroes' shared perspective, the warriors appeared to have materialized out of the night itself, dark and silent. Erika counted an even twenty of them, all armed with rusted swords and axes and flails and clad in armor assembled from individual elements of disparate styles and materials and conditions — the arms and armor of scavengers of the dead. Erika's nose picked out of the air the merest taint of decay; these men were either very freshly risen or exceptionally well-preserved.

"The Deathless Legion," Adolphus said. "My own creation and soon, along with the lad, my gift to Lord Habbatarr — his new elite warriors. Now, before you start in with the threats against me, you should know that I've given them their orders, and they will execute those orders regardless of my condition."

"And those orders are?" Derek said.

"To take the boy, of course." Adolphus raised a hand, stopping cold Derek's response before it could form. "Now now. I'm not an unreasonable man. I am willing to make you an exceptionally generous offer: turn the Reaper over to me and the rest of you will be allowed to leave, alive and unharmed."

"Yeah, right," Felix said.

"Friend, do you have any other choice?"

Felix drew his sabers by way of an answer.

"If you think we're just going to hand him over so you can kill him..." Derek said.

"Kill him?" Adolphus said, his voice rising a half-octave. "No no, sir, you mistake my intentions; I'm not going to kill him. That is not for a lowly servant such as I. No, I plan to bring him to Lord Habbatarr that *he* might have the satisfaction."

"Oh, well, when you put it *that* way..."

"Derek, stand down," Erika said. Derek hesitated then released Adolphus. Erika stepped in and brought her sica up under Adolphus' chin. "Give me your word. We give you David and you let the rest of us walk."

The explosion of shocked and furious protest began with Derek and leapt to the others like a wildfire jumping from tree to desiccated tree — yet this wave of outrage never spread to young David, who was instead gripped by an almost euphoric sensation of separation, feeling like a spectator to this bizarre turn of events rather than the central subject.

"You can't seriously —" Derek sputtered.

"Derek," Erika said, "you need to shut up and back off...and for once in your life, dammit, follow your orders."

He gasped as though Erika had kicked him in the crotch — and in light of the confidence he'd shared with her three nights past, a foot to the balls would have hurt far less.

"Erika?" David said, his voice barely working anymore.

"Well?" Erika demanded.

Adolphus raised his hands to proclaim his confirmation. "We go our way with the Reaper," he said, "you go your way with your lives." Erika nodded and lowered her blade. Adolphus gestured. One of his Deathless Legionnaires came forward, his stride as smooth as that of a living man, no hint of impediment by rigor — and still, there was something to his movements, an indefinable wrongness that marked him as not exactly human.

"What in the Gods' name are you playing at?" Derek said.

"You need to let this happen, Derek," Erika said. "You need to trust me."

Derek would have found trust easier in coming had Erika been able to look him in the eye.

Felix and Winifred turned to him, seeking guidance as the piecemeal warrior approached. *Fight?* their faces said. *Flee?*

David was rooted to the spot and rigid with horror. He didn't move. He didn't speak. The Legionnaire reached out for him.

"Derek," David whimpered.

*No.*

Derek lowered his shoulder and crashed into the Legionnaire like a runaway bull. He snatched up David, shouting orders. The horses, responding more to the urgency in his voice than his words, raced off. The companions dashed into the inn as the Deathless Legion charged, their unholy silence more terrifying than any battle cry.

"Gods DAMN it, Derek!" Erika roared.

Only the rumble of heavy footsteps on the front

porch registered. Derek dropped David — he fell to his knees, trembling — and reached out to throw a deadbolt that was not there. "Get him upstairs!" he shouted as the first Legionnaire burst through the door. Momentarily bereft of his sword, Derek punched the warrior in the face. His nose flattened with a wet crunch and noisome blackish-red sludge splashed down his lips and chin, yet pain never registered on his face. The impact drove him back a few steps, causing a brief but valuable jam in the doorway; Derek loosed his sword and stabbed, skewering the noseless Legionnaire and one of his allies like piglets on a spit — again to no visible effect. These Deathless Legionnaires were aptly named.

Derek weaved and bobbed through the miniature maze of tables and took the stairs three at a time. Felix shouted a warning. Derek ducked in the nick of time under a flying chair. Winifred pitched a second chair over Derek's head. Felix emerged from a nearby guest room carrying a squat nightstand, which joined the chairs to form a crude blockade at the foot of the stairs — crude, but effective. One of Habbatarr's minions attempted to clamber over the clutter and pitched face-first onto the steps.

"David! The furniture! Ignite the furniture!" Derek said, but David had gone utterly blank. "Winifred! Get him into a back room!"

Winifred grabbed David by the arm and dragged him down the hallway, clearing precious space for the fight to come. The hallway was two people wide with a low ceiling — not a lot of room to swing a longsword, but their assailants, once into the stairwell, would be even more confined.

The Legionnaires cleared the blockage and began their assault. Derek rammed his sword home, sinking it to the hilt in the lead warrior's chest, to the same non-effect as before. A second, third, fourth Legionnaire pressed behind the first. Derek leaned into the scrum, but the combination of his weight, gravity, and leverage could not overcome the sheer brute force of now seven men advancing as a single unit to conquer the summit of the Forest's End Inn's lone stairway.

In this instance, Felix and his short sabers were better suited to the tight environs, so Derek withdrew and allowed his partner to take point. A scissor-slash across the throat deprived the lead Legionnaire of his head, and a double pincer-stab to the temples shredded the brain of the second. Felix stumbled back as he wrenched his blades free and Erika bounded into the fray, her sica sliding through lifeless flesh and bone as easily as the air itself. A second head thunked to the floor, its face as expressionless now as before.

She braced for the next man, but nothing came. It was not what one would consider a conventional retreat; the remaining Legionnaires simply turned around and stalked away as though they had lost interest in the fight and wished to find a greater challenge. The companions listened as the Legionnaires' footsteps crossed the inn and faded away.

"What just happened?" Derek said.

"Don't knock it, man," Felix said. "Not that I'm complaining, but they were pretty stupid for 'elite' warriors."

*Were they?* Derek wondered. Adolphus was audacious and brazen, no question, but he did not strike Derek as a fool.

"Winifred," he said. "Where'd she go?"

He'd sent Winifred to a back room, and that is where they found her: in the farthest room, on the left-hand side of the hall, rolled into a tight fetal position, her arms cocooning her head. Felix screamed her name and shoved his way in. He knelt and gingerly pulled her arms away. Her blonde hair had been dyed a dark pink on the left side, stained by the blood flowing freely from a small but ugly wound a few inches above her ear.

David was nowhere to be seen. The bed was on its side, ruling out any chance that the boy might be hiding underneath. That left the lone window, the remnants of which crunched under Derek's boots as he crossed the room. It looked out over the porch roof and into the empty street.

"She's hurt bad," Felix said.

"David's been taken," Derek said.

"Did you hear me? Winifred's hurt!" Derek righted the bed and helped lift Winifred off the floor. She whimpered as Felix explored the area around the wound with his fingertips, feeling for signs of a skull fracture despite having no concept of what that might feel like. "I — I need light. I need to see how bad it is."

"Do you think she'll be able to move?"

"I don't know!" Felix spat.

"Then figure it out! We have to go after David!"

"No we don't!" Erika said. "And if you'd listened to me in the first place she wouldn't —"

One of the first things Erika realized about Derek Strongarm was that, despite his ferocity in battle, he was not a violent man — not in the same way that she was a violent woman. He was at his core a gentle soul, level-headed and easy-going, someone who would have to be pushed very hard before he let anger take over.

Pinned against the wall now, with Derek's hand encircling her throat, Erika knew she'd achieved something rare.

"I'm done listening to you," he growled. "You let a boy — a *boy* — get taken away to his own execution, and if you think for a second I'm going to let that happen —"

Erika tried to speak, but her words were reduced to breathless croaking sounds. "Please," she managed, and for a moment she thought Derek hadn't understood her mangled gurgle — or worse, understood but didn't care.

His grip relaxed, ever so slightly. The rush of fresh blood made her light-headed.

"This was what was supposed to happen," she rasped.

"What are you talking about?"

"This was the mission. Remember? We were supposed to bring David to Hesre and that's where he's going."

"What, we were supposed to drop him off on Habbatarr's doorstep and that's it?"

"Yes!"

"And what about bringing him back? You were supposed to bring him home afterward, right?"

"..."

"Right?"

"No. High Lord Ograine told me to bring David to Hesre then return to Oson. Alone."

Derek's hand fell away from Erika's throat, leaving behind faint shadows of his fingers. "But...but that doesn't make any sense," he said. "Why would Ograine tell you to leave David behind?"

"Because he doesn't expect David to survive," Felix said. His declaration hung there, heavy and ugly.

"There was part of the prophecy High Lord Ograine never told David," Erika said. *"The Reaper shall deliver the Decaying King into the arms of the Gods...and thus ends the Reaper, who shall belong to the ages."*

"Were you ever going to tell *us* that part?" Derek said, his voice thick with emotion.

Erika averted her gaze.

"Of course she wasn't. She couldn't use us if we knew what was really going on," Felix said bitterly. "Story of our Godsdamned lives."

"Not this time," Derek said. "Felix, patch Winifred up as best you can. I'm going to go find the horses, then we're getting out of here. We're finding the bastards that took David, then we're going to Hesre and we're killing Habbatarr. All of us."

"We can't," Erika said. Derek rounded on her. It took on her part a supreme effort of will to hold her ground. "David has to do it alone."

"Says who?"

"The prophecy! The prophecy doesn't say the Reaper *and his friends* face Habbatarr. For all we know our interference could screw up everything, and there's too much at stake to risk that."

Derek wanted to hit her. It was a loathsome thought, an irresistible impulse, but he wanted to hit her — not because she was wrong but because she was irrefutably right.

"I'm sorry, Derek," Erika said. "I am. But the

prophecy says David fights Habbatarr alone."

"No," Felix said. He was sporting that crooked smile of his, the one that appeared whenever he had a brainwave and was about to show the world how fantastically brilliant he was. "No, that's not what it says."

"Felix..."

"That's not what it says. The prophecy says that the Reaper will, and I quote, *enter the Decaying King's towering tomb in the Dead City, armed only with his strength and his stealth and his heart and his hate.*"

"Yes. Exactly: the Might of the Shattering Hand. It's in David's pack and he —"

"Or!" Felix said, raising a finger for emphasis. "Or: his strength..." He pointed at Derek. "...his stealth..." He pointed at himself. "...his heart..." At Winifred. "...and his hate." At Erika. "And maybe that riff about the end of the Reaper and belonging to the ages means that after Habbatarr's dead, David's job as the Reaper is done and the insufferable little shit gets to spend the rest of his life with the whole world's lips forever attached to his ass."

Felix waited for this to sink in. Then he waited for the accolades.

"I could kiss you," Derek said.

"That would be awkward, man."

"No, that's — that isn't — you're completely twisting the prophecy," Erika said.

"And?" Felix said. "Prophecies get interpreted and reinterpreted and misinterpreted constantly. I'm merely offering my interpretation, and who's to say mine is wrong? You? Gods, until Matron Delsina told us about Artemisia Renn's armor, you were ready to march David into Hesre with nothing more than his rakish charm!"

"You don't —"

"Believe in prophecies, I know. But like I said: *you do*. And if your interpretation is wrong and the four of us are supposed to be there, David dies and he dies for nothing."

"And the rest of the world follows," Derek said. "We can't afford not to be there. If you're right and we don't matter, then David will kill Habbatarr with no problem and we get to bring him home to a hero's welcome. But if he needs us..."

"Those aren't my orders," Erika said. "That wasn't what I was told to do."

Felix spat a profanity at his erstwhile employer. Derek waved him silent. A dozen speeches rolled through his head, all of them variations on a theme: appeals to the lifelong servant to shrug off her shackles of honor and do what she felt was right rather than what she was told — but he could not convince himself that anything he said would yield results. This woman was not interested in seizing the moral high ground and to hell with what consequences may come; her will was not so strong.

"Then stay out of our way," Derek said.

Bravia and Titania, smart and loyal steeds both, had escaped to the edge of town to await their masters; Derek found them loitering near an empty public stable.

He returned to the inn, horses in tow, where Felix tended to the wounded Winifred. He'd rounded up and lit several oil lamps and now sat at the bar, inspecting Winifred's head under the flickering pale yellow light. She was conscious but her face was a blank mask; her ever-present, ever-comforting smile was conspicuously absent.

"How bad?" Derek asked.

"She got real lucky," Felix said. He grabbed an unmarked bottle off the bar and tipped some pungent liquor into a rag. Winifred winced as he dabbed at her scalp. "Best guess is one of those bastards caught her with a glancing blow from a mace or a flail. Scalp wounds, always look worse than they are."

"Says you," Winifred said. She sounded drunk.

"Yeah, says me. You bled like a stuck pig but it's a small gash. Couple inches lower and...well."

"Winifred, this is very important," Derek said. "They took David. We're going to go after him. Can you travel?"

She nodded unconvincingly.

"Give me a minute to patch her up," Felix said.

Winifred haltingly talked him through concocting a poultice of the liquor and some herbs from her kit. He pressed the resulting paste into the wound and secured it by wrapping Winifred's head with her own bandages.

"Nice job," she said.

"Learned from the best."

Erika followed them out of the inn, trailing at a distance. Felix mounted Bravia, and Derek hoisted Winifred up to him before climbing onto Titania.

"What about me?" Erika said.

"What about you?" Felix said. "What, you wondering how you're supposed to get home?"

Erika gestured in the affirmative.

"Boy...isn't that ironic?"

Erika Racewind had, in the truest sense of the word, been alone for most of her life, and that was how she generally preferred it. She sought out isolation and carried it with her, wrapped herself in it like a favorite quilt, warm and quiet and comfortable. It was her element, her country, her religion. And in this moment, as she watched her former companions race off into the night on their fool's errand, leaving her behind like a bad memory, Erika Racewind hated her solitude as she had never before hated anything.

## NINETEEN
**Secrets Laid Bare**

Bravia and Titania valiantly pressed on until mid-morning, when exhaustion claimed them, and they refused to go another step. The roadside yielded spots of green grass stubbornly refusing to be snuffed out, but the land was mostly barren, so Derek let the horses strip what was available before breaking out the sack of oats. He felt oddly like an executioner delivering a final meal.

"What do you think?" Felix said.

"About what?"

Felix shrugged. "Whatever, man. I just need me some of that ol' reliable Strongarm optimism. I'll take whatever flavor you got."

Derek looked around. "Winifred seems to be doing all right," he offered. She was moving around — stiffly, like a woman stretching out the kinks after a terrible night's sleep, but that she could stay on her feet without swooning was a positive development.

"Yeah. Told me she has a killer headache and she's had a couple of mild dizzy spells, but, you know...could've been worse."

"Hm. I think that's our leitmotif."

"Yeah," Felix chuckled. "'Hey, guys, how was the trip to Hesre?' 'Eh...'"

"'Could've been worse,'" Derek chimed in, and the two friends laughed for the first time in what felt like forever, or very close to.

They laid the map out on the ground and tried to figure out where they were. By Derek's estimate they'd covered fifty miles since last night, maybe sixty but certainly no more. That placed them approximately halfway between Aley and Hesre — but the more pressing question, for which they had no answer, was how far behind Adolphus and his Legionnaires they were. The Legionnaires were not constrained by a prophecy-ordained deadline; they had no reason to hurry, save to bask in their lich-lord's accolades all the sooner.

"I think our best bet is to give the horses an hour or two, let them rest up, then push hard for Hesre," Derek said. "With luck we can catch up to Habbatarr's men and intercept them on the road."

"No, we can't just catch up to them," Felix said, "we need to get ahead of them. We need to set up an ambush."

"Yeah, good thinking. We're looking at six-to-one odds..."

"Not what I was thinking. I'm thinking if we don't take out the brains of the outfit first, he might kill David. Betcha he'd rather kill him on the spot and risk pissing off Habbatarr than lose him."

A grim prospect but a realistic one, Derek thought. Felix's strategy was sound, but how were they to flank an opponent whose location was a mystery? By the time they resumed their desperate charge two hours later, they had yet to arrive at a solid answer.

Despite their protracted respite, the horses were unable to resume their previous breakneck pace; the rigors of cross-continent travel were taking a toll, and the beasts could not sustain a gallop for more than a few minutes at a stretch. By noontime their pace had dropped from a steady canter to a brisk trot.

Soon thereafter, the trio encountered the remnants of a ramshackle hamlet that did not appear on their map — the ghost town of Avoy, one of the first to be fully abandoned by its denizens. Its houses — huts, more accurately — were scattered about with little rhyme or reason, the mark of a young township comprised of settlers who decided to plant their stakes in the first convenient bare patch of ground. The homes were in advanced stages of disrepair, with roofs caving in upon themselves and walls rotting away in patches like gangrenous flesh. As they approached the center of town, the residences fell into a vague order to create a de facto main street, and at the end of this road stood a fairly impressive meeting house — much too large for the town's pre-exodus population Felix thought, making an estimate based on the number of homes. Wishful thinking on the part of the town fathers? A dream of a booming future with a bustling, thriving populace expressed in stone and wood?

"There has to be a well around here somewhere," Derek said, thinking aloud. A cursory scan revealed nothing.

"I'll go take a look from the bell tower," Felix said, nodding toward the meeting house. He dismounted and helped Winifred to the ground. "How're you doing?"

"All right," she said with forced cheer. "Head-ache's a little better."

"Keep an eye on her," Felix said to Derek.

"I'll be fine."

Felix nodded and, throwing Derek a look that said *You heard me,* made for the meeting house. Derek smiled; it was heartening to see Felix legitimately taken with a woman rather than viewing her merely as a spot of fun for the night.

"He's very sweet," Winifred said.

"He's a good guy," Derek said, harkening back to a time in their partnership when he couldn't say that with a whiff of sincerity.

"DEREK!"

Felix sprinted out of the meeting house. A trio of soldiers — human soldiers — clad in coats of plates and brandishing arming swords pursued him. Derek leapt off Titania and drew his sword. Winifred struck a convincing enough en garde, but Derek knew she wasn't up to snuff, not by half; a stiff breeze would knock her over.

The man at the head of the charge came at Derek with a wild windmill strike, which Derek deflected with ease. His opponent wore over his armor a simple surcoat, quartered in red and blue and emblazoned over the left breast with a disembodied hand parenthe-sized by gold scrollwork.

"Wait! Stop!" Derek shouted, throwing his hands up as if in surrender. "Stop! Erika Racewind! Erika Racewind!"

"What about her?" a sharp, authoritative voice

said. It belonged to a stern-faced woman who led another dozen plus six soldiers out of the meetinghouse. Derek held up his sword, showed it to the woman, and made a show of planting it in the ground and stepping away from it.

"Felix, drop them," Derek said. Felix hesitated, but upon reviewing the decidedly lopsided odds, placed his sabers on the ground.

"What about Erika Racewind?" the woman said. She approached Derek and inspected him head to toe and back and sniffed disapprovingly. She was a good two feet shorter than he, but Derek sensed that she did not consider that a detriment.

"We've been traveling with her, helping her protect David. I mean, Lord Ograine."

Her expression was inscrutable. "What happened to her escorts?"

"They were killed outside of Ambride. She hired me and my friends to replace them."

"Then where is she? And Lord Ograine?"

"Erika's...we had a parting of the ways back in Aley," Derek said, "and Dav— *Lord Ograine* was captured by one of Habbatarr's necromancers. We've been trying to catch up to them."

The woman nodded. "I see. Or maybe? You're a bunch of mercenaries who killed both of them and are now heading back to Hesre to receive your reward."

"Huh?"

"Or maybe they're assassins sent to find —" one of the soldiers said, but his commander silenced him with a gesture.

"Maybe," she said. "Maybe. Take them!" She stood aside as her men surrounded our heroes, forming a razor-sharp ring of swords.

"No! We're not working with Habbatarr!" Derek said. "We're friends!"

"We'll see."

They learned that the woman in charge of the unit was named Captain Helena Greystone, and they were obviously soldiers in High Lord Ograine's service, but all else remained firmly within the realm of wild speculation as Greystone and a half-dozen of her soldiers escorted the companions to — well, that was for the nonce part of the mystery. Suffice it to say they were escorted out of Avoy...and by escorted, I mean they were deprived of their weapons, bound at the hands, placed atop three of the soldiers' horses, and carted off.

"Are we there yet?" Felix said.

"No," Greystone said.

"Are we there yet?"

"I just told you —"

"Are we there yet?"

"Will you shut up?"

"Will tell us where we're going? No? Okay then. Are we there yet?"

"Felix," Derek said.

"I can keep this up all day, man."

"And I can break your jaw," Greystone said.

"Try it, honey."

"Felix!" Derek said. "Not helping!"

"No, what's not helping is these dumbasses taking us prisoner! No, sorry, correction: *you* letting them take us prisoner!"

"Excuse me?"

"You were the one who told us to put our weapons down! We could have taken these goons."

"Not with Winifred still hurt we couldn't have."

"You couldn't have even with her help," Greystone said defensively.

"Oh no," Winifred said, "we could have beaten you very easily."

"See?" Felix said. "Told you? We could have kicked their asses and gotten back on the road, but nooooooooooo, we had to play nice..."

"They're High Lord Ograine's soldiers!" Derek said. "I'm not going to kill them!"

"I didn't say *kill* their asses, Derek, I said *kick* their asses — why do you never listen to me?"

"I listen to you."

"Barely. You listen to me and then decide my ideas are no good and we end up doing what you say, and now look where it's gotten us! Sometimes I feel like we're not equal partners here, that this is all about you and I'm just along for the ride."

"Felix, I...that's not true," Derek said, twisting in his saddle to face Felix. "You *are* my partner. And I do listen to you and I do value your opinion...and I'm sorry if I ever make you feel like I'm ignoring you. I know I can be bossy sometimes and, well, if I ever get like that again, I want you to tell me."

"Yeah? Seriously?"

"Absolutely. I don't want to argue like this again because we're not communicating. Okay?"

"Yeah. Okay...I'm sorry I snapped at you."

"It's all right."

"No, it's not..."

"No, really, you've been under a lot of stress. We

both have."

"Still not an excuse."

"Are we good then?"

Felix smiled. "Yeah, we're good."

"All right. Excuse me? Captain Greystone?"

"What?"

"Are we there yet?"

They were not there yet for several hours. They arrived after sundown.

They passed through a small patch of forest and emerged into what could be most accurately described as a military encampment. Makeshift checkpoints had been established along the camp's perimeter every twenty-five yards, each one manned by two soldiers armed with halberds and crossbows. Past this first line of defense sat a ring of heavy wagons — Wensley Grandes emblazoned with the Ograine crest — interspersed with large transport carts meant to be pulled by a team of draft horses. Gaps between the conveyances were few, far between, and never wider than the width of a single man. Beyond this improvised bulwark lay a sprawl of two-man pup tents, dense canvas over wooden A-frames, row after row of them — standard issue for traveling armies, and this was indeed an army. Soldiers, some still in their armor, some in just their clothes, were hunkering down at bonfires to take their evening meal. Their mood, Derek noted, was one of subdued joviality: the mood of men and women the night before they were to lay down their lives for whatever cause their lord or lady had embraced — men and women trying to smother whatever feelings of doubt or fear gnawed away at their resolve and not wholly succeeding.

Captain Greystone led her prisoners to a grand pavilion tent in the center of the camp. Not one but two pairs of armed guards flanked the entrance, and they saluted Greystone as she dismounted. Her men helped their captives down from their horses and directed them at swordpoint into the tent.

"My lord," Greystone said to the small robed figure hunched over a table, apparently in consultation with a pair of high-ranking soldiers in highly polished plate armor.

"What is it, captain?"

"Oh my Gods," Derek gasped. It was impossible. "David?"

The boy did a double-take echoing Derek's. "Do I know you?" he said. Derek, stunned, could but stammer incredulously. "Captain, who are these people?"

"We encountered them at our outpost in Avoy. They claim to have been traveling with Erika Racewind," Greystone said, uttering Erika's name as though it were a mild profanity. "I suspect they may be assassins sent for you."

"Hold on. You think Habbatarr may have sent us to kill him," Felix said, nodding at the boy, "so you thought the best thing to do was *bring us right to him?*"

"..."

"Gods, you're stupid."

The boy crossed his arms, his mouth puckered sourly, and if there had been any question left as to his identity, that erased it. "You're Alexander," Derek said, and he was the spitting image of his older brother — negligibly older, unless Derek missed his guess.

"A twin brother?" Felix marveled. "Are you serious?"

"Someone better start coughing up some answers," Alexander said, "or I'm going to order up some executions just so I don't have to worry about any of this crap."

"Oh yeah, they're brothers," Felix said.

"Lord Ograine," Derek said, "As I tried explaining to your captain here, David's entourage was ambushed en route to Ambride. All his guards were killed. Erika hired me and my partner here as escorts. We were ambushed by Habbatarr's soldiers in Aley and David was captured. They're taking him to Hesre right now, to Habbatarr."

"I see," Alexander said, glancing over his shoulder to his advisors. They turned to one another, whispering.

"We were trying to catch them when your men here captured us," Derek continued. "I think we're only a few hours behind, if you let us go right now we —"

Alexander raised a hand. "Captain, cut them loose."

Greystone held her protest and motioned for her men to do as bidden.

"Thank you."

"Now take them back to the outpost and send them on their way."

"Wait, what?"

"Problem?"

"David's still —"

"Why are you still worrying about him?" Alexander said blithely. "He played his part."

"His — excuse me? His *part*?"

Felix's mouth went slack in dawning horror.

"Ohh..."

Alexander shuffled over to the fire burning in a stout iron brazier. He eased himself onto a padded bench and sighed wearily, the firelight highlighting his sallow complexion, pronouncing his sunken cheeks. He had in an instant transformed from a young man to a boy growing old before his time. That was the final piece of damning evidence.

"He's the older brother," Felix said. "David isn't the Reaper. Alexander is."

Alexander spread his hands expansively: *Of course I am.*

"No," Derek said, but it was an empty, reflexive protest. It made sense — Gods help him, it made terrible, ruthless sense. How better to protect the Reaper from life as a human target than to conceal his identity behind an ersatz Reaper in the form of his younger twin brother, raised to believe he was the genuine article? How better to mask the true Reaper's march on Hesre than by not-so-secretly dispatching his decoy on a false campaign?

"*Ohhhh*...Racewind didn't tell you?" Alexander said. He laughed and shook his head. "That woman is a piece of work."

"Yeah," Derek said, his voice tight. "She sure is."

Greystone returned the party's weapons, offering by way of an apology a quick meal by the fire and some warm mead. They accepted, picking listlessly at a thick beef stew that smelled marvelous but not so much so that it could overcome their utter lack of appetite. Their stomachs felt as though they'd been replaced by giant knots of betrayal and recrimination.

"Racewind," Felix muttered, throwing his bowl

to the ground.

"I know," Derek said. "I know."

"No. I mean she's here."

Erika rode into view atop a handsome stallion with coal-gray hair — the former property of the Deathless Legionnaire Erika had deprived of his head, abandoned at Aley. She took no notice of her companions until Felix called out to her.

"Felix? Derek?" She jumped down. "How did you —?"

She went down tasting blood. A second punch sent a bolt of electric pain shooting through her left eye and through the back of her skull.

"You BITCH!" Felix bellowed. "You heartless fucking bitch! I'm gonna break your Godsdamned neck, you —!"

Derek pulled him off. Felix kicked and screamed and spewed bile and hatred and demanded release that he might finish his work. Why Derek did not comply he did not know, precisely.

"What the hell!?" Erika spat.

"How long did you know?" Felix demanded. "Huh? How long? Were you in on this sick scheme from the day he was born? It was probably your idea, you piece of shit!"

"*What scheme?* I don't know what you're talking about!" Felix lunged for her, but Derek held him back. "Derek..."

"Enough," Derek said. "No more lies, Erika. We know. About David and Alexander and the plan..."

"Alexander...? Alexander *Ograine?*"

"Yeah, Alexander Ograine."

Erika blinked at him with her good right eye; her

left had already swollen shut and was turning an ugly blackish-purple to match the handprint on her neck. "What does Alexander have to do with anything?"

Derek told her.

He expected a vehement denial of complicity. In his heart of hearts, he hoped it would also be an expression of sincere ignorance. He feared she would confess her role in this most vile plot, showing no trace of remorse, perhaps even take the credit for conceiving of it. What he received was this:

"Huh."

"That's all you have to say? 'Huh'?"

"If I said I thought it was a brilliant plan you'd probably try to snap my neck again."

"If he won't," Felix said.

"Did you know about it?" Derek said.

"No," Erika said.

"Horseshit," Felix said, and he found himself suddenly face-to-face with the elf; one second she was smack on her ass, the next she was close enough that Felix could smell the coppery tang of the blood oozing down her chin.

"I admitted I knew I was carting a teenage boy to the ass-crack of Asaches to get killed by a lich," she said, "and you already think I'm scum of the earth because of it. Why would I bother to deny anything else?"

Felix had no answer to this but could not let the moment pass without retort. "I'm not sorry I hit you."

"Didn't think you were."

"Enough," Derek said. "What I said before still stands: we're going to Hesre. We're going to save David. Stay out of our way. If you try to stop us —"

"You see where we are, Derek? In the middle of

High Lord Ograine's army," Erika said. "If I really wanted to stop you, all I have to do is give the word and every man and woman within earshot will hit you like an avalanche."

"But...if you're not here to stop us...?"

"Mount up," Erika said. "We've got an obnoxious brat to rescue."

## TWENTY
## Into the Land of the Dead

Erika made a quick stop at the camp armory to replenish her supply of arrows. She grabbed a quiver's worth for Felix as well, to show there were no hard feelings — even though there were, but knocking his teeth down his throat could wait; it was all about priorities now. As per Winifred's request, Erika also grabbed a shaft intended as a replacement for a polearm. Winifred preferred open-hand fighting, but given her condition, she thought it wiser to arm herself.

From there Erika went to the stable area to arrange for fresh horses and then to the quartermaster for enough food and water to sustain them for the short jump to Castle Relok — short being a relative measure. After the many miles they'd covered over the past weeks, the half-day's journey to Habbatarr's lair would feel like a leisurely stroll. A leisurely stroll into the mouth of Hell itself, granted...

No one thought to question Erika as she did her shopping. No one was that brave.

Captain Greystone graciously relinquished custody of her former prisoners to Erika, happy to be rid of the lot of them, and Erika in particular. The feeling was quite mutual. Greystone wished them a safe and swift journey home as an empty courtesy then crawled into a tent left empty by its rightful occupants, who were on guard duty, to get a full night's sleep before returning to her outpost in the morning. This was a cruel if unintentional taunt; the companions had been without a proper night's sleep for close to two full days, and their exhaustion was like a weight upon their chests, crushing them, stealing their breath and snuffing their will to move.

It was midnight, on the dot, when they left the camp.

They rode northwest, plotting a course that intersected with the northeastern edge of the Dead City of Hesre; they were in agreement that avoiding the city entirely was preferable, but time was at a premium, and they could not afford the luxury of circumnavigation. Tracking north, Erika reasoned, would minimize the risk of an encounter with Habbatarr's minions without extending their trip, and she predicted they would by daybreak arrive at the base of Mount Relok. That theory, however, did not translate into practice; they had no moon by which to navigate, only a diffused glow pressing in vain against a pervasive cover of craggy gray clouds, and the want of illumination slowed their progress.

Hesre itself, given its mythic mystique, was an anti-climax, and at first they'd not realized they'd crossed its borders. The stories they'd all heard since childhood had led them to believe they would be entering a vast necropolis on par with fabled Wihend, but what they found was no more impressive than your typical abandoned quarry. There was nothing within sight that resembled, distinctly or in passing, a manmade structure. Asaches had reclaimed the Dead City of Hesre and would surrender no secrets.

They exited Hesre proper as they had entered it: unknowingly and without incident, yet none of the companions regarded this as a promising portent.

By the first hints of muted dawn, they had yet to emerge from the strip of dead forest that comprised the final barrier before Mount Relok. The party dismounted for a brief rest and a quick breakfast of dried fruits and lightly salted nuts, and over this humble meal, Winifred raised a question that had yet to be considered.

"How are we getting into Castle Relok?"

"We'll have to figure that out once we get there," Erika said, finding this prospect highly disagreeable.

"Not so," Felix said, snapping his fingers at Derek. "Let me see your pen."

Derek handed over the box containing his pen and ink. Felix spread the map out on a flattish patch of ground, blank side up, and began to sketch.

"What's this?"

"Little Lord Alex apparently had some of his men running reconnaissance on Mount Relok," he said, "because he had a very detailed map of the area spread out on his table."

"He did?"

"Uh-huh." Within a few minutes Felix had reproduced from memory a version of Alexander's map — cruder for his middling skill as an artist but accurate. "On our current track we'll come out here," he said, pointing with the pen to the western edge of the forest.

A no man's land of indeterminate size separated the woods from Mount Relok, and looking at his finished product, Felix now realized that Mount Relok sat in a deep valley shaped, eerily, like a giant boot print, the no man's land forming the heel and arch.

An outer curtain wall riddled with wide gaps marked the base of Mount Relok, which was in fact more of a high hill with a broad plateau than a mountain in the traditionally accepted sense. Castle Relok was situated along the western edge of the plateau, left of center as viewed from above. This orientation placed even more ground between their entrance and the castle, and for a large army, the eastern forest was the only way in; a second, denser stretch of woodlands formed a natural fortification that ran from the northeastern point of the compass to the south point.

Felix pointed to a thick black crescent he'd drawn on the western face of the mountain. "That's the mouth of a cave that runs under the castle," he said.

"I've seen designs like this before," Derek said. "Castles built on top of cave systems use them as a giant cesspit; all the garderobes empty into the cave."

"Ew," Winifred said, summarizing the general sentiment among the party.

"Gross," Felix agreed, "but clever. See this big chunk of nothing between the backside of the hill and the river? Betcha that's old farmland."

"What makes you think that?" Erika said.

"This river here," Felix said, pointing out the wavy line paralleling the western tree line, "is your handy water source, and the cave-slash-cesspit is your handy source of manure."

"That squiggle's a river?" Derek said.

"Don't be such an art critic."

"Now that you've given us the guided tour," Erika said, "get to your point."

"You wanted a way in? That could be our way in," Felix said, tapping the cave. "There might be an access hatch in the castle's lower levels. We circle around using the trees for cover, go in through the cave, come up through the lower levels, and my guess is that Habbatarr will be in this top tower. Seems like the kind of place an evil dead guy would hang out."

"And why in the world would we want to slog through a cave full of shit to sneak through an access point that might or might not exist when we can just go straight up the center?" Erika said, drawing with her finger a line up the eastern face of Mount Relok.

"Because the map said there are enemy forces all over the place," Felix said.

"How many?"

Felix uncorked the ink bottle, submerged the nib, and flicked the pen over the map.

"About that many."

"*Hmph.*"

"I know. Decisions decisions, right?"

They reached the edge of the unnamed forest an hour later, the ruins of Castle Relok peering at them through the scatter of withered trees. They secured the horses out of sight and crept on hands and knees toward the tree line, crawling over emaciated roots exposed by generations of erosion, until they reached the lip of the valley and beheld Castle Relok in all its aged and ragged glory. The entire structure appeared sagging and crooked, like a sandcastle constructed of basalt compressing under its own weight, waiting for one last wave to erase it from the world. A central tower thrust skyward from the center of the fortress, a defiant finger damning the Gods.

This, however, was not the sight that caused an uneasy chill to snake through our heroes' bones. No, it was the many, many figures pockmarking the valley and the visible face of Mount Relok: ghouls, dozens if not hundreds of them. Curiously, there was little discernible movement among them; the ghouls wandered the grounds listlessly, like sleepwalkers.

"This is wrong. These things shouldn't be out like this," Derek said. True, the sky was but a roiling black ceiling through which no sunlight could escape...

"We can use this," Erika said, her voice so low that Derek, sprawled on the ground next to her, could barely hear her. "We can make a straight shot for the main gate, charge right between them."

"And then what?" Winifred said.

"What do you mean, 'And then what?' What did we come here to do?"

"You're assuming David is in there now, but we don't know that for certain."

"She has a point," Felix said. "If we did beat Adolphus and his goons here, we'd be storming an empty castle."

"Empty except for Habbatarr," Derek corrected.

"Even worse. And if David *is* in there, what're the chances he's still alive?"

"Felix..." Erika snarled.

"No, he's right," Derek said. "Habbatarr didn't survive all this time because he's stupid or careless. The smartest thing he could do is kill David on the spot."

"Derek," Erika said, measuring her words, "we

have nothing but lousy choices here. No matter what we do, it's probably going to end badly."

Derek, who had some harsh experience in no-win scenarios, could not dispute this.

"You know what I say? I say screw it. Screw playing it safe, screw the prophecy, screw High Lord Ograine, screw Alexander — I say we go in there and we start killing and we don't stop until Habbatarr's dead or we are."

"Sounds like a real fun party, but we don't have to be so suicidal about it," Felix said. "We still have an unguarded back entrance. If we sneak in — "

"Through a cesspit..."

"Unnoticed!"

"No time," Winifred said urgently. "Look!"

Their journey had been an ordeal like none of them had experienced in their lives. They had traveled hundreds upon hundreds of miles, knowing full well that every step brought them ever closer to the greatest evil known in this or any age, one step closer to their likely demise, faced along the way all manner of petty hardships, perilous challenges, and mortal dangers — and in the end had their righteous cause, that which sustained their flagging spirits in the darkest of hours, stripped from them so cruelly by a callous young noble. Their capacity for hope had been depleted, drained dry until naught but dust remained in their souls.

But now, upon spying the dark coterie galloping up Mount Relok and into the castle through its yawning main gate, one lone human in the lead, his horse tethered to another bearing a precious young cargo — hope burned anew.

"I guess this means we're going through the

front door after all, huh?" Felix said with married relief and apprehension.

"We are. Hell bent for leather," Erika said.

David awoke, for want of a better word; he had not truly slept. It would be more accurate to say that as he laid upon the cold, unforgiving ground beneath a thin wool cloak, graciously provided by his otherwise inhospitable captor, he drifted in and out of consciousness over the course of the night — and even in those precious stolen moments of oblivion, he remained painfully aware of the coarse hemp rope lashed about his wrists and ankles.

"Ah, you're awake," Adolphus said brightly. "Rise and shine, my lad. We'll be moving out soon."

A necromancer. A traitor to the living. A kidnapper of young boys. And worst of all, a morning person. Truly a man of boundless evil.

David rolled onto his rear. Adolphus smiled a thin smile in David's general direction and jostled a small cast-iron frying pan over a campfire. His Deathless Legionnaires were precisely where Adolphus had left them last night, in a loose circle surrounding the campsite, unfailingly vigilant.

"No dawdling," Adolphus said, sliding a thick slab of piping hot bacon onto a length of cheesecloth, which he used to sponge away the grease. He noticed David eyeing the meat. "Oh no. Bread is good enough for you, my young friend."

"But," David said. He hated himself for what he was about to say, but the bacon smelled so marvelous and looked so delicious. And he was so hungry. "Don't I get a last meal?"

Adolphus considered this and, with a dispassionate shrug, tossed the bacon to David. His fingers, numb and paralyzed, could not grasp the meat, and it fell to the ground. David stared at it accusingly. Then he picked it up, rubbed the dirt off on his pants, and shoved it into his mouth.

He refused to cry. He willed the tears to stay hidden inside him. He would not show weakness to this bastard. He would not despair.

He failed miserably on all counts.

"Now now," Adolphus said, retrieving a fresh piece of bacon from his crate of provisions and dropping it into the pan. "Dignity, my lad, always dignity. No matter how low a man sinks in life, he is never lost if he retains his dignity."

David's breakfast muffled the profanity.

"Sorry, didn't catch that."

"Nothing," David said.

Adolphus chased his breakfast of bacon, eggs, and strong coffee with a pinch of a spicy-smelling tobacco, which he smoked in a simple clay pipe while the Legionnaires tended to the menial task of cleaning up the campsite and packing the horses for the final leg of Randolph David Ograine's journey.

Two Legionnaires untied David's ankles, clumsily hoisted him onto a horse of his own — once the property of a comrade recently rendered truly dead by Derek Strongarm's sword — then re-secured his legs to the stirrups. Two Legionnaires rode in front of David's steed, one on each side, and two in the rear. He had the nagging feeling the zombified warriors were not there to protect him from harm from without but in case he figured out a way to do himself in and deprive

Habbatarr of any satisfaction.

They rode at a leisurely pace through a forest of tall, pale, leafless trees along a disused dirt trail. Adolphus was humming a tune David recognized but could not put a name to. It was supposed to be a jaunty melody, a song well-suited for happy drunkards at the local tavern, but his captor's basso profondo voice turned it into a dirge. It had a soporific effect, and David drifted off into another false sleep.

The horse bucked, and David awoke — hours, days, maybe weeks later, he knew not — and he choked on a scream. The undead were everywhere, everywhere he looked, all around him, as far as the eye could see — and the ghoulish contingent was staring back at him, hungrily. He wrenched his gaze away and instantly regretted it because now Castle Relok loomed large in his sight — his tombstone, his sepulcher, a titanic monument to his imminent demise rendered in ancient weathered stone. The blood drained from his head, and the world wobbled and pitched.

Adolphus said nothing as he led David and his men into the inner courtyard through a high arched main gateway; the gate itself had long ago transformed to rust and crumbled away. He dismounted and ordered the Legionnaires to pull David down. They did so, indelicately, and passed custody of the boy on to their master. They remained behind as Adolphus, his hand hard on David's arm, led his prize into the main keep, into the great hall. A single staircase climbed along the wall to David's right and disappeared into the high ceiling. At the base of these stairs, they were met by a heavyset man with a rat's face, pointed and suspicious.

"What's this? What's this?" he said, and Adolphus made a vaguely annoyed gesture.

"Calm yourself, Greeley. I bring the master glad tidings and a very precious gift," Adolphus said, giving David a shake. Greeley's eyes darted between Adolphus and David, uncomprehending. Adolphus sighed and brushed passed his fellow thrall. "Out of the way, dolt."

With each step David's feet grew heavier, his legs stiffer, and by the top of the stairs Adolphus was nearly dragging him. Greeley trailed them, clucking nervously.

They emerged onto the roof of the keep. Debris that once comprised a mighty trebuchet littered the area. Its ammunition, a collection of ten rounded stones, each of them weighing as much as David thrice over, were stacked in a tidy pyramid, just as they were when prepared countless ages ago. David twisted around to see the eastern valley spread out before him, and some distant, disconnected corner of his mind admired the strategic brilliance of this location. Anyone launching a siege campaign against the castle would have to weave their army through constricting woods, cross a wide-open plain, and then fight their way uphill as arrows and stones rained down on them.

Only the most foolish of fools would ever try to storm Castle Relok, he thought.

Wide battlements unfurled to David's left and right, but Adolphus guided him across a center bridge connecting the keep and the main tower. They entered a vast circular chamber where stairs spiraled up the wall and carried them through several more identical chambers, each successive level colder than the last.

David's heart thundered like a war drum as he beheld the horrors of the penultimate room: Greeley's workshop, which upon casual inspection could have passed for that of a skilled butcher — or an inept surgeon. The air tasted thick and rank and coppery. One wall boasted what looked like a carpenter's bench and tool rack — if said carpenter dealt exclusively in the reduction of large pieces of wood into smaller pieces, for every tool was a saw or chisel or hatchet, and every one appeared to be caked with heavy rust. A section of a heavy banquet table, commandeered from the dining hall for Greeley's grisly responsibilities, dominated the center of the room, and it cast upon the floor an amorphous blob of a shadow, the outline of which did not at all match the table's plain rectangular shape.

"Worry not, my lad. This is not your destination," Adolphus said. David found a grain of comfort in this when it dawned on him what the rust and shadow truly were.

That dubious nugget of consolation slipped through his numb fingers when he entered the uppermost chamber.

It was freezing here, impossibly so. A light glaze of frost coated the walls, and the floor glistened with moisture. This room appeared to be one part library and one part chemistry laboratory, both sides fighting for dominance, neither side wishing to live harmoniously with the other. A discarded robe, heavy yet threadbare, was piled into a high-backed throne in the center of the chamber.

"My lord," Adolphus said with giddy anticipation, deep respect and, David sensed, more than a little fear. "My name is Adolphus Drakemore. I am now and forevermore your loyal servant, and I have brought you something."

The robe stirred. "Who...?" it said. The sound was like bone scraping on stone.

"Adolphus Drakemore, master." He swallowed hard.

The robe rose, and a pair of white hands, tinged the palest of green, peeled back the hood.

There is only so much terror any one soul may endure. When it becomes too much to bear, the entire world ceases to lose all meaning, good or ill or in-between. Color is turned off, and everything fades to shades of gray. Sound becomes silence. A gentle touch is no different than a violent blow. Joy, sorrow, anger, hate — these all become meaningless, abstract concepts. It is all the mind can do to cope: shut down and reject all input.

Randolph David Ograine, for all intents and purposes, in all ways that matter, ceased to be in the moment he beheld the face of Habbatarr the lich-lord — or, more precisely, the face Habbatarr had most recently appropriated. The flesh had taken on a leathery quality, sagged slightly around the eyes and mouth, and was teasing the beginnings of putrefaction but was in all other ways disturbingly unremarkable.

Habbatarr moved toward David, head cocked like a curious dog puzzling out an unfamiliar noise. "What?" he said. "What is it? Tell me, tell me what it is?"

Having no answer, Greeley went silent and still. Adolphus bowed his head in reverence — or perhaps because he did not wish to see his master's reaction should his gift fail to please. "This," he said, "is your nemesis, my lord. I present him to you that you may see the face of your enemy before you destroy him."

"The...no. He? The...?"

"The Reaper," Adolphus whispered.

The cold stone walls amplified the lich's roar to an earsplitting explosion. Habbatarr flailed away, falling into his throne. "TAKE IT AWAY!" he screamed, clawing at the air. "The destroyer! Assassin! Assassin! Take it away!"

Greeley rushed to his master's side, pleading for calm. "Fool!" Greeley spat at Adolphus. "I told you to slay the Reaper!"

"He's helpless! He can do you no harm, master! I swear it, he cannot harm you!" To prove his point, Adolphus hurled David to the lich's feet. Habbatarr squealed like a housewife cornered in the kitchen by a passing mouse and hid behind his thrall. David did not rise, did not squirm. "You see? You see?" Adolphus said.

And Habbatarr did see. He saw a wisp of a boy prostrate at his feet, his power gone, his resolve stolen, and at this, the lich-lord uttered a nervous laugh.

"*Heeeeehhh*...on its feet, thrall," Habbatarr said. "On its feet!" Greeley and Adolphus did as bade and righted the boy. Habbatarr grinned a lopsided grin and wagged a finger in David's face. "You. Yes. You. Heh. No harm. Not from you, no, no."

"Just do it," David said in a bland monotone. "Kill me and be done with it."

Habbatarr blinked mechanically and said with a rare clarity, "I'm doing you a favor, you know. Killing you. Sparing you. A mercy, really."

And this lifted David, at least slightly, from the

black void into which his mind and soul had retreated. "Sparing me?"

"*Yeeeeessss*. Tell me, Reaper: The power — how does it feel? Hm? To know, to know that you, you can take that which the Gods created and bend it to your will. Hm? It is *delicious*," he said, confident that he had answered accurately on David's behalf. "I know. Yes. I know. But what price?"

He pulled back one sleeve to reveal Greeley's journeyman stitchery running up the inside of his arm. With his other hand he grasped the seam at the wrist and pulled, peeling the skin off his hand as though removing a glove.

"This flesh," he said, presenting the now-empty sheathe to David for inspection. "Why do I wear it?"

"It...it's how you stay alive," David said, anger and disgust flickering within his chest. "You kill people and wear their skin to stay alive."

Habbatarr barked, a sick parody of a laugh. "Life? Life?! No! Not life. Not life," he gibbered, his lucidity waning. "Not life. Life remains, always. Power. Yes. Power. Not life. This! This, boy, this, young wizard, is your future," he said. He waggled his naked fingers, displaying to David bone and sinew and muscles that had withered and shriveled and by all rights should no longer function. "This is the price. This is the price!" he roared, throwing his flesh-glove in David's face. It hung there for a moment, like the image of a slap suspended in time, then slid off and fell to the floor, leaving a bloody contrail.

With nothing in his stomach, David had nothing to vomit up.

"That is why I will do you a mercy," Habbatarr

said. "I will spare you this. You will die, yes, but unlike me, at least you will die."

"Like hell!" Felix said as he drove an arrow straight through Habbatarr's throat, right under the bend of his jawline.

The ghouls noticed nothing at first.

As stupefied as they were in the subdued daylight, it took them a moment to notice the distant thunder and sense something was amiss. They turned toward the forest and listened, jaws working silently as though warming up for a lengthy feast.

Erika rode in the lead, bent low over her saddle. Winifred, Felix, and finally Derek followed in a tight single-file, shouting at their horses, driving their heels into their flanks, pushing the poor beasts for every last ounce of speed they could muster.

The ghouls snapped out of their trances. They swarmed to intercept Erika, forming a hideous unliving blockade that would tear her and her steed to ribbons before she could break through. She saw two major clusters of ghouls forming: one large scrum at her ten o'clock position and a smaller one at high noon. She broke left toward the larger mass. Her comrades followed with military precision. As hoped, the second smaller group followed their track while the first held its ground and, as one, howled in hungry anticipation. The end result was one very large wall of ghouls dead ahead — and a clear path to their right. Erika waited until the last possible moment and banked hard toward the opening. The ghouls, as if acting with a single mind, lunged at the intruders and smashed into one another, falling over in a tangle of limbs. A few ghouls broke free from the knot and gave chase but were unable to gain ground on the speeding steeds.

The companions dismounted once they reached the inner gate, meeting the Deathless Legionnaires right where Adolphus had left them. The ersatz knights, acting purely on base instinct, moved to intercept the intruders.

"Punch through!" Erika shouted. She dropped back a step and let Derek take point, and he hurled himself into the Legionnaires with the delicacy of a renegade rhino making short work of a flower garden fence.

They weaved through the castle guided only by what little they'd gleaned of the layout from outside, until they reached the stairway in the central keep. Reasoning that they pointed in the general direction of the main tower — up - Derek decided they were as good a choice as any.

They reached the roof, the central tower looming before them. Derek let Erika again take the lead, and he fell back to rear guard position for the mad dash across the bridge. He paused and saw the Legionnaires coming up behind them, far faster than the dead had a right to move.

Habbatarr above, Legionnaires below — a war on two fronts.

Derek drew his sword and planted himself in the tower doorway. "Go!"

"Wha—? Derek!" Felix said.

"Don't argue, Godsdammit, just GO!"

"You heard the man!" Erika said, slipping past Derek, drawing her blades, and throwing herself bodily at the oncoming Legionnaires.

Felix and Winifred bolted up the stairs, chased by the sounds of steel slapping against steel, of flesh and bone being rent asunder — no screams, but the thief and the elf were not necessarily comforted by that.

Felix drew his bow and, moving more cautiously, checked each new floor for danger lying in wait before allowing Winifred to follow. They rose, rose, rose...

"Oh, shit," Felix muttered, catching his first glimpse of Greeley's personal abattoir.

"What? What is it?" Winifred said and received in response Felix's hand waving for silence. He tapped an ear, then his throat, then pointed to the ceiling. Winifred listened then nodded in understanding.

"I think this is it," Felix said.

"It would appear so," Winifred said, squeezing her quarterstaff.

"You ready?" Winifred shook her head. "Me neither."

She grasped his shirt and pulled him into a kiss, long and soft. "If we survive," she said, "I plan to have vigorous sexual intercourse with you."

Felix smiled. "Honey," he said, "you just gave me the best reason in the world to keep on living."

The Legionnaires that survived the initial attack surrounded Erika and Derek, corralled them, and pressed them back to back. For living soldiers this would have been a prelude to toying with their opponents, but there was no contempt here, no malice or perverse joy; they were but automatons doing their job with cold and ruthless efficiency.

Thirteen of them left. Armed. Hard to kill.

Hard, but not impossible.

"Hey. We good?" Derek said.

"Yeah. We're good," Erika said.

And then the slaughter began.

Greeley cried out and threw David aside in his haste to aid his master. David rolled onto his back to see the lich-king clawing at the shaft jutting from his neck.

Adolphus did a frantic two-step as the gears of his brain disengaged, granting Winifred the opening she needed to lay her quarterstaff across his head, striking with enough force to snap the shaft in two. He staggered, a galaxy of stars dancing in his eyes, and Winfred put him down with a roundhouse kick that dislodged teeth and splintered bone.

Wailing like a bereaved widow, Greeley hurled himself toward Felix, his arms pinwheeling, but instead of delivering a series of punishing hammer blows that would batter this cursed interloper into a gooey paste, Greeley caught an uppercut to the point of his chin. His head rolled as though it was mounted on a spring, and he collapsed into a heap.

Felix grabbed David and dragged him clear. "Winifred!" He tossed his knife to her. "Cut him loose and get him out of here!"

The lich-king locked eyes with the thief and Felix froze. Habbatarr pointed accusingly and made a gurgling sound, which jolted Felix from his stupor. He nocked another arrow and fired, aiming for the sweet spot in the center of Habbatarr's forehead, but halfway between points A and B the laws of physics turned traitor; the arrow reversed course and found a new home in Felix's ribs. His leather cuirass, road-weary and worn thin in spots, kept the arrowhead from achieving full penetration, but there was enough of the point in his side to rob him of breath. He was vaguely aware of Winifred calling out his name. He yanked out the arrow and felt blood saturate his shirt at an alarming rate. He tried to speak, tried to warn Winifred not to get close to Habbatarr, for the love of the Gods don't try and attack him with nothing but his hunting knife, but all that escaped was an agonized gasp.

Habbatarr caught Winifred's arm and she screamed. She jerked it away and staggered back, a blackened imprint of the lich's hand marking her pale skin: instant frostbite. He motioned and a force swept across the chamber, picking both adventurers off their feet and hurling them into the wall to pin them there. No, not a force: a hurricane wind, emanating from Habbatarr himself. It was crushing them, squeezing the breath from their lungs...

The lich dropped his hand. The gale died as suddenly as it had whipped up. The warriors pitched face-first onto the floor. Habbatarr advanced on them, his mouth fixed in a leering rictus, and it struck Felix that the lord of Hesre had done all this without uttering a single spoken incantation.

*That's impossible...*

Habbatarr reached for the thief, arcs of blue light dancing between his undead fingers.

Derek's longsword bit deep into the lich, cleaving through his shoulder and several upper ribs — alas, Derek had meant to split the monster's skull. Habbatarr glanced down at the blade jutting from him and released a drawn-out hiss that sounded distinctly like a sigh of profound annoyance. He laid his buzzing fingers on the steel and Derek stiffened, a scream trapped behind his clenched teeth. There was a pop, like a thunderclap in miniature, and Derek flew backward, sliding across the floor and nearly dropping through the stairwell. Erika leapt over him, touched down, and lunged in a single fluid sequence. The tip of her sica slid under Habbatarr's solar plexus and found a home in the black knot that was once his living heart — a purely symbolic lethal blow.

She drew back for a slash with her dagger, intending to take out his eyes. Habbatarr flicked his fingers. A large tome, one of many bound collections of his research through the ages, hurtled across the room. Erika caught the flash of motion out of the corner of her eye and instinctively threw her arm up. She prevented the missile from taking off her head, but sacrificed the bones in her forearm to do so. Pain exploded up her arm. She stumbled, her feet sliding out from under her on the icy floor.

Moving like a man with all the time in the world, Habbatarr pried Derek's sword loose and tossed it away. His arm, dangling from his bifurcated torso, continued to move by sheer force of will. Somewhere in the recesses of his fragmented mind, memories of similar intrusions roiled — would-be heroes on a mission to end his existence, invading his home and interrupting his work, and why? In the name of aborting a prophecy he cared nothing about. What good would come of destroying the world? How would that return true life to his body? All he wanted was to be left alone to work in peace, but fools like these...!

And then it all made perfect sense.

If he wanted solitude, complete and everlasting,

he would have to force it upon the world. There was nothing quieter than a graveyard.

"I have suffered you long enough," Habbatarr spat, "and today, I will end you. End you all! My wrath will cover the world like a shroud! My rage will bury you in the earth! And none will remain — none but I, Habbatarr! The Decaying King! Lord of Hesre! I am become death, and you cannot stop me! *You cannot stop me!*"

And in that moment, an ancient prophecy that was in truth no more than words carried across time by believers and skeptics alike, with no sway over fate but that which mankind granted it, took a step across the thin line separating fiction from fact — and the people who had unwittingly nudged myth into the realm of reality were helpless to stop it. Derek Strongarm, Felix Lightfoot, Erika Racewind, Winifred Graceword, they were but people — remarkable in their courage, their nobility, their indomitable will but simple mortals nonetheless. They were not the one person who could avert a global apocalypse: The fabled Reaper, the Bane of Habbatarr, the Savior of Asaches, the boy born of noble blood who was destined to enter Hesre and slay the lich-king — and that boy was not here.

Randolph David Ograine, however, was.

And he was *angry.*

"*Igi aus'um.*"

The Decaying King's robe ignited with a flash and a deep pop that rattled our heroes' very bones. A scream rose from his throat and just as quickly died as supernatural flame devoured his stolen flesh. The walls hissed as their frosty coating flash-boiled away. His panicked flailing threw embers onto the worktables, where the fire claimed new victims in the form of Habbatarr's accumulated knowledge in the mystic arts. Within seconds, his chamber became a crematorium.

The unliving bonfire careened toward David, arms outstretched to scoop him up in a scorching embrace — Habbatarr's dying, desperate bid to take his foe with him to Hell. Derek reached out, grasped the lad's shirt, and pulled him quite literally out of the line of fire. Habbatarr crashed headlong into the workstation reserved for concocting his arcane potions and elixirs; staggered back; and at long last fell, never to rise again.

"Do I still have eyebrows?"

Derek squinted at his partner. "Looks like it, yeah."

"Hooray," Felix said.

The companions, reunited, sat in one of the lower chambers of Habbatarr's tower, letting the chill settle into them, soothe their many wounds. Erika grunted as she forced her radius and ulna back into alignment. She flexed her fingers and gingerly rotated her wrist, testing her joints.

"But will you ever be able to play the piano again?" Felix said.

"I don't play the piano," Erika said. "Oh. Joke. Got it."

"Yeah, I'm a funny guy."

"Hysterical."

"Shouldn't we be, I don't know, celebrating or something?" Derek said.

"Probably. Maybe later," Felix said. "I just want to sleep."

"Ohhh, sleep would be wonderful," Winifred said. "I want to take a hot bath and crawl into a warm feather bed and sleep."

"I want a beer. A beer and a steak as big as my head. Then the bath and the sleep."

"You know what I want?" Derek said. "A nice cold glass of milk."

"Milk? Seriously?" Felix laughed. "Gods, you are such a bumpkin."

"Screw you, you lousy thief."

"I'm an awesome thief, pal, and don't you forget it."

"What about you, Erika? What do you want to do when we get out of here?"

Erika gave him a look. "You mean once we fight our way past the hundreds of ghouls waiting for us outside?"

"Oh. Yeah. Forgot about them."

"Well, shit," Felix said.

Not that there was an abundance of jubilation to be found among our heroes to begin with, but the realization that their victory had not yet cleared the slavering jaws of defeat snuffed out the few remaining feeble embers of their morale.

"It's not fair," David said.

"No," Derek agreed. "It's not."

"Our world and welcome to it," Felix said, forcing his legs into service.

"What are you doing?"

Felix threw his hands up. "Hey. If we're going to get torn apart by the undead we might as well get to it."

"Yeah. Suppose so," Derek said. "Good times."

"Hell yes, man."

Winifred took Felix's hand. "I'm sorry we'll never have the opportunity for that lovemaking I promised."

"Back at you."

"Did I miss something?" Erika said. "No, scratch that, I don't want to know. Derek?"

"Hm?"

"...You're the least annoying person I've ever met."

Derek smiled. That surely had to have been the nicest thing Erika ever said to anyone.

"Thank you," David said in a small voice. "Thank you for...everything, I guess. For protecting me. Believing in me."

"Putting up with you," Felix suggested.

"Putting up with me. So. Yeah. Thanks."

And with that, the companions descended the tower, at peace with themselves, with one another, and content in the knowledge that, though their names may vanish into the mists of history, the fruits of their heroic deed and selfless sacrifice would change the face of Asaches, indeed all Ne'lan, forever and ever.

Yet none of them found reason to complain when they were met at the bridge by a team of a dozen armed soldiers, marching toward them briskly in a tight defensive formation around Alexander Ograine.

"Alex?" David said, agog.

"Randy?" Alexander said, equally agog.

"What are you doing here?" the brothers said in perfect unison.

"Did...did father send you to come get me?" David asked.

"Uh...well, uh..." One of Alexander's guards — Derek recognized him as one of the commanding officers he'd seen in Alexander's pavilion — said something into his lord's ear. "Yes. Yes, of course. Randy. I have, uh, I have something to take care of, won't take a minute, we'll be right back, so why don't you and your friends, you know, wait here. Be right back."

He gestured to his men, who pushed past the companions and filed into the tower. David tried to shout out a warning, but Felix clamped a hand over his mouth.

"He'll figure it out soon enough," Felix said.

David turned toward Erika. "I don't understand. What's going on? What's Alex doing here? He did come to escort us back home, right?"

The elf felt a bomb of guilt go off in the pit of her stomach. "David," she said, "there's something you have to know."

She laid out in ruthless detail the truth behind David's mission then braced for a reaction: tears, screaming, a punch thrown in her direction — but all she saw was a blank mask. She found the utter non-expression disconcertingly familiar; she was sure she'd worn that same mask on too many occasions.

"Let's just go," David said. "I want to go."

"Hold on," Felix said. "Kid, you got seriously screwed over by your own family. Your father made you march through hell so you could play sacrificial lamb to a crazy lich so your prick of a brother could have a clear shot, and in a few minutes Alex is going to realize that his actual destiny is as empty as your fake destiny because you did the job he was supposed to do...and you're telling me you *don't want to stick around to see the look on his face?"*

David considered this. "Yeah, all right."

It would be a fleeting moment of guilty pleasure, yes, but as a wise man once said, sometimes it's all about the little joys in life.

# TWENTY-ONE
## Homecoming

David and his guardians made the trek back to Oson in the company of High Lord Ograine's army — which is to say they traveled with the army as they marched down the Grand Avenue, the route by which they arrived in advance of David and his guardians. Felix was not above lobbing an *I told you so* at Erika upon learning this. They trailed the troops at a respectable distance, however, and the casual observer would have drawn no connection between the impressive army and the bedraggled quintet. At night they set up their own annex camp well outside the main encampment. They steadfastly refused Alexander's offers to avail themselves of the army's ample stores, instead relying on Felix's bow for their meals.

They did all this at David's request; he wished his presence to remain a secret from the rank and file, but declined to explain his reasons. He spent the journey buried in a hooded cloak, saying little — although in this instance his silence was concerning rather than welcome. Alexander approached his brother a few times during their first week on the road, hoping to discuss what had transpired in Hesre, hoping to explain his role in the grand scheme of things, but was roundly rebuffed. On his last attempt, Erika intervened and advised Alexander in the strongest possible terms to refrain from further entreaties. This led to one brief confrontation between Erika and Captain Greystone, who rejoined her comrades as they passed through Avoy. The women had never been cordial and were happy to capitalize on any excuse to express their mutual displeasure. Erika, broken arm notwithstanding, proved more expressive. The army accommodated the party's desire for solitude from that point on.

A month passed.

It was dark when the army returned to Oson — not nighttime, but an extraordinarily gray day, as dreary as any given day in Hesre. There was no heroes' welcome to greet them, no fanfare. Citizens on the streets stopped to watch the procession, some of them recalling the troops' departure under unknown circumstances in the opening days of spring. They thought nothing of it then, and they thought nothing of it now. They saw no carts bearing the enshrouded bodies of soldiers slain in battle, no horses trotting in with empty saddles, none of the flags were flying at half-staff. Whatever campaign they'd been on, they reasoned, it must have been uneventful.

They paid even less mind to the individuals straggling behind the troops.

Alexander led the men and women into Castle Ograine in the ceremonial position traditionally reserved for the commanding general. A guard on duty at the western gatehouse spotted the young lord and raced to the main keep to deliver the news. High Lord

Ograine came out to meet his son in the courtyard. He retained his composure long enough for Alexander to dismount and then threw himself on the boy, weeping with relief, with joy, with shame and guilt that could no longer be held in check.

"Father," Alexander said.

"Father," he said again — yet this time his voice seemed to come from elsewhere. High Lord Malcolm Ograine opened his eyes and felt his blood turn to ice water.

"Nothing for me?" David said.

David always loved the family library. He was not much of a reader — his father favored history books, which he found excruciatingly tedious — but he loved the atmosphere. He loved curling up on the low-backed couch in front of the cavernous fireplace to bask in its warmth. The room always smelt faintly of smoke, smoke and that indescribable perfume of old, dusty books. He spent so many nights in here with his father, just the two of them, talking about David's destiny, his future as High Lord of Asaches. His father often re-marked what a fine leader his son would be one day, how proudly he would carry on the family name.

Lies. All of it.

High Lord Ograine eyed the ragged foursome that accompanied his second-born. They stood close to the boy, like his personal guard...or personal assassins, awaiting their master's kill order — and eagerly so, judging by their cold stares.

"I would appreciate it if I could speak with my son in private," Ograine said, though in truth he hardly knew where to begin.

"No," David said. "They stay."

"David — uh, Randolph. Lord Ograine," Derek said, "maybe we should —"

"No. You're staying. All of you." David stared at his father. "You're the only people I trust anymore."

"Randolph," Ograine said. "You need to understand, what I did — what I did was necessary. I took no pleasure in it whatsoever..."

"Didn't stop you, though," Felix said.

"I don't know who you are," Ograine snarled, "but you have no cause to speak to me like that. You have no idea what I've been through, how much torment I've endured —"

"Oh, fuck you," Felix said, relishing the fact that this might be the only time in his life he could speak so to a lord and walk away unscathed. "You don't get to have hurt feelings, pal, you sent your own kid out to get killed."

"I made a sacrifice in the name of the greater good! Habbatarr threatened to exterminate every life in Asaches — for a start — and I did what I felt I had to do so Alexander could fulfill the prophecy."

"Except Alexander didn't," Erika said. "He did."

Ograine scowled at her for making such a tasteless joke — and then recalled that Erika Racewind had no sense of humor. "Randolph? You...?"

"Yes," he said. "No. We killed him. My friends and I."

"The point remains that Alexander didn't do the job. Lord Ograine did," Erika said, "which means the prophecy was complete..."

"Horseshit," Felix suggested.

"Horseshit! All of it! You could have sent your

army into Hesre years ago and none of this —"

"And how was I to know that?!" Ograine thundered. "I believed the prophecy! So did you! What was I to do? Ignore it and pray that whatever I did instead would be enough? I had no choice!"

"Yes you did. You could have chosen not to throw your own child to the wolves!"

"Stop," David said. "Erika. Everyone. Go outside now. Please."

The companions reluctantly filed out of the library, leaving father and son to face one another.

"I had no choice," Ograine repeated, with no more heartfelt conviction this time around than the first.

"Neither did I," David said.

Ograine raised his hands as if in surrender. "Randolph. Son. I've wronged you terribly. I know that. And I'm not asking for your forgiveness because I have no right. I *am* asking that you understand why I did everything I did, why I couldn't place the life of one person, even my own flesh and blood, above the lives of millions. One day you'll know what it's like to face an untenable decision, and maybe you'll then appreciate —"

"Except I won't know," David said, "because I'm not the first-born. Alexander will become High Lord someday, not me."

"No," Ograine said, shaking his head. "As far as anyone outside this castle knows, you are my first-born, and that is how it shall remain. You are the true savior of Asaches, and thus you are the rightful heir. I'll announce tomorrow —"

"I don't want to be the rightful heir. I don't want

your title or your responsibility."

"Then what? Tell me, Randolph," Ograine said. For a moment David thought his father was going to fall to his knees in supplication. "What do you want? Anything, it's yours. Just tell me."

David thought for a moment then said, "Erika Racewind. She performed the task you set for her, so you'll honor your agreement with her. Release her from her contract."

"Done. Done."

"And the two men, Derek Strongarm and Felix Lightfoot. I wouldn't have survived without them. They were promised payment for —"

"They'll get it. Whatever they were promised."

"And Winifred."

"Of course, yes." He waited for David to go on, but the boy said nothing. "But what about you?" Ograine took a cautious step forward, another, and laid a hand on David's shoulder. The boy did not withdraw. Ograine smiled. "What about you? What does my son want?"

David did not meet High Lord Ograine's gaze when he spoke in a thin, tiny voice, a single tear sliding down his face.

"I don't want to be your son anymore."

Two days later the whole of Oson, every man, woman, and child, lined the streets to attend the funeral of Lord Randolph David Ograine.

Word of the young man's heroic demise spread like wildfire following High Lord Ograine's tearful announcement the previous morning. A little more than two months earlier, Lord Randolph David Ograine, who had spent all of his tragically short life honing his skill in the magical arts, departed Oson with a full regiment for Hesre, where he met his destiny head-on. The soldiers cut a swath through an equal if not superior opposing force of the undead and carried the Reaper into Castle Relok, where he ordered his men to hold position that he might face his legendary foe alone and put no other man at risk. That was the last time anyone saw Randolph David Ograine alive.

An hour passed before General Montague Alastaire, the army's commander, dared breach Habbatarr's tower. He climbed to the uppermost chamber where he found a conflagration of such fury he thought he had stumbled into Hell itself. Within that pyre he found Lord Ograine, dead, no doubt struck down by the lich-king even as the Reaper delivered his killing stroke. General Alastaire refused to let his lord go to his final reward this way; he dragged the body clear and carried it home, that Lord Ograine might receive a sendoff worthy of the savior of Asaches. However, the intense flames had done their damage; the tradition of placing the body to lie in state for a full day was, for the sake of decency, foregone. His remains were placed in an ornately carved mahogany casket for the procession through Oson. That Lord Ograine was saved from incineration only to be carried home for proper cremation provided the masses with ample reason to remark upon how cruelly ironic the world could be.

A dozen high-ranking mounted soldiers led the procession through Oson's winding, labyrinthine streets. High Lord Ograine, his wife Samara, and their remaining progeny, Lord Alexander, the newly appointed heir apparent, rode inside the family's personal Moste Grande, its shutters open that the populace might see their stoicism in the face of such unimaginable loss and emulate their courage. That their stately resolve was in fact gut-churning guilt was — like the official account of the Reaper's demise — a secret that the bereaved family vowed to take to their own graves. The hearse, a flatbed carriage drawn by Bravia and Titania, on-loan for the occasion, followed the family. Banners in the family colors flew at each corner, waving lazily, and behind the hearse, marching in precise formation on foot and on horseback, came the regiment dispatched to Hesre, now assigned to complete their task of escorting their lord home.

The casket rolled under an arched stone bridge, from which our heroes surveyed the proceedings with all due respect and reverence.

"This is pretty damned cool," Felix said. "I've never seen a funeral like this. I'm used to people getting wrapped up in cloth and thrown on a bonfire. Or in a hole."

"Funerals among my clan are more celebratory," Winifred said. "They commemorate a life well-lived and the soul's journey into the next world, to join the Gods."

"I like your version better. But given a choice? I want one of these suckers. Parade, color guard, streets lined ten people deep with mourners — pomp and circumstance out the ass. And lots of booze."

"You're a class act, Lightfoot," Erika said.

"Don't I know it."

Derek offered David a comforting pat on the back. "They love you," he said. "Look at their faces.

They truly loved you."

David peered out from beneath his hood and scanned the crowd, and he knew Derek was offering a polite lie. He saw no love among the multitude. He saw people lamenting the loss of a life cut too short, empathizing with parents who had just lost their child, but love for him? He'd spent his life sequestered in the castle, so very rarely leaving its protection, and certainly never intermingling with the common man. To the people of Oson, indeed all of Asaches, he existed as the central subject of a popular rumor — he was a concept, not a person. How could any of them feel personal loss for someone they never knew?

"I guess they did," David said. "Can we go?"

"Sure, pal. Whatever you say."

"Yeah, let's blow this place," Felix said. "I've got a heap of gold burning a hole in my pocket, and I still owe myself a steak dinner. And a room in an upscale inn with private baths and nice, thick, soundproof walls," he said, snaking an arm around Winifred's slender waist.

"Hold onto some of that money, partner," Derek said. "We have some debts we need to pay off."

"Like what?"

"I promised Mother Delsina we'd make a donation to the temple, for one."

"*You* promised *we'd* make a donation?"

"Wasn't my life the sisters saved," Derek pointed out. "Then there's the mess we made at Miggis's house. And the damage at the End of Aming Inn. And —"

"Are we going to have *any* money left over?"

"Some."

Felix sighed. "As usual."

Derek passed a small leather sack to Winifred. "That's for Mother Delsina, with our gratitude." She accepted the gold with a bow. "And there's a little extra in there for a horse, so you don't have to make the hike on foot."

"Ohh, that's so kind of you, Derek, thank you," Winifred beamed, but Derek shook his head. "His idea," he said, nodding at Felix, who accepted both the redirected credit and Winifred's grateful kiss in silence.

The companions pushed through the shoulder-to-shoulder crowd and, once clear, headed west. They were to put up their feet for a while in a secluded tavern and await Captain Greystone who was to deliver Bravia and Titania after they had finished their official duties. And from there...

"Where *are* you two going, anyway?" Derek inquired.

"Haven't given it any thought, honestly," Erika said — apprehensively, Derek thought. "I've never had my life to myself before."

"Me neither," David said, the vague concept of starting life anew, free from the tethers of destiny — real or imagined — becoming frighteningly real.

Derek glanced at his partner: *You mind?*

Felix rolled his eyes, nodded: *Go ahead.*

"Then how about you come with us?" Derek said.

"Where are you headed?" Erika said.

"Wherever life takes us."

"Is that your poetic way of looking at life as a hobo?" David said.

"It's an honest way of saying I don't know what

tomorrow will bring," Derek said, "but whatever it is, we'll roll with it. That's what life as an adventurer is all about."

"An adventurer, eh? Fine then," David said, taking the lead, as he felt he should. "If that's the case, I need an adventurer name."

"An adventurer name?"

"I can't use my real name anymore. And, as absurd as this sounds, it would be idiotic if we were to bill ourselves as Strongarm, Lightfoot, Racewind, and David."

"David?" Derek said. "Not Randolph?"

The boy paused. "Randolph Ograine's dead, Derek. We just came from his funeral. Remember?"

"Of course. My mistake, David."

"All right. So," Felix said, "an adventurer name."

"Right," David said. "Something distinct and dramatic, something that captures my essence."

"Captures your essence, huh? How about David Whiny-Brattington," Felix suggested.

"Excuse me?"

"It's hyphenated."

"No."

"Okay. David McAnnoyingson, then. David Von Jerkface? David Painintheassfield."

"Stop it," Derek said. "We have to give him something decent. Maybe something that reflects his magical abilities?"

"Yes!" David said. "There you go. Something like that."

"I got one: David Doomfinger."

"Doomfinger?"

"Sure. You know: *fwoosh!*" Derek said, miming the spell that brought down the Decaying King.

"*Doomfinger?*"

"No, huh? David, uh...Deathdigit?"

"David Flaming-Phalange," Felix said. "Hyphenated again."

"David Hothand."

"David Pyropointer?" Winifred tried.

The boy sighed. "Just call me David..."

And thus was a new fellowship born, a small but courageous band of heroes that would in their time face many a dastardly foe, discover countless wonders, and pull back the veil from great mysteries that have confounded the races throughout time immemorial. Their names and deeds would become the stuff of legend, and their exploits would leave the world of Ne'lan forever changed.

But these, as we say in the narration game, are tales for another time.

I bid you, my friend, farewell.

For now.

## ABOUT THE AUTHOR

Michael Bailey was born in Falmouth, Massachusetts and raised on a steady diet of comic books, *Dungeons & Dragons*, Saturday morning cartoons, sci-fi television, and horror movies…which explains a lot.

An effort to parlay his love of geek culture into a career as a comic book artist failed when he figured out he wasn't that good, so he turned to writing as means of artistic expression. Since then, Michael has written several scripts for New England-area renaissance faires, as well as a number of articles based on faire culture for *Renaissance Magazine*.

In 2013, Michael left his job of 15 years as a reporter and blogger for his hometown newspaper, the Falmouth Enterprise, to pursue his writing career. His debut novel, *Action Figures – Issue One: Secret Origins* made its debut in September 2013.

Michael lives in Massachusetts with his wife Veronica, four cats, an English bulldog, and a comic book collection large enough to warrant its own room.

Visit Michael online at www.innsmouthlook.com, and find him on Facebook, Twitter, Tumblr, Pinterest, and Goodreads.

Made in the USA
Charleston, SC
21 December 2015